The Sunset Rule
A Southern Horror Story

Beverly Peace-Kayhill

This novel is a work of fiction. Names, characters, places, and incidents are the product of the author's imagination or are used fictitiously. Any resemblance to actual events, locations, or persons, living or dead is coincidental

Cover design by Mars Robinson

The Sunset Rule. Copyright © 2019 by Beverly Peace-Kayhill
All rights reserved. No part of this book may be reproduced or transmitted in any form or by any means including photocopying, recording, or by any information storage and retrieval system without the written permission of the author, except where permitted by law.

Printed in the United States of America

Library of Congress Control number: 2020904531
ISBN 9781098306083
ISBN 9871098306090 (e-book)

For Mom
I miss you every single day.

"True redemption is when guilt leads to good."

Khaled Hosseini

Chapter 1

1931
Forsyth County, Georgia

The bright rays of the sun couldn't pierce the leafy canopy that shrouded Dead Man's Alley. The creatures that called this length of road home thrived in the steamy surroundings. The dank atmosphere preserved the animals and strange plant life that relied on the somber darkness and dread that kept most people out.

Portly trees and thick vines suckled on the hazy brume that hung in the air and lent a sense of foreboding to the path named by superstitious locals.

"Dumbass!"

The toe of her shoe was dusty and scuffed from the rock she had kicked along the way. The last and hardest kick sailed it into the weeds.

"Stupid girl!"

"Walked all this way for nothing. Now I gotta make it home by supper."

It would be chicken and dumplings, her favorite. She smiled and sucked her thumb to soothe her nerves. Emma Lee had told Mama she was going to see Sarah's new colt, but she had already seen it last week, brown with a snow-white bib standing next to its mama on wobbly stick legs. It was so cute.

"Why'd he even tell me to come?" she muttered.

Emma Lee thought about the boy she had met in town that morning. He'd been standing outside the hardware store when she came out and sat in one of the rockers. Daddy was still inside bickering with the Jew.

"What's your name?" he'd asked.

He was older, probably sixteen or even seventeen, handsome as all get-out and she couldn't believe he was talking to her.

She'd turned her head away, her thoughts tumbling every whichaway. She didn't know him. He was a stranger; he had some nerve talking right at her like that.

"You gonna tell me your name? I ain't got all day."

"Emma Lee." Dang it! It had just fallen out of her mouth. She hadn't meant to tell him.

He'd looked straight at her. She'd felt his eyes moving over her hair, taking in her face, her body. She squirmed in the rocker, cheeks burning, and peeked at him from under a forehead of frizzy bangs.

"I'm Cory," he said.

"Cory. What kind of name is that?"

"It's the name my mama gave me. You got a problem with it?"

Emma Lee twisted the hem of her dress around one finger. If she smiled she might giggle and older girls didn't giggle, but it was hard looking at him looking at her with those grown-man eyes.

"How old are you?" he asked.

"Fifteen."

"Girl, you ain't fifteen. Thirteen, I bet."

"Wrong! I'll be fourteen next month."

"Why you lie?"

"How old are you?"

"Seventeen."

He was deeply tanned from laboring under the hot sun. A tattered straw hat sat back on his head. Wheat-colored strands rested on his neck. His eyes were ocean-blue, severe, piercing, and mysterious.

"I bet you're a daddy's girl."

She'd wanted to suck her thumb so bad, a nervous habit from forever. Instead, she stuck her hand into the pocket of her yellow gingham, her favorite dress. It had a keyhole opening at the neck that showed the locket Daddy had given her for her birthday last year. Her lips folded inward, and she smoothed the sunflowers on her skirt and wished Mama hadn't put pigtails in her hair.

"You live around here?" she asked.

"Naw, working as a farmhand for a few weeks."

"Where?"

"Miller farm."

"Out near Dead Man's Alley?"

"Yup."

"My daddy knows Mr. Miller. Do you go to school?"

"Not anymore," he said. "You got a boyfriend?"

"A boyfriend?"

"I guess that's a no," he chuckled.

She'd giggled and to resist the urge to suck her thumb held her hand tightly in her lap.

"Ever been courted by a boy?"

"No."

"If your daddy approves, I'd like to keep company with you. Do you think he'd be agreeable?"

Her thoughts danced a little jig. What would Sarah say when she told her a seventeen-year-old boy wanted her company? She couldn't wait to tell Sarah.

"I don't know you."

"You could get to know me."

"How?"

"I have to go, but can you come out to Miller's later so we can talk some more? Then your daddy might let me take you to a picture show. I'll even come to your house and ask him."

A picture show? Emma Lee's heart skipped. Oh, God! Suppose he wanted to kiss her?

"You know where the Miller farm is?"

"We pass it every time we come to town."

"Can you meet me at five? I have something special I want you to see."

"Something you want me to see?" she asked, skeptically.

"Yes, Emma Lee. But you gotta come if you wanna see it."

"What is it?"

"Something real important to me."

Emma Lee's eyes lit up with excitement. She slid off the rocker and stood against the wood post. "I'm not sure."

"Why? Your mama won't let you?"

"I don't need permission. I go where I want."

"You sure?"

"What time did you say?"

"Around five, when I get off."

She teased a pebble with the tip of her shoe and mashed it into a crack in the wood.

"Oh, come on! It'll be worth it. I promise."

"Maybe."

Cory reached over and tugged one of her pigtails, "Okay, pretty girl, maybe I'll see you, maybe I won't." He winked, and strode down the sidewalk, thumbs hooked in his belt loops, his boots cracked against the wood walkway. He looked back, his eyes sparkling as he touched his hat.

"See ya at five."

Cory hadn't been at the Miller farm when Emma Lee arrived. She had waited at the gate for as long as she could, and now she walked back through the gloominess of Dead Man's Alley, alone.

The alley was shaded by a dismal horde of fat tree limbs that reached across and around one another in dizzying twists and turns. With every generous breeze, a shower of leaves fluttered down, and Emma Lee waded through the ankle-deep foliage. In the distance, a smidgen of bright light winked at her, and she picked up her pace anxious to leave this gloomy tunnel behind and feel the warm sun on her face.

As she walked along, she heard the sparrows bickering and the woeful call of a lonely owl from somewhere in the darkness. Tree shadows reached like spooky fingers all around her and fear quickened her heartbeat. She had made a mistake coming all this way alone to meet a boy she didn't even know. She continued her way up the dark path; her thumb jammed in her mouth like a bottle stopper and her eyes focused on the light ahead.

"Emma Lee."

She stopped and looked around.

Cory appeared beside a huge Magnolia tree, its limbs hanging heavy with cabbage-sized blossoms. The sparrows continued to fuss at one another from behind a leafy screen.

"You came." He said, surprised but clearly elated.

His long legs quickly crossed the road and then he stood directly in front of her. She smiled and opened her mouth, but before she could utter one word a rock crashed into her face knocking out her front teeth and crushing one eye into a bloody pulp. He hit her again, cracking her forehead. She felt herself falling, but then she was floating and he was carrying her. Cory dropped Emma Lee into a nest of pinecones and minty weeds. The strong scent of woods drifted through the broken cavity in her face. Her thoughts tumbled amidst a flurry of pain. Hundreds of scenes flashed forward like the reel on a picture show. The new film Dr. Jekyll and Mr. Hyde was showing in Cumming. She wondered if Daddy would let her go. Then she saw the baby deer standing up next to its mama, it vanished when pain clenched her brain in its unrelenting grip leaking tears from her one good eye.

Emma Lee thought about Mama and she remembered it was suppertime. A slim essence of simmering onions drifted past her nose and the savory aroma of Mama's chicken and dumplings emerged, and it was wonderful. This had to be more than a memory, she thought.

There was a thickness in her mouth that must be the gravy. It leaked over her lips and drizzled down her chin, but something wasn't right a bitter taste scoured her tongue. Where was the spicy chicken flavor Mama was famous for?

More chicken broth, Mama.

Twilight glazed the forest with a golden patina and the air was filled with the drowsy, earthy fragrance of pinecones and dried leaves that seeped into the hole in Emma Lee's face. Her remaining eyeball shifted and followed the dizzying surge of a stately pine until the treetop poked a drifting cloud with its crown. She wondered how a tree could grow so high.

Cory loomed over her; his blue eyes vacant as he ripped her favorite dress down the front. She winced when he tore her petticoat and his dirty fingernails sliced into her small breasts. He was awkward and frantic as he struggled to remove her underclothes.

"Shit!"

There were several more tugs and now she was naked. He hauled her body toward his. Her cries gurgled blood in her throat causing it to seep over her lips like an overfilled sink, and then she saw Cory's face. But instead of the handsome boy she'd met in town, his mouth was twisted into an angry sneer and his eyes were as lifeless as a broken doll.

When Emma Lee tried to lift her head, shards of pain raked her forehead like barbwire and pushed her back down into the weeds. She peered through one eye at Cory's grinning face as her body battled against the heavy weight of sleep that wanted to take her to another place. But her heart was pumping a mile a minute and her senses were not yet willing to let go. Thoughts of escape were a whisper that her arms and legs ignored. Latched firmly to the ground, her limbs were as weak as a newborn kitten.

And then, as blood pooled in her throat she gagged and coughed so violently, it racked her brittle body and splattered Cory with crimson globs, startling him from a state of psychotic sloth.

Cory's hand flew to his face and wiping her blood with disgust, he said, "Fucking bitch!" Enraged, he slapped Emma Lee, a blow so savage it dislodged what was left of her broken eye. He watched humorously as her eyeball slipped out of its socket and dangled on a thin cord of flesh.

"You ain't a pretty girl no more," he sneered.

Cory fumbled in his trousers; he removed himself and then snatched Emma Lee's legs apart stealing her virginity with brute force. Her body jolted against the pain that seared her tender skin like burning hot liquid and she cried out for Mama. Where's Mama? She was always right there when Emma Lee was hurting.

The only witnesses to the assault were the frightened animals hiding in the brush and the startled birds hopping from branch to branch screeching in protest. Emma Lee heard the little birds crying out. She wanted to find them and tell them to fly away but she was growing very tired.

After savoring his pleasurable release Cory rose from his knees and with a contented sigh he pulled up his trousers and tucked his shirttail in. As he fed his belt through the loops and synched his waistband tight he gazed up at the clouds drifting past the treetops with a satisfied smirk. Using Emma's dress, he cleaned the blood from his hands, tossed it into the weeds and smoothed his thick blond hair back from his forehead. When he raised his arms stretching the kink in his back, another gratified moan escaped from his perfectly formed mouth. Cory's blue eyes sparkled when he breathed the crisp country air and he couldn't help but smile. However, when he looked down at the fitful rise and fall of Emma Lee's chest, his smile vanished as fear slithered like a putrid slug into his consciousness.

She was still alive. With quickness, Cory searched the surrounding bushes kicking rocks along the way and then plucked one from the ground. He tested the rock's weight by shifting it from hand to hand.

"This should do it," he muttered. He raised the rock high over his head and brought it down with such brute force it smashed what was left of Emma Lee's face into a tomb.

When Emma Lee didn't come home for supper, her daddy, Beasley Taggart, went to her best friend Sarah's house. He was certain they were yakking the way girls did, and she'd probably forgotten all about suppertime. He planned on giving her a stern talking-to about being late. But when Emma Lee wasn't at Sarah's, an alarm sounded inside Beasley's head. He checked a couple more places that she would likely go, and then the daylight faded and he knew he needed help.

He stopped by his wife's cousin Donny Anderson's house, who left his own supper table to join Beasley in the search. Donny took the wheel of Beasley's Ford Model A work truck, so Beasley could jump out right quick at the houses of Emma's friends. They also checked inside the stables and barns along the way. They came upon little Henry Hayes walking on the road with two mangy dogs, one heavy with pups.

"I seen Emma Lee walking up the road. I hollered out 'Hey' and she waved."

"Which way was she headed?"

"Thataway," he said, pointing north. "But ain't nothin' up that road but Dead Man's Alley."

Beasley and Donny exchanged anxious glances and Donny mashed the gas pedal to the floor. Dirt and rocks shot up from under the wheels as the truck skidded and took off.

The setting sun had surrendered to nightfall as they drove into the dark stretch of road that was Dead Man's Alley. "Pull over there," said Beasley; nodding at the right side of the road and Donny pulled the truck to a stop. As the men stepped out of the truck they were taken by the silence hanging over the Alley. Only an occasional flutter of leaves revealed the creatures hiding in the trees watching mutely from a safe distance. The light was sparse; even the brightness of a full moon couldn't defeat the shroud that covered Dead Man's Alley, so Beasley and Donny each walked by the light of a lantern. They searched all night, from the start of the alley through the dense trees and brush, over piles and piles of fallen leaves. The forest remained still throughout the search, not a peep from the critters that dwelled there as though they sat in silent regard of another mortal tragedy.

The morning sun was burning through a murky cloud cover when Beasley spotted a pink sweater lying among the pinecones. As he stepped closer, he wanted so badly to dismiss what he saw as something else, a patch of wildflowers, anything. But his heart was thundering like the hoof beats of a wild herd, and he knew he was walking into his worst nightmare. Beasley fell to his knees and picked up the sweater, he buried his nose deep into the soft wool inhaling the sweet scent of rose toilet water that his daughter loved so much. Tears blurred his vision as he got to his feet and pressed on. He followed a trail of disturbed weeds and broken branches deep into the woods, and there, lying in a nest of burly weeds, he saw his daughter, Emma Lee. Her clothes had been ripped from her body and tossed aside. Her legs were splayed, thighs stained with dried blood. Beasley hurried to her side dropped down and covered her exposed body with the sweater, and then, he looked at what was left of her face. Beasley didn't recognize the wail as something that could exist within him, but it did. The grisly sound sailed up from his gut past his lungs and leaped from his throat like a wounded animal shattering the silence and startling the birds into flight. Donny was so alarmed by the cry that he tripped and fell over a log but quickly got to his feet following Beasley's choking sobs.

When Donny reached Beasley and the sickening scene, his face blanched with horror, and shock rooted him to the ground. Beasley was cradling Emma Lee's head, his tears dripped onto her bloody face, and his eyes were fixed on the heart-shaped locket he had given her. A thin strand of light had found an opening in the leafage and the gold locket glinted under its touch. He thought of his daughter's gap-toothed grin when she'd first opened the box. Her small arms had flown around his neck like tender vines and her kiss had been sticky jelly on his cheek. He willed himself to focus on the locket and not on what was left of Emma Lee's face.

Finding some resolve, Donny stepped closer. "Is she alive?"

"No, she's gone." Beasley's voice was barely a whisper.

He scooped his daughter from her wooded grave carrying her in his arms like a newborn. Donny followed closely and then hurried ahead and opened the passenger door.

Beasley got in the truck with Emma in his lap and Donny hurried around the truck and slid in behind the steering wheel. Beasley sat trembling, swatting the tears that kept coming. His voice cracked as he rocked his child in his arms. His face was cloaked with desperation when he looked at Donny. "Her face, Donny. I can't even recognize my baby girl."

"Here, use this," Donny said, as he quickly removed his own shirt handing it to Beasley, and then watched as Beasley covered Emma's slaughtered face.

With a dismal nod toward the road, Beasley uttered, "Let's go."

Donny's hand shook as he turned the key and pushed the gearshift into first, his foot hit the gas and the truck lurched forward picking up speed, leaving Dead Man's Alley to cling to its hidden skeletons.

In the daylight, they passed spacious fields and plantations that yielded hearty crops and were peppered by wildflowers, their colorful blooms a patchwork quilt that blanketed the ground. The morning air was chilly and dew teased the meadow with a first sip before the rising sun chased it to another day.

"I know who done this," muttered Beasley.

Donny looked at him, and then at Emma's blood seeping through his shirt.

"Look over there," Beasley nodded at a vast cotton field where dozens of Negro workers were arriving for the day's picking. "I always said white girls ain't safe in this county."

"You think it was one of them?"

"No white person would do a white child like this. Niggers are savages!"

Before the start of the Civil War, the Taggarts had been among the first settlers to break ground in Piney, Georgia. Beasley's father, Samuel Taggart and his brother George had fought in the war and Beasley honored them by displaying the Dixie flag from his porch railing. Samuel often told his son that even after the war ended there was unrest. Some Union soldiers-turned-outlaw invaded the town, looting and ransacking homes already devastated by war and stealing what little there was left from starving families. Those who stood up to the soldiers were either beaten or in some cases shot. Beasley saw the pain in his father's face when he spoke of his brother George standing up to the outlaw soldiers and being shot dead in front of his wife. Beasley, who wondered why freeing Niggers was worth his uncle's life readily absorbed his father's bitterness.

After Samuel's death, Beasley left Piney when he was fourteen years old. He found work in the town of Cumming, the County Seat of Forsyth County, Georgia. It was there he met his wife Mary-Ann and their daughter Emma Lee was born. Over the years, Beasley's hometown of Piney had become a working town of farmers with growing families, and Beasley moved his own family back to Piney. So remote was the small town, that officials in Cumming took their time appointing a Sheriff, which was fine with the citizens of Piney, who lived by their own set of rules, and were in no hurry to have a Sheriff enforcing laws.

As Beasley stood on his porch looking out over the growing town, two Negro men riding in a horse-drawn wagon passed his house. Both men nodded and touched their hats as they drove by. Beasley was shocked and so offended by their gesture, his jaw tightened and the veins in his neck bulged.

"Mary-Ann!"

The screen door squealed when she pushed it open. His wife stood by his side wiping her hands on her apron. "What, honey?"

"You see that," he said, scowling at the Negro's in the wagon.

"Uh huh."

"You make sure you keep an eye on Emma Lee. You hear me?"

"She don't go nowhere but to school and Sarah's house!"

"Do as I say!"

"I will," she replied, calmly.

"Seems like there's more of them moving to Piney every day," he griped, glowering at the wagon as it disappeared up the road.

Mary-Ann's hand touched her husband's arm but his eyes had gone cold, his mouth a jagged crack. Resignedly, she went back into the house.

Now, his daughter was dead. The Taggart home was a place of mourning, with family and neighbors stopping in to sit with Mary-Ann who broke into fits of hysterics, screaming for Emma Lee and then collapsing into an anguished faint. This went on for days until Doc Perkins mixed a powder of phenobarbital with water to render her unconscious for the duration of the funeral. In the parlor, Emma Lee's body lay in the pine coffin Beasley had assembled. She was dressed in her favorite Sunday frock, her body resting on a bed of rose petals that Donny's wife Cora had pulled from her own garden. The coffin was carried to the church graveyard, and Beasley watched as they lowered his daughter into the ground. Even after everyone had gone, Beasley stood staring at the grave. Tears stung his eyes as anger swelled in his chest, his fists clenched so tightly his fingernails pierced his skin.

The Piney General Store provided supplies to the community and served as a meeting place for the Piney Men's Association, a group of like-minded neighbors who gathered to discuss policies for the growing town. Since the County Seat had yet to appoint a Sheriff, the men leaned toward the most outspoken member for guidance, that member being Beasley Taggart.

A week after Emma Lee's funeral, Beasley joined the men in the back of the general store. "My baby is in the ground, and its time the killers were brought to justice," he said.

"You know who done it?" asked Buford Barnes, the owner of the general store.

"There's a plantation next to Dead Man's Alley," replied Beasley.

"Plenty of Nigger boys work that farm," added Buford.

"It had to be a Nigger, maybe more than one," said Donny, nodding his head with certainty.

"They musta drug her in that place; ain't no way any girl would go in Dead Man's Alley all alone," offered Buford.

"I told ya'll that Niggers were dangerous when they started settling in Piney," Beasley argued, "But no one wanted to listen to what I had to say, and now, my daughter's dead. What the hell ya'll plan to do about it?"

Deliberation among the men spurred Doc Perkins, the town physician, to speak up. "Not sure what they done, but Gus Porter got some Niggers locked up in his barn. Let's start with them."

The morning held a chill in the air for those who got out of bed early to witness justice for little Emma Lee. Under an ash-colored sky, Beasley Taggart and members of the Men's Association stood silent amid a bank of placid oak trees. Three Negroes had been lynched. A woman in the crowd cried out when she recognized one of the bodies as a child. A little colored boy hung alongside the two men. His small body swayed more than the others. The ropes, taut with strain, had bloated their faces into hideous purple masks with eyes bulging out of the sockets, lips blackened, their tongues lagging from their mouths. The wind played tag with the bodies twisting them on the ropes and swinging them back and forth like grisly tree ornaments.

"That's a child!" the woman screamed. She stumbled away from the trees and vomited into the dirt. Her husband guided her away from the sickening display. Angered by the woman's cries, Beasley climbed into the back of his truck and stood up shouting at the onlookers. "Emma Lee was a kid, too! My girl was thirteen years old. Me and my wife will never see her grow up and get married. In fact, my wife is so broken she don't get out of bed no more. Niggers have torn my family apart. And you!" he yelled, his angry eyes found the woman and his accusing finger pointed her out, "You cry for a Nigger? Do you have a daughter?" he asked. Then he spat at her.

"If so, how do you, or any of you with girls," he scanned the crowd, "plan to keep them from being raped and murdered by savages? Don't think what happened to my family can't happen to yours, not as long as Niggers live in Piney!"

Beasley's words hit deep, inciting fear and rage. The crowd surged forward, surrounding Beasley's truck. Voices rose up in anger and fists pumped the air. With rifles held high overhead, the people screamed revenge for Emma Lee. Then, somebody shouted, "Beasley, what should we do?"

Beasley snatched up a lantern holding it in the air. "Burn," he said, "Let's burn them out of our town!"

That night, the citizens of Piney had little Emma Lee on their minds when they followed her father to the Negro section of town. Once there, they raided homes and ran through the streets like crazed lunatics. Unrestrained by the lack of law enforcement, they grabbed anything they could use as weapons, beating Negroes to the ground with sticks and rocks. Beasley's men used gasoline to ignite intense fires, incinerating Negro homes and property and sending flames leaping into the night sky, illuminating the darkness like a meteor shower. Terrified Negroes ran in fear for their lives as the fires tore through their homes, devouring the wooden shacks with blistering greed. The violence and vandalism went on for the rest of the night as Negroes hid in the fields watching their homes explode into flames and sending their meager possessions up in smoke.

The morning sunrise exposed the festering remains of Negro property as white residents picked their way past the burned down shacks. Along with daylight, the rising sun brought a stagnant heat wave that increased the torridity of the fire to sweltering. The acrid stench of gas and charred wood was caustic, and those who ventured out covered their faces with rags, but even so, the falling ash stuck to their clammy skin like a flaky rash.

As the white residents returned home, Beasley Taggart and the Men's Association remained behind to oversee the departure of the Negroes. They watched as the Blacks crept out of hiding, packing what little they could find onto the backs of mules.

Beasley leaned out the window of his truck and yelled, "ya'll got until sun down to get outta Piney. I wouldn't dally if I was you." His face was void of emotion as he sat back holding his rifle on his lap.

"They got a long walk ahead of them," remarked Donny, who, seated next to Beasley, cradled his own rifle.

The terrified Negro citizens grabbed up whatever they could find and took to the road, hushing their crying children and tugging the reins of stubborn mules, all the while watching the sky in fear of the deadline Beasley had set.

"Where we gonna go?" cried Tandy, a housemaid whose husband, Booker, had a nasty burn from the fire. Tandy ripped the hem of her petticoat into strips and wrapped Booker's burned skin—he winced in pain. Along with the other Negroes, the two had hidden in the field and watched as the house Booker built for them burned to the ground.

"We jus gotta git outta the county," Booker said, "Den we can think on what to do."

"C'mon now, finish up quick," he urged, as Tandy wrapped the strip around his arm. "Put the chirren in the wagon and let's go!"

The procession began, as dozens of Negroes walked for miles in rancid heat and wet-rag humidity, past the farms and the plantations where they worked. An ill-boding cloud of dust dredged under their feet and they walked the entire way shrouded in a dingy fog. Beasley and his men took to their trucks, riding alongside the Negroes, guns cocked and ready for anyone attempting to turn back. That day, as Negroes exited the town of Piney, in Forsyth County, Georgia, Beasley Taggart settled a score for his father.

In the months that followed, the officials in Cumming approved funding for a jail to be constructed in Piney, and soon after that, a Sheriff was appointed for the town. The Sheriff, Joe Fuller, Jr. was born and raised in Atlanta, Georgia, and boasted about being related to a famous Confederate General. It only took one slug of whiskey to get him babbling on about his distinguished kin without ever naming the man, much to the chagrin of his listeners.

As the Sheriff settled in, Beasley requested a meeting to introduce the Men's Association. It took a few days before Sheriff Joe could find time, as he was in the midst of building a house for his pregnant wife. The house was located on the outskirts of town, and Sheriff Joe had little opportunity to come to the jailhouse for anything but official business.

But soon enough, a day and time was agreed upon, and Beasley and eight members of the Association arrived at the jail. They were impressed by the solid structure of the building and the Sheriff's personal office with a sturdy oak desk and matching swivel chair. The men were also treated to a tour of the four new jail cells. Sheriff Joe didn't have enough chairs for everyone, so most of them stood against the wall.

Beasley Taggart stepped forward and explained to Sheriff Joe that Nigger savages had murdered his daughter Emma Lee.

The Sheriff removed his hat, saying, "I humbly offer my condolences, Mr. Taggart. I can't even pretend to know the ache that must live in your heart at the loss of your baby girl."

Beasley was touched by his kind words, and the unexpected gesture of sympathy caused him to lose his train of thought. Everyone waited while Beasley composed himself before continuing.

"Gus Porter had three Nigger boys locked up in his barn," said Beasley.

"For what?" asked the Sheriff.

"Stealing," said Gus. "Caught them red handed with two of my chickens."

"For all we know, one of them coulda killed Emma," added Donny Anderson from the back of the room.

"That's right," said Beasley. "Theft and murder—that calls for lynching."

All of the men nodded in agreement.

Sheriff Joe sat back in his chair, his arms crossed, his face taut with observation. A tall man, he was not accustomed to having his legs under a desk so he sat with his limbs stretched out, boots crossed at the ankle.

"So, let me get this straight. After you lynched the three Negros, ya'll decided to burn down the shacks of the rest, and run 'em out of Piney."

"Yes sir; that's right," said Gus.

"It was the only way to keep our women and children safe," added Donny.

"I'm not in favor of men taking it upon themselves to act as the law," said the Sheriff. "However, being that Piney had no official law at the time of this horrendous crime against a white child, I think we can overlook the actions taken here."

Beasley nodded at that decision and decided right then and there that Sheriff Joe was a perfect fit for the town.

The Sheriff, however, was not done talking. He stood up reaching his full 6'2" height; his steely blue eyes scanned the faces of the men. Beasley Taggart was silent, and as he waited to hear what else Sheriff Joe had to say, he looked the man over. The Sheriff was taller than any man in the room, his face was ruddy from the sun, and he had a high forehead. Bristly eyebrows crawled above his eyes and a horseshoe mustache added to his sober proclivity.

The Sheriff walked around to the front of his desk. His tan uniform was starched and ironed, and his badge gleamed on his shirt pocket. He pushed some papers aside, and sat on the corner of his desk.

"Ya'll done run out your own workers."

He waited for the rumbling in the room to die down, and with his eyes pinned on the faces in the room, said, "On my way in, I seen farms with crops sitting idly in the hot sun. Ya'll know we in the midst of summer dog days, I hope ya'll got enough men to haul everything in before them crops turn to dust."

"We can hire workers from Cumming, can't we?" Beasley asked, looking around at the men.

Thomas Hughes, who owned a cotton farm, was sitting down but quickly got to his feet.

"Them pickers cost a pretty penny as it is, and when they know our Niggers are gone, they gonna raise the prices even higher."

"Didn't nobody think of that when you ran them Negros outta town?" Sheriff Joe cleared something in his throat and hocked it into a tin cup.

"So let's see—ya'll don't want Negros in your town, but ya'll still need the labor." He paused, letting his conclusion settle.

"Have you ever consider using the Sunset Rule?" he suggested.

"The what?" asked Gus.

Tom Hughes piped up, "I heard of that rule. Niggers can work in town during day hours, but they gotta get out before the sun goes down."

"Is that a real law?" asked Donny.

Sheriff Joe stood up, he hitched his pants up on his waist, saying, "Truth is—there ain't nothing in the law saying it can't be done, and a lot of small towns are keeping Negros from settling down by using the Sunset Rule."

There was a sudden sense of expectation about the upcoming harvest, and the level of discussion in the room rose to a lively banter.

"Ya'll need to chew on that for a spell; see if it suits you. I gotta get back to my wife, so I'll let you boys handle it from here," the Sheriff said.

As the men filed out of the jail, each one shook the Sheriff's hand. The last to leave was Beasley Taggart who said, "I appreciate your good advice, Sheriff."

The Sheriff placed a hand on Beasley's shoulder, "I know it pains you, Mr. Taggart, but we gotta get the Negros back if this town is gonna survive and grow."

"I understand," said Taggart. "At least, now we can keep Niggers from living in Piney permanent."

"I'll tell you what," added Sheriff Joe, "From what I can see, the Men's Association is a good group of civic-minded citizens. I'll let ya'll be in charge of making sure Negros follow the new rule."

Beasley was hard-pressed not to break into a grin; instead, he kept his respectability, saying, "I'm sure the members will be agreeable to seeing that justice is served."

The Sheriff stuck out his hand, saying, "I'll do whatever's necessary to keep the town safe. It's the least I can do for your little girl."

Beasley gripped his hand in a firm handshake.

In less than a month after meeting with Sheriff Joe, the farmers traveled outside the county, picking up Negro workers and bringing them back by the wagonload. The workers were distributed among all of the farmers, and soon crops were being harvested and loaded into wagons. The farmers decided that the Negroes should arrive by 5:00 a.m. and work until 4:00 p.m., giving them plenty of time to leave Piney before sunset.

However, it wasn't long before the workers found themselves burdened with work that held them past the deadline. Jonah, an older Negro man who had worked at the Woodson farm before the fire, spoke up for the workers. "Excuse me, Mr. Woodson suh, the sun is moving down quick and we shoulda been gone before now."

Woodson barely looked at Jonah; his eyes scanned his field of cotton plants. "Ya'll just get that last row of cotton in," he said, with uncaring eyes, "You can go after that."

The sun had already set as Jonah, and four Negro men stepped cautiously through the field. If they walked on the road, they would be seen in Piney after dark.

"Ya'll follow me," said Jonah, "Stay low and keep quiet."

As they crept along through the brush, they came upon a post with a sign nailed to it. The men stopped and looked over at Jonah, the only one of them that could read.

"What it say Jonah?" asked the youngest, a boy of fourteen, named Corn.

Jonah read the uneven scrawl.

"Nigger don't let the sun set on you in Forsyth County."

He looked back at the nervous faces behind him, "It means we gotta keep moving if we wanna stay alive."

"We should go through the Hillard farm," said Corn, "It's quicker."

"No," said Jonah, "We need to stay together keep in the bushes."

"Jonah's right," said Burroughs, a long-time picker. "We need to stay low."

"Ya'll too slow, I'm going through Hillard's," said Corn, and before Jonah could stop him, he took off in another direction.

"That boy's head is hard as a dang rock!" Jonah bristled.

The next day, the men arrived for work at 5:00 a.m. and Jonah looked around for Corn. "Where's the boy?" he asked.

"He ain't never made it home last night," said Burroughs, with a dismal shake of his head.

Chapter 2

1965

Eleven-year-old Vicki Taggart sat on her bed; the collar of her cotton nightgown wet with tears. Her sobs fell in stilted hiccups as she pulled her knees into a tight embrace. Her bottom lip trembled, and she wanted so badly to cry out, but her hand covered her mouth, holding her misery at bay. The whimpers that escaped through her fingers provided some relief, but Mama could hear a mosquito pissing on a cotton ball, so she clamped her free hand on top of the other one. She sniffed back her tears, wiped her nose with the back of her hand and looked out her bedroom window. Sunlight warmed the room; it was going to be another hot day. She could see the cornfield from where she sat the burly stalks standing tall and still like gatekeepers.

Vicki stared in horror at the blood in her underwear. Mama had told her that one day she would get a monthly visitor, but she hadn't said it would be blood coming from between her legs and an awful pain in her stomach. Mama was never very good at explaining things, so she had asked her friend Mattie Campbell about it. Mattie had three older sisters and was more than happy to fill Vicki in on what to expect.

"It's so nasty. Blood is gonna pour out of your pee-hole for five days every month."

"You're such a liar," said Vicki.

"Just wait," said Mattie with anxious glee. "You'll see."

Vicki had to admit that Mattie didn't lie. She went to her dresser and removed a clean pair of underwear and then went into the bathroom. A wad of toilet paper stuffed between her legs would have to make do until she told Mama, whose reaction would probably raise the dead. Vicki worried that Mama would tell Big Daddy and then Baby Mitch would find out. Her face flushed with humiliation at the thought of her brother's grinning face. Oh, God! Who else would Mama tell? The mailman, the lady she chatted with at Piggly Wiggly?

"My daughter just got her monthly on."

That settled it; she would keep this from Mama for as long as possible.

But that wasn't as easy as Vicki thought it would be. At the breakfast table, Vicki was miserable. A dull ache throbbed against her forehead, and she was certain there was a tiny mule kicking against her insides.

Her oatmeal had stiffened and sat cold in the bowl.

"Ain't you gonna eat?"

"I don't feel good."

Mama's hand caressed her daughter's forehead.

"You ain't hot. What hurts?"

"My stomach."

"Hold on, I'll get some aspirin." Mama's slippers flapped against her dry heels as she hurried from the kitchen.

"Ow." The mule kicked harder this time. "Mama!"

The slippers flapped again and Mama was back holding a pair of panties with a dark red stain.

"Oh no, Mama," Vicki winced, and hid her face.

"You got your cycle on; no wonder you ailing. Lord, I knew this day would come," Mama said, slippers flapping as she paced the kitchen floor. "I got my cycle at the same age, but I hoped you would be older. Now, you gotta go through this for the rest of your life. And boys, oh Lord the boys—your body can make a baby now."

Her slippers flapped nervously all around the kitchen as she opened the cupboard searching for aspirin.

"Did they teach you anything in school about your cycle?"

Ugh, cycle. Vicki already hated the word.

Mama gripped the back of Vicki's chair her eyes big and worried. "Well, did they?"

"Oh, Mama, stop!" Vicki blurted, holding her aching stomach.

"Here, take these," Mama said, dropping two aspirin in Vicki's hand." She set a glass of water on the table and watched Vicki swallow the pills.

"Now, go in the bathroom and look under the sink. Behind the bag of Epsom salt, there's a king-size box of Kotex pads," Mama said.

Mama fished around in the kitchen drawer and then handed Vicki two safety pins. "Use these to fasten a pad in your underwear."

"Oh, God!" Vicki groaned, and rolled her eyes to the ceiling.

"Don't use the Lord's name in vain. This is His punishment to women for the sin that Eve did to Adam in that Garden."

"Yes, ma'am."

"This will happen every month. It's a curse we have to suffer with."

"Yes, ma'am."

Vicki took the safety pins and went to the bathroom.

It was a less than a minute before Mama's voice seeped through a crack in the door. "You okay in there?"

"Yes, Mama."

When Vicki returned to the table, Mama sat a cup in front of her.

"Here, drink this tea. It's got lemon and some cinnamon and mint leaf. That will help relax those cramps."

Vicki sipped the hot tea and with the thick pad pinned in her underwear she felt certain she was sitting higher in her chair.

When Big Daddy snatched the screen door open, the hinges squealed like a frightened piglet. "Bertie, I'm taking Baby Mitch with me to Cumming to look at some of them pigs they got for sale."

"Pigs? What we need pigs for?"

"I didn't say I was buying. I said I was looking!"

"Okay, okay," she murmured resignedly, and turned her attention back to the sink and the pot she was scrubbing.

"We'll be back in time for the meeting tonight."

The screen door squealed again, then eased slowly on a broken hinge enough time for Vicki to jump up and slide through before it closed. She wanted to go with Big Daddy to see the pigs but not if Baby Mitch was going, so she watched them get into the truck.

"What the hell we need pigs for?" Mama mumbled, as she dried a pot and set it on the stove.

Outside, Vicki sat on the back steps. The ache in her stomach had lessened, and she adjusted the pad in her underwear. She pulled her knees up shaded her eyes from the sun and peered across acres of dried corn husks and ragged weeds. Her gaze shifted to Big Daddy's Air Streamer motorhome sitting on bricks at the far end of the property. The Georgia sun had long ago bleached the robin's egg-blue finish to stark white, and the silver trim to dull pewter. At one time, Vicki had wished she could ride far away in the motorhome, but it hadn't been moved since Vicki and Baby Mitch were little. In fact, she couldn't remember ever riding in it, even though Mama said she did. Now, it was only used for Big Daddy's special meetings and Vicki wasn't allowed inside. That didn't bother her; she avoided the strange cylinder-shaped vehicle. It was creepy—like a tomb.

That night, Mama tucked Vicki into bed. "Girl, this room is a mess," she said, plucking clothes from the floor and stuffing them into the drawer.

"Mama, don't touch my stuff!"

But Mama paid Vicki no mind as she moved things around on the dresser making it neat, when a sudden thought occurred, she paused, and still holding one of Vicki's shirts, she searched her daughter's face.

"What's going on between you and your brother?"

"Nothing," Vicki lied.

"Brother and sister don't need to be bickering."

"We ain't bickering," Vicki said. Her innocent tone was enough to send Mama back to tidying the room.

Vicki glanced at her mother from behind an Archie comic book and was annoyed when she saw her opening and closing drawers. Her eyes crawled over Mama's drab appearance. She was wearing her everyday housedress; the sunflowers had faded into large white splotches on a dingy blue background. Her slippers were a Christmas gift Mama got for Big Daddy. He never wore them, so she did. It didn't matter they were a size too big and sent her sliding and flapping up and down the hallway. At least Vicki knew when she was coming. Mama always wore her dark hair twisted up and held in place with bobby pins; gray strands peppered her forehead and temples. When she was little, Vicki recalled hearing Mama laugh but the disappointing years and a mouth full of rotten teeth muted even a smile.

There was no way that Vicki would tell Mama the truth because she wouldn't believe it. The truth was that Baby Mitch had been bothering her. At first he talked dirty talk, but soon after he tried to touch her privates. When she shouted for Mama, he would dash out the room like a cat running from a water hose. Vicki knew that Baby Mitch was crazy. She saw it in his eyes, eyes deader than the road kill Mama made her sweep out of the driveway.

She recalled the time they were sitting on the porch steps, when all of a sudden, he blurted, "You my girl!" He had put his arm around her shoulder like they were sweethearts and said, "One day we gonna run away together and get married."

"Brothers and sisters don't get married, dummy."

"They do in Egypt. I seen it one time in a book."

"Shut up and move away from me. You stink!"

"See this?" he nodded at a bulge next to his zipper. "I got the hot's for you." His lips made a kissy sound.

"Ew!" she shoved him hard. "Get away from me!"

His laugh was a pig's snort as he stumbled off the steps, nearly falling over. "You should've seen your face."

"If you bother me again, I'm telling Big Daddy. I ain't playing, fool!"

Baby Mitch's pants flapped like flags around his skinny legs when he ran to the Air Streamer. His gleeful braying cracked the evening calm until he pulled the metal door of the trailer shut, sealing himself inside.

Even though Vicki never told Mama about Baby Mitch, she did tell her friend Mattie Campbell who was in her class at Piney Elementary. Mattie took Vicki to her house to see her three older sisters. In a back bedroom that Mattie shared with fourteen-year-old Kitty, the girls huddled and spoke in whispers. "Your brother is a nasty dog," said Kitty.

"What should she do?" asked Mattie.

"He's gonna come after her again; they always do," added fifteen-year-old Gladys.

The oldest sister Evelyn, who was seventeen, sat on the bed. One leg pulled up, she leaned against her knee, painting her toenails. Her attention was razor focused on her big toe as she carefully painted the nail with bright red polish. Evelyn never once looked up from her task when she said, "All she has to do is jerk her knee into his balls."

The girls all looked at each other wide-eyed; with shock, their cheeks flushed. Kitty laughed first and then a giggle fit struck and they all fell to the floor rolling around with childish laughter. It was quickly decided Evelyn's plan would solve Vicki's problem.

That same night, Vicki took a bath and climbed into bed. Mama had dropped an unexpected chore on her and she found herself raking and weeding the front lawn all afternoon. It was a hot and sweaty job and she was glad to finally relax in bed. Not long after she had clicked off her lamplight, she heard her door creak and she closed her eyes and pretended to be asleep. Baby Mitch was as sneaky as a weasel. He crept up to her bed and pounced on top of her pressing his hand so hard against her mouth she had tasted the dirt and grease that lived in his skin. Vicki bit down on one of his fingers and at the same time jerked her knee up as hard as she could into his balls. "Fuck!" he yelped, and rolled onto the floor.

Leaning over her bed she whispered, "Go ahead and scream, idiot. Wake Mama and Big Daddy, so they can catch you in here holding your balls."

"You little bitch."

"Stay outta my room and keep your dirty thoughts away from me." She watched him crawl out on all fours. After that, Baby Mitch hardly spoke to his sister, and when he did there was nothing dirty in their conversations. Vicki was glad that she had gone to the Campbell sisters, who had given her some real good advice.

Now, as she lay in bed watching Mama fussing around her room, Vicki assured herself that her lie was necessary. No sense telling her something that would upset her. Vicki lay on her back, her hands clamped behind her head, waiting for Mama to leave. Soon enough, she was done straightening up and now she stood over the bed and pressed her palm against Vicki's forehead. Vicki leaned away. "I'm okay!"

"You're not hot. Just take an aspirin if you feel any aching down there." Vicki rolled her eyes and let out an exasperated breath.

"Okay now," Mama said, looking around the room at her handiwork. "Call me if you need anything."

Her slippers flapped to the door.

Vicki sighed with relief and pulled the cover over her head, but then, she asked, "Where's Big Daddy?"

"Still getting them pigs, I suppose. Go to sleep; he'll be back soon," she said, pulling the door closed behind her.

Vicki listened to the sound of Mama's slippers and then the hallway light went out.

Outside, the full moon shimmered and illuminated the field behind Vicki's house. Its gleaming spotlight penetrated her window and brightened her bedroom. Vicki peered overhead at the moon and tried to imagine it had a face. Soon, she grew tired and settled back on her pillow staring at the pink rosebuds on the curtains until they grew smaller and she could no longer keep her eyes open.

Baby Mitch sat in a chair staring at Vicki through large doll eyes. She viciously kicked him between the legs, but he couldn't scream because he had no mouth. Pimply white skin took up the space under his nose. Vicki's fingernails were long and razor-sharp. She clawed at his eyeballs popping them from their sockets. She threw the eyeballs through the screen door and watched as a herd of cats fought over them.

"Stop!"

Vicki's eyes jerked open. The room was dark, but a white light glowed on her dresser, lighting up the Kewpie doll she'd won at the fair and gliding over a jar of pennies. The light sailed around the wall and up to the ceiling, where it hovered liked a flying saucer and then it was gone.

She sat up and threw the covers back, climbed out of bed, and went to the window. Another bright light was shining on the Air Streamer. She squinted through sleepy eyes at sheets sailing around the yard. Had Mama's sheets come off the line? Her heartbeat picked up as the thought of ghosts brought her fully awake. Her eyes widened as she clutched the grainy rosebud curtains and slid down the wall onto the floor, where she sat shaking, too terrified to move an inch.

Then, suddenly, she heard Big Daddy's gravelly voice call out.

"Stop! You going too far over, fool!"

Car doors slammed, and there were other voices.

"Don't they see the ghosts?"

Vicki turned around and got to her knees. Her fingers gripped the windowsill, and she pulled herself up to eye-level.

It was the headlights from a truck that shone in her window.

"What the hell?" she muttered, and then she saw legs walking under the sheets. It wasn't Halloween; she never missed Halloween. No, this was something else.

Big Daddy barked orders, but she didn't know which sheet he was under. Other voices were laughing and saying things she didn't understand.

"Get them out!"

The sheets moved to the rear of one of the trucks and let the tailgate down. She could see a pair of feet and a body was hauled out. Vicki had seen dead animals on the road and even a dead deer in the yard one time. She peeked through the curtain; she had never seen a dead man before.

A rope was wrapped around a Negro man's neck. His eyes bulged from his head in a fixed stare. Now Vicki squeezed her own eyes tight to block the dead man's face. She didn't want that in her dreams. The second body was a colored man, too. He didn't have a rope, but the hole in his chest oozed blood. She listened closely as the men argued.

"Shit; this Nigger done got blood all in my truck!"

"Shut up and get him out."

The men pulled both bodies from the truck.

"Get them in the field."

Two of the men hoisted one of the bodies and carried it toward the cornfield.

"I ain't doing the digging this time; it's your turn."

"Yeah, yeah."

"You got the shovel?"

"Aw, shit!"

"Go get the shovel outta the truck, dummy!"

All of a sudden, the man holding the shoulders of the dead man tripped, and the Negro's head hit the ground and cracked like a watermelon.

"Damn it, fool; now look what you did!"

"It's alright. He don't feel nothing no more. Besides," the man fussed and snatched his sheet off, "I can't work with this on, it's too damn hot!"

"You ain't supposed to take that off when we doing official work."

"Ain't nobody out here but us, and I can't dig wearing this thing."

"Mitch, can we take this stuff off now? It's too fucking hot!"

"Yeah, go ahead, we about done." Big Daddy pulled his own sheet off.

From the window, Vicki watched as the men all pulled the sheets over their heads. She recognized Buford Barnes from the general store, and Cecil Miller, the Fire Marshal. Tate Jones and his son Robert were there, along with two other men she didn't know. Then, she saw Baby Mitch, standing next to Big Daddy, grinning like he'd just found the prize in a Cracker Jack box.

"Idiot."

Vicki watched for a few more minutes as the men lugged the bodies into the cornfield; then, she climbed back in bed and pulled the covers up around her neck.

"I wonder if Big Daddy got them pigs," she muttered.

When Mr. Crawley's rooster Rusty crowed, Vicki's eyes popped open and she sat up.

"Good morning, Rusty," she stretched her arms with a satisfied moan and looked over at her window. Memories of last night rushed back as she recalled the light shining in her room, the men wearing sheets, and the dead Negroes. When Rusty crowed again, she smelled bacon grease. Mama was making breakfast.

Vicki left her bed and looked out the window. The daylight provided a much different scene. The cornhusks glistened with dew and blackbirds glided on the morning breeze. No ghostly sheets and no dead bodies; only Big Daddy's pickup parked in the usual spot next to the Air Streamer. However, she knew what she'd seen last night wasn't a dream. There were plenty of boot prints to prove it.

An abrupt burst of water splattered the window scaring her, and she jumped back hearing Baby Mitch's taunting laughter. He was using the hose to wash the bloodstains.

Vicki had plenty of chores to do that day, and she was glad to have things to focus on. After breakfast, she sat at the kitchen table popping string beans while Mama fluttered around the kitchen like a mother hen.

"Be sure to pop them beans close to the ends."

"Yes, ma'am."

"How's your stomach feel?"

"Fine."

"When you change that pad, wrap it up tight and put it in the trash pail outside, you hear me?"

Vicki rolled her eyes up to the ceiling. "Yes, ma'am."

The screen door creaked and Baby Mitch came loping in. He was covered with sweat, his pale white skin blotchy with sunburn.

"Mama, Big Daddy wants to know where's the rake."

"He lent it to Clement last week. I told him not to do it. Clement don't never bring nothing back."

Baby Mitch grinned down at his sister then plucked a string bean from the bowl and popped it into his mouth.

"Get your filthy hands outta that bowl, boy!" Mama scolded.

Baby Mitch laughed and pushed through the screen door. "Okay, I'll tell him." The door cracked shut behind him.

Mama turned the fire down under the pot and hurried to the door.

"Will ya'll be back for supper?"

"I guess so." Baby Mitch called out.

Vicki focused on the sound of the peas popping under her fingers.

"You mighty quiet, young lady," Mama said, wiping her hands on her apron. "What's on your mind?"

"You hear anything last night?"

"I was dead to the world."

"When did Big Daddy get home?"

"Late, Vicki, very late. You were fast asleep."

"Something woke me."

"What was it?"

"Some men moving around in the yard."

"You were dreaming. There wasn't no one in the yard last night."

"You sure?"

Mama bristled. "What you mean, am I sure? Don't question me."

She moved to the sink, opened a cupboard, and took down a bowl. "We're out of eggs. Take this bowl and walk over to the Crawley place and get some. Free eggs is the least he can do for us putting up with Rusty's cockadoodling every dang morning."

"Yes, ma'am."

Vicki pushed back from the table, picked up the bowl, and walked through the living room but not before taking the opportunity to sit in Big Daddy's lounge chair. It was an enormous monstrosity of cracked vinyl frayed to the cotton by Big Daddy's three hundred pounds. She pushed the head back and kicked the legs up just as Mama appeared in the room.

"Get outta that chair. I need them eggs now, not later."

Vicki frowned as she slid from the lounger and walked through the front door onto the porch. Not yet noon, the morning was already as hot as a griddle as the sun inched toward its highest peak. She shaded her eyes and jumped off the top step landing flat-footed on the ground and then walked along on the shady side of the road, avoiding fire ant mounds in the patchy grass.

She skipped her way along the road, careful not to drop the bowl until she came across a glade of majestic weeping willow trees. Their limber branches dangled over a tranquil pond, and she imagined they were women washing their hair. Hundreds of dandelions peppered the grass and her imagination took her to a place of fairies and elves. She stopped, crouched, and plucked a hearty stem. Vicki ballooned her cheeks and puffed the dandelion into tiny spores, sending her wish into the universe.

"I wish," she said, "Baby Mitch would die."

Leaving the glade behind, Vicki continued up the road. She wasn't far from the Crawley farm now. Clutching the bowl, she kicked an old can and dragged a stick along a chicken wire fence.

"Wish I coulda seen them pigs," she mumbled, coming up to a cotton plantation. Negro workers were bent over pulling balls of cotton from the stalks and tossing them into bags they dragged along the ground. Vicki recalled hearing Big Daddy say that Crawley hired Nigger day laborers to work his field.

"As long as they get out before sundown," he had said.

Vicki's foot connected with the can, sending it sailing across the ground, it landed in a trench beside the fence.

"Hi."

Startled, her eyes followed the voice over the chicken wire to a girl the same size as her. She was colored. Her skin was bronze and her face round like a pie. Her eyes were almond shaped and they lifted at the corners when she smiled. She had dark curly hair twisted into two pigtails and tied with blue ribbons. Her smile took up half her face.

"What's your name?" the girl asked.

Vicki was stunned, and at the same time taken by the girl whose smile was so friendly and her voice so sweet. While Vicki had seen many colored children playing on the farms, she had never spoken to any of them.

"I'm Ella," the girl said. "How old are you?"

Nervously, Vicki looked around. She was alone on the road. And then she stepped down into the trench and moved closer to her side of the fence. She looped her fingers in the chicken wire and leaned in, saying. "I'm Vicki. I'm eleven."

"I'm eleven, too!" Ella said, happily.

"Do you live in that big house over there?"

"Naw. That's the Crawley house. I live thataway." Vicki pointed back the way she came.

"Can you play?"

"Huh?"

"Look." Ella held up a red plastic ball. "I'll hit it over the fence and you hit it back 'til one of us misses."

Vicki placed the bowl down on the ground and backed up.

When Ella hit the ball over the fence, Vicki took off running and slapped the ball with all her might and watched as Ella bolted after it. Her arms high in the air Ella smacked the ball back over. But this time, Vicki jumped and hit the ball hard enough to send it flying past Ella's head.

"Wow, that was a good one," Ella said. You won that time."

"Can I play too?"

Vicki looked through the fence at a boy walking toward Ella. His skin was bronze like Ella's, but his hair was different; it was as red as a bowl of cherries. As he approached the fence, she caught sight of his eyes, light brown and golden. They brightened when he smiled. His eyes reminded her of the tiger's eye gemstones she saw in a book of rocks at school.

"No, this game is not for boys." Ella announced. To Vicki she said, "That's my brother, James."

"Hi!" he said as he approached the fence.

Vicki blushed when he looked through the chicken wire into her eyes.

"You live in that big house?" He asked.

"No, dummy," said Ella, pointing, "She lives back thataway."

"How old are you?"

"She's eleven, like me," Ella answered, and then turned back to Vicki, "James is twelve, 'bout to be thirteen in two weeks."

"What are ya'll doing over there?" Vicki asked.

"My Daddy and Uncle are working in the field," said Ella.

"You work in the field, too, James?"

"Naw, my Daddy won't let me, but I help them load the cotton in the truck, and they pay me a quarter."

"That's a lot," Vicki said.

"I'm gonna save ten dollars to send for a telescope I seen in the Stargazer magazine."

"He wants to be an astronaut," Ella explained.

"An astronaut?"

"They fly in space ships to outta space," James said.

"He's the smartest in his class," added Ella, "He gets all A's on his lessons, and Daddy said he's going to college."

"I never heard of a colored astronaut before."

"I'm gonna be the first Negro to fly way up in the sky through the clouds to outta space," James said proudly, pointing up.

Looping her fingers into the fence, Vicki leaned her head all the way back and looked at the sky. "I don't see nothing but them black jays way up there."

"If you wanna see the stars, you have to see them at nighttime," said James. "I can show you the Big Dipper and the Little Dipper."

"You can?"

"Yep. When I get my telescope, I'll be able see the planet Saturn, too."

"A real planet?"

"Uh-huh. Do you want to see the Dippers?"

"When?"

"Can you come back later?" he asked.

"James," Ella cautioned. "You know we gotta be gone before the sun goes down."

"The sun don't set 'til around seven-thirty or so. We can meet here at seven. I can show you the Dippers right quick before we leave."

"I'm coming, too!" Ella blurted.

James approached the fence. "So, do you want to come, Vicki?" His smile was lopsided, his eyes bright.

She looked into his tiger-eyes and thought about the gemstones.

"Uh-huh, I wanna see the Dippers."

"Okay, meet here at seven on the dot," said James.

"Bye." Ella hopped back from the fence and with the ball tucked under her arm, she ran toward the barn. But James, however, walked backward, a grin spread over his face, waving his arms back and forth over his head. Amused, Vicki chuckled and picked up the bowl. When she looked back, she could still see him and he made a funny face and did a silly dance. Vicki laughed and she wanted to make a funny face too, but then decided against it. Instead, she hurried to the Crawley farm.

Vicki sat quietly at the supper table, watching Big Daddy spear a hunk of beef with his fork. He sank the meat into a mountain of lumpy mashed potatoes and shoveled the whole thing into his mouth. Mama's slippers flapped against her dry heels as she moved back and forth across the kitchen. She set a plate of food in front of Baby Mitch.

"We gonna have to replace those shingles on the front roof tomorrow," said Big Daddy, spewing bits of chewed potatoes across the table. "I'm gonna need you to go over to Weinstein's and get some of them shingles he got for sale."

"We dealing with that Jew now?" Baby Mitch shoveled his own fork full of potatoes and meat under an awning of buckteeth.

"He sellin' 'em for a nickel apiece," Big Daddy replied. "We can get enough to mend that spot over the fireplace for less than a dollar. So yeah, we dealing with that Jew. So go'n over after supper and get what we need."

"Yes, suh."

Vicki sat quietly staring into her plate and poked at her food with her fork. She hated sitting across from Baby Mitch and looking at his stupid face.

"What's wrong, Vicki? Ain't you hungry?" asked Mama.

"Big Daddy, how do you get to be an astronaut?" Vicki said, ignoring Mama's question.

"An astronaut? Who do you know wants to be an astronaut?" Big Daddy said, not looking up from his plate.

"No one," she said. "I just wondered."

"Well, not you, that's for sure," Baby Mitch said, through a mouth full of food.

"Quit spitting, pig!" hollered Vicki.

"Will you two stop?" Mama said, adding, "An astronaut is a mighty big job. You have to be pretty smart for that job."

Baby Mitch glared at Vicki as he heaped more food onto his fork and scooped it into his mouth.

She put her fork down and propped an elbow on the table and rested her head against her palm. "I guess I don't feel that good."

Baby Mitch drained his drink glass, smacked his lips, and belched an obnoxious gas not once, but twice. The legs on his chair screeched against the linoleum when he pushed away from the table.

"Might as well go on over to see the Jew," he said, stretching his arms to the ceiling, exposing his rat-nest armpits. He stuck his pinky nail in his front tooth picking at bits of beef stew.

"I'm done here, too," Big Daddy said, as he pushed his chair back and stood.

Both men left through the kitchen door.

Mama went to the sink and filled a glass with cold water, brought it back to the table, and set it in front of Vicki. "You want an aspirin?"

"No, ma'am. I think I'm gonna sit outside."

"Sun will be going down soon."

Vicki shrugged and went out anyway. As soon as she sat down, a skinny orange cat appeared and jumped onto her lap.

"Hey there, kitty!" She rubbed her hand along its boney spine as the cat caressed her knee.

Mama cracked the door and tossed pieces of fatty stew beef onto the porch. The cat quickly abandoned Vicki's lap and pounced, gnawing fiercely at the leathery meat.

She squinted at the sky. The sun had left streaks of fiery orange in the fading daylight. "I gotta see them Dippers," she muttered.

"Mama," she called, "what time is it?"

"Almost seven," Mama replied.

"Going to Mattie's, Mama." She jumped from the porch onto the ground and hurried around the house and down the driveway.

When Vicki reached the Crawley farm, she followed the chicken wire fence, and when she saw the old can she had kicked into the weeds, she knew she was at the right spot, but James and Ella where nowhere to be seen.

The sun was not yet setting and she hoped James would get here soon so he could show her where to look with enough time for him to get back. She waited as the light slowly disappeared behind a line of evergreens that bordered Crawley's property. Their tall shadows reached across the field. As twilight took the sun's place, the crickets and katydids sprang to life in the grass, their chirping and buzzing as familiar to Vicki as her own voice. A mosquito landed on her arm. She slapped it into oblivion and then wiped away the bloody remains on her shorts.

They must have left by now she uttered, as darkness crept across the field.

"Hey!"

Vicki looked up and far in the distance saw a stick bouncing toward her. Then, she saw that the stick had arms and legs. It was James, running zigzag through the field. His lopsided grin came into view as he barreled to a stop just at the fence. He bent over, grabbing his knees, panting hard like a racehorse coming off a full-on gallop.

"You're late. Where's Ella?" Vicki asked.

"She couldn't come and I had extra chores, so we gotta hurry. They about to leave."

"Well, where are the Dippers?" Vicki asked, her hands perched on her hip gazing up at the sky.

"Hold your horses," James said, as he moved closer to the fence. "It really ain't dark enough yet to see everything, but I'll show you the spot and you can look later, okay?"

"Uh-huh."

"You see right there?" he said, pointing up. "You gotta look north to see the Big Dipper."

James looped his fingers into the chicken wire to steady his legs on the slope.

"You can just about make out the handle from here."

"Where?" Holding onto the fence she leaned back and stretched her neck looking straight up.

"See that star right there, it's kinda hard to see right now, but that's Alkaid. It's the leader because it's at the beginning of the handle."

Vicki squinted at the sky.

"The next one, dang it, you can barely see it, but it's called Mizar and it's really a double star that connects the handle to the bowl of the Dipper."

Vicki's eyes followed his pointing finger.

"Look, Vicki, look over there . . . ."

"Hey, boy!"

Vicki froze.

Seemingly out of nowhere, a horse sprinted across the field and the rider yanked the reins pulling it to a stop next to James.

"Hey, boy! What you doing out here talking to that white girl?"

The man was dressed in a dingy white shirt with black suspenders and a bowtie. He wore round spectacles and was perched on a chestnut brown horse. He was mostly bald with tufts of gray hair stuck to the sides of his head like sprouting weeds.

Vicki had seen this man before. Mr. Ernest sold cotton candy at the spring fair every year. Generous with every pink cloud his candy machine spun, he always said, *this one is gonna be bigger than your head, kiddo*. His smile was always warm, but today it wasn't.

"You sneaking 'round messing with white girls, huh, boy?"

Just as suddenly, a black stallion charged up and ground to a halt beside Mr. Ernest. The rider was a ranch hand. Silver spurs clinked on his boots and he spat a stream of tobacco at the dirt.

"What you got here, Ernest?" he said, looking down at James and then over at Vicki.

"I found these two sneaking around out here, Owen."

Owen snatched his hat from his head, waving it like a fan in front of his face. The hair on his chin was like a dried patch of white rice growing under a thick handlebar mustache stiffened by dirt and sweat. He studied James through spiritless eyes and his wormy lips spread open, revealing ragged teeth inside a jack o' lantern grin.

Vicki backed up through the brush; the prickly weeds stung her legs. Suddenly, the man named Owen said, "Hey, hold on, I seen this girl before. You Taggart's youngest?"

"Yes, suh."

"Well ain't that some shit. I wonder what your daddy would say about this. You want I should tell your daddy?"

She looked at him through dim tearful eyes, and said, "No, suh."

He looked over at James. "You got some hell of a nerve, boy; don't he, Ernest?"

"You give 'em an inch and they take a yard," added Ernest. "You know you supposed to be gone before now, dontcha, boy?"

"Yes, suh."

"You know what, Owen? I bet this boy can't even read signs. Can you read, boy?"

"Yes, suh."

"Then you know the signs say Niggers gotta get out before sunset. Ain't that right?"

"Yes, suh."

"Where you work, boy?" shouted Owen.

James pointed to the large cotton field in the distance.

"What you doing way over here for?" barked Owen.

"Ernest, you thinking what I'm thinking, is this boy trying to get with a white gal?"

Owen scowled and spat another wad, dribbling tobacco juice on his chin.

"Good thing we come up on 'em," said Ernest.

Ernest looked over at Vicki standing on the slope. "You, girl! Was this boy messing with you?"

Vicki stood in quiet desperation too panicked to speak.

"Don't be afraid. Tell me the truth!"

"I ... uh."

"Talk, girl! Ernest shouted. "Tell me now! Was he messing with you?"

With tears of panic in her eyes and her fear growing by the second, Vicki grasped for self-preservation when she answered.

"Yes!"

"I knew it!" Ernest growled, his mouth puckering with anger.

Owen reached behind his saddle and pulled out a coiled rope. He shook it loose.

"I'm feeling kindly tonight, boy, so I'm gonna give you one chance. You grateful for a chance, ain't you, boy?"

"Yes, suh," James uttered as tears of panic and fear overflowed.

A full moon lit up the field and Vicki saw that James was trembling and his voice choked with tears when he asked, "Can I go to my daddy?"

"Where's your daddy at, boy?"

With a shaky arm James pointed across the field at the barn.

"In the barn?" asked Owen.

"Yes, suh."

"Well gwan, run boy, run to your daddy!"

James stumbled forward, but the horses were blocking his way.

"I said run, Nigger!"

Terrified, he tripped and fell in the dirt as the horses sensing his fear began snorting and stomping the ground. Stumbling to his feet James ducked past them and ran. Owen pulled back on the reins of his horse steering it in the boy's direction. He whirled the rope high over his head like a rodeo cowboy and then launched it at James.

Vicki crouched low. Her eyes followed the rope as it flew easily over James' head and snapped tightly around his waist. Unable to look away, she watched as Owen yanked the rope, wrenching James from his feet. The horse whinnied with pain when Owen rammed his spurs into its flanks and it took off galloping. On it charged, kicking up clouds of dirt in its wake as it dragged James through the field.

Mr. Ernest was angry when he steered his horse around and found Vicki hiding in the bushes. "Git home, girl!" he yelled.

Vicki crept from under the brush and took off running down the road. When she paused to catch her breath, she heard the depraved voice of Owen shouting, urging his horse forward as it burst with untamed speed and the horse ran as though the devil himself was the rider. At the same time, Vicki looked up into the sky, and there, right over her head, shimmering in the darkness, was the bowl of the Big Dipper.

Chapter 3

As the summer came to a close Vicki was excited about going back to school. All she could think about was making friends and playing in the new school playground. She loved driving by the school with Big Daddy, watching the playground being assembled, and now it was finished and open. Each Saturday afternoon, precisely at one o'clock, Big Daddy left the house and wobbled over the weeds and gravel toward his truck for his weekly in-town run.

"There he goes," Mama said, peering out the kitchen window, Vicki's cue to dash out of the house, beat Big Daddy to the truck, and climb into the passenger's seat. She was nestled back into the cushion when he flung his door open.

"When did you get here, Sweet Pea?" he said, feigning surprise.

She giggled saying, "I've always been here."

Big Daddy stood at the door panting hard from the walk to the truck. His face was a rain shower of sweat as he waited for his breathing to catch up. After a slight reprieve to satisfy his pounding heart, he hooked his fist onto the steering wheel and grunted as he attempted to pull himself up into the truck. However, the barrel that was his stomach wasn't having it and he slipped back onto the ground. He heaved again and again and Vicki was fearful he would pull the steering wheel clean off, but then he adjusted his weight and gained the momentum he needed to swing his mountain-sized belly up into the driver's seat and shove it under the steering wheel.

"Yay!" Vicki cheered and clapped her hands when he mashed the seat pad flat as a pancake.

The school playground had been erected over the summer with funds raised by the Women's Garden Club. There had been pie sales, raffles, and even a fair at the Post Office courtyard. They'd also received a large donation from the Women with Southern Pride Association, which enabled them to add two slides instead of just one.

Vicki felt pure joy at the sight of the brand-spanking-new slides gleaming in the sunlight and the large swing set with six swings. She could already see herself swinging high enough to touch a cloud with her toes. Vicki saw Mr. Rastus, the colored janitor, tossing hay straw on the ground.

"What's he doing that for?"

Big Daddy glanced out the passenger window.

"Oh Rastus, he just putting hay straw down so you kids don't crack your heads on the cement."

When they arrived at the General Store, Big Daddy pulled the truck to a stop, yanked the break and cut the engine. Vicki sat back in her seat as he struggled to unhinge his gut from under the steering wheel. While waiting, she popped open the glove box and fished around until she found a pack of Wrigley's spearmint gum. She unwrapped one green-colored stick and relished in the gum's minty aroma just before folding the gum into her mouth. The silver tin foil became a Band-Aid around her finger.

"Stay in the truck," Big Daddy said, and then shoved the door with his shoulder until the latch caught.

She watched him waddle on horseshoe shaped legs to the General Store. Mama told her that Big Daddy had leg disease when he was a baby before they invented the right medicine. Vicki felt sorry for him rocking from side-to-side and she wondered if he ever got seasick.

He made it to the storefront joining the men who were obviously waiting on him. They all shook hands and some slapped him on the back. Baby Mitch was there too. At fifteen, he stood taller than the grown men in the group. His red hair stood straight up like a rooster and he was shaking and moving like a marionette under the control of a nervous puppet master. He just couldn't be still. Mama said he had ants in his pants, and Vicki had giggled at the thought of little ants running around in his dirty drawers. Ever since he had felt the force of her knee against his thing he had kept a wide breadth between them, watching her warily through angry eyes but never approaching.

The group of men filed in the front door. She could see their movements through the storefront window, arms waving, heads shaking, scowling, and some laughter. She figured they must be having a good old time with all that lively talking they were doing. She watched the men for a few minutes more until the sound of childish laughter tinkled in her ears. She looked at the playground and saw a girl pushing a little boy on the swing. It was his laughter that Vicki heard. Boredom was setting in so Vicki tented her fingers and played the church and steeple game.

Vicki's bare feet were propped up on Big Daddy's dash. She wiggled her toes in the dust particles that swirled around in the sunlight and imagined that the dust specks were tiny fairies that only kids could see. More time passed and the warm breeze rustled the white blossoms of the flowering pines. The honey-scented Magnolia bushes planted all around the property were enough to lull Vicki into an afternoon nap.

"Wake up, baby girl!"

Big Daddy stood at the driver side window. The rusty hinges creaked when he pulled the door open and Vicki sat up. He grabbed the steering wheel and locked his fingers into the side of the seat. His face turned beet red as he pulled his hippo-like torso in a direction it didn't want to go. Vicki rubbed the fairy dust from her eyes and watched as her father once again lurched up and onto the seat and then, jerking his stomach back around he shoved it underneath the steering wheel.

"Whew!"

She waited silently until he collapsed back in his seat huffing through his nostrils like a charging bull. When Big Daddy's breathing calmed, he looked over at Vicki. His forehead leaked water into his eyes.

"Don't look like you going to school this week, Sweet Pea," he said, as he slid his key into the ignition. The engine grumbled and turned over.

Suddenly fearful that this was the last she would see of the playground, Vicki burst into tears.

"Don't you start that bawling; it's for your own good. They're trying to get colored kids in your school. We got to work on stopping that," he said as he backed the truck up, nodded at a man walking past, changed gears, and drove down the road.

The old truck lurched past the playground, and Vicki, crying loudly now, watched it disappear in the rear window.

"It won't be long, Sweet Pea. They ain't gonna keep it closed long. We got say in this town, you can believe that."

Chapter 4

On what was supposed to have been the first day of school, a sizable protest was held in the town of Piney. Big Daddy, one of the organizers, brought Vicki with him to the demonstration.

"We got rights," he told her, "And we aim to make sure you kids are safe in this town."

"Safe from what?"

The anger that flashed in his eyes was frightening and Vicki regretted her question. She shrank away from him in fear. However, Big Daddy saw his daughter's terror and quickly changed his demeanor.

"You remember how we talked about your ancestor Emma Lee Taggart?"

"Uh huh."

"And do you remember what happen to her?"

"She was killed by Niggers."

"That's right. She was a young girl just like you when she was snatched up and taken to Dead Man's Alley by Niggers and killed in a horrible way."

"That's why we gotta fight to keep Nigger kids from going to white schools. If they do, then we'd have to allow Niggers to live in

Piney and we can't let that happen. So you gonna have to wait a little while longer for school to start, just until we get all this mess sorted."

"Yes, suh."

Big Daddy's meaty hand patted Vicki's head harder than he knew and she shirked under his touch. He climbed out of the truck while Vicki got out on her side. She stood back watching him pull a sheet over his head, but this time he didn't put the hat on.

Vicki followed Big Daddy who was joined by other men wearing sheets and she found out the sheets were called robes and the hats were called hoods. He pulled her aside, saying, "You stay back until this is done, Sweet Pea." Vicki joined a group of women and kids who were more excited about the event than she was.

All of a sudden, Vicki heard laughter and people were pointing. The object of everyone's amusement was Mr. Calvin, who was stringing up a dummy on the school crossing sign.

It's from the ladies' boutique, she heard someone say. The dummy had been dipped in black paint and a patch of sheep's wool was stuck to its head. The amused crowd traded jokes as Mr. Calvin fastened a noose around the dummy's neck and tossed it up over the sign, wrapping the ends around the pole, and pulling it tight. When the dummy was in place, a wooden board was propped next to the pole with the words, Nigger-free school zone. The crowd cheered and Mr. Calvin took a bow.

Sheriff Alton Collier, who had traveled from Cumming and was there to ensure a peaceful rally, laughed along with everyone else.

When the rally started, a man dressed in a Rebel uniform and holding a Dixie flag shouted into a megaphone, "The federal government ain't gonna tell us who our kids should go to school with! It don't matter if these are the only schools in this town. Whites should be with Whites. That's how it's been, and that's how it's always gonna be!"

Others stepped up to voice their opinions, and when one lady stated that things were changing all around the country, she was shouted down before she could say one more word. Her husband grabbed her and pulled her away before the jeers turned to violence.

Vicki stood on tippy-toe to see and then moved closer when Big Daddy made his way to the front. He walked proudly, leading a group of men wearing hoods and robes. Big Daddy raised the megaphone to his mouth, cleared his throat, and shouted into it.

"Good folks. We all gotta remember the real reason behind this protest today is not only against integration. It's because of a little Taggart girl, who years ago, was raped and mutilated not far from here by a band of black Nigger savages. Now, I know that 1931 was a long time ago, but that don't mean we forget my ancestor Emma Lee Taggart and what they done to her—my family never will." He cleared his throat and continued. We can't let these animals live among us, and we will never allow them to go to school with our children. Our brave forefathers put the Sunset Rule in place to keep Niggers from living in Piney. Now, the Government is trying to get in our business and make changes. But by sticking together," he yelled, "we can keep Piney safe for its white citizens!"

The crowd burst into cheers as the Klansmen stood in formation next to Big Daddy. A line formed and the townspeople happily pumped the hands of the men whose identities were hidden under hoods. Big Daddy was the only member who wasn't afraid to reveal his face to the crowd.

A lady holding a baby turned to Vicki. "Ain't you proud of yo' daddy?"

"Yes, ma'am," Vicki replied, beaming.

"This town sure is lucky to have Mr. Taggart and the Men's Association," the lady continued. "We can rest easy in our beds at night."

However, everyone wasn't in agreement with the Sunset Rule and the handling of Negro workers. Ned Preecher and his wife Lily owned several acres of farmland just on the other side of the Taggart cornfield. The Preechers were known to hire Negro sharecroppers to live and work on their expansive farm. These Negroes were permitted to own some of the crops they grew for Preecher, which they could sell for a profit. Preecher had continued this practice for years. According to him, he had a calling from God to help the coloreds. In truth, he paid them very little for the work they did, and he rented some of his workers out to other plantations. This practice did not sit well with Big Daddy and the Men's Association. but no action was ever taken against Preecher.

Baby Mitch sat on the open tailgate of his truck smoking a cigarette and drinking beer he had stashed in a cooler. He had purposely parked his truck away from the protest so as not to be seen by Big Daddy, who would for sure make him put on a sheet and stand out in the hot sun with the others. "No fucking way," he said to his friend Terry, who was fishing in the cooler for a beer.

"This shit is boring," he said to Terry, who had snagged a beer bottle and popped the cap off on the rim of the truck.

"What did you expect? This ain't nothing but another church social with a message about Niggers."

"That Nigger dummy that Calvin strung up was a hoot, though," snickered Baby Mitch. He chuckled and flicked his cigarette butt into the dirt. "But I got a better idea."

"Shit, Mitch, what you up to now?"

"You do know that Ned Preecher still has Niggers working and staying overnight on his property, don't ya?"

"Yeah, well, Preecher was always like that. He ain't letting nobody get in the way of his money."

"But why should he get a pass for his Niggers?"

"What you talking about doing?"

"Suppose his barn was to burn down, you think he'd get the message?"

"Oh man. I don't want no parts of that, Mitch. Leave it alone."

"I was just thinking out loud, that's all." He said, smirking. "But I wonder what Big Daddy and them other fools would think if someone really did something instead of bumping gums all the time?"

"I don't know, Mitch, that's not a call we can make."

Baby Mitch popped another cigarette on his lip and flicked his lighter against the tip it glowed red-hot when he inhaled and he sent a stream of smoke over his head.

After the protest ended and all the beer was gone, Baby Mitch left Terry behind and made his way to Silkys bar. His friend Jody was the bartender that day and had no problem serving beer to some of his underage friends. Baby Mitch liked sitting at the bar tossing back beers and talking shit with Jody. A glance through the window turned his mood sour when he spied Preecher's truck parked in front of the General Store. Preecher sat behind the wheel as two colored workers loaded the pickup with supplies.

"Well, ain't that some shit," Baby Mitch said, his anger piqued.

"What?" asked Jody, as he wiped the bar down.

"Over there," said Baby Mitch, nodding across the street, and Jody craned his neck looking out the window.

"Don't get so prickly," said Jody. "It ain't sundown yet."

"Gimme another beer."

Jody uncapped a beer bottle and set it on the counter. Baby Mitch gulped the beer and watched the men finish loading the truck. When they hopped in the back, Preecher started the engine, pulled away from the curb, and drove in the direction of his farm.

"I'm so sick of that cracker giving us all the middle finger. He's outright disrespecting my family. Who the hell does he think he is anyway?"

Jody, seeing Baby Mitch's anger flare, set another beer in front of him, adding, "that's gotta be your last one. Sheriff Collier's in town, and I don't need him coming in here talking shit about serving minors."

"Who says I'm a minor?"

"The law, stupid."

"Fuck the law," Baby Mitch said.

Jody chuckled and swirled a bar towel around the counter top until all the water spots were gone.

"You do know that Preecher has one of the biggest farms in Piney and his money built that church over on Sycamore Street."

"So?"

"So. Ain't no one gonna tell him what to do."

Baby Mitch cut his eyes at Jody, stood up, drained the beer bottle and burped.

"You leaving?"

"Yeah, I got some important business needs doing."

"Alright now, don't go getting yourself in no trouble."

"Trouble?" he said, and laughed. "What the fuck you talking about, I live for trouble."

It was dark when Baby Mitch pulled into the gas station. Inside, he bought a pack of gum, some cigarettes and paid for a container of gas. Back at the truck, he set the container on the floor behind his seat, climbed behind the wheel, and unwrapped a stick of gum and folded it into his mouth. "How you doing, baby doll?" He said to the plastic hoola doll stuck to his dash. He plucked the doll with his finger and watched it sway back and forth. "It's time to teach Preecher a lesson."

Hunkered down in the bushes outside the Preecher house, it only took a few seconds for Baby Mitch's eyesight to adjust to the nightshade, and soon he was able to see everything by the dim rays of the moon. He sighed impatiently and observed the blinking fireflies hovering above his head. A peeper since he was a kid, he easily spied on Ned and his wife Lily through the windows of their home. When Lily came outside and got into the truck, he squatted down behind the bushes. Ned hustled down the stairs and slid in behind the wheel. Ned and Lily exchanged some words and the engine started up.

It was Wednesday, the day every church-going person in Piney attended Bible study, and Ned Preecher was no exception. In fact, he and his wife taught the classes.

Baby Mitch smacked a bug that landed on his arm then scratched the spot. The later it got, the louder the crickets chirped, and he guessed they were hollering at him to get going. The odor of the gas was strong and he turned his head away from the smell. He only meant to set a small fire in the barn and he figured one gallon of gas should do the trick.

He snickered and adjusted his butt on the ground while going over the plan in his head. Once he set the barn on fire, he was certain that Preecher's Niggers would come running and put the fire out before

Preecher got back. And when he did come home and see his burned down barn, he would recognize the fire as a warning.

Baby Mitch knelt down next to the gas can grinning with anxious glee, and when he accidently snorted fumes from the can, he choked and coughed hard enough to spit. "God, that's nasty," he muttered, as he crept to the side of the barn. The horses, alerted by his presence, snorted and whinnied, and he hurriedly splashed gas against the wood frame, lit a match and tossed it. A blue flame flared and in seconds fire was traveling along the length of the barn. The fire erupted so quickly, Baby Mitch panicked.

"Shit!" he said, as the reflection of the growing flames danced in his eyes.

Baby Mitch snatched up the empty gas can and dashed to his pick-up. He looked back just as the flames reached the roof incinerating the cheap asphalt shingles in seconds. Black smoke poured from the burning structure and the stench of burning asphalt filled the air. He quickly climbed into his truck looking back for Preecher's boys to come running. "They gonna be here any minute," he told himself. But he didn't wait around to find out. He pushed the key into the ignition and turned the engine over, released the brake, and took off up the road.

However, what Baby Mitch didn't know was that until recently, Ned Preecher only had one Negro worker that lived on the farm, and by the time Minter Saul woke up, the barn was fully consumed by fire. The horses ran in panic and knocked over a blazing bale of hay that ignited the porch and caught the house on fire. The fire raged so fiercely, it lit up the sky and could be seen for miles.

Sheriff Alton Collier was still in town that night; he was having a beer at Silkys when he and the other patrons noticed the sky ablaze in the distance. Stepping into the street, they were struck by the smell of smoke, and that led them to jump in their trucks and head out in direction of the fire. When word spread that the Preecher farm was on fire, the whole town arrived and took to passing water buckets and hooking up hoses to quell the flames. By the time they got the fire under control, the house and barn were reduced to smoldering rubble. Preecher stood back with his wife Lily who wept uncontrollably in his arms.

It didn't take long to figure out who the culprit was. Baby Mitch's friends Terry and Jody were quick to remove any suspicion on them by revealing all they knew about Baby Mitch's anger at Preecher. Soon after, Sheriff Collier arrived at the Taggart house and spoke to his friend Mitch Taggart.

"Your boy done burned down Preecher's house Mitch," he said. "Do you know where he's at right now?"

Big Daddy sucked in a quick harsh breath and his jaw clenched with anger. "That damn fool," he said, tightly.

"Where's he at, Mitch?"

"Probably in the trailer out back."

Sheriff Collier walked around back to the trailer with Big Daddy, who hammered the door with his fist. "Open the door, boy!"

Baby Mitch stood in the doorway looking like a wild man, eyes bloodshot and stretched wide, hair standing up like weeds and the stench of gas and smoke seeped from his clothes.

"Let's go, son." said the Sheriff, waving Baby Mitch out of the trailer.

"Where you taking him?"

"To the County Seat. He's gotta go before Judge Barnes."

Big Daddy beckoned the Sheriff to the side. "You can take care of this for me, right?"

"No Mitch. Preecher's pressing charges."

The very next day in the Cumming Court house, Big Daddy stood next to his son in front of Judge Barnes, who just so happened to be a member of a chapter of the Men's Association in Cumming. The Judge was enraged by the boy's heinous act and didn't seem to care that Big Daddy was an associate.

"Arson, Mitch?" he barked, looking at Big Daddy.

"This is a straight case of deliberate arson. What the hell is wrong with your boy?" he yelled.

Big Daddy fumed at being spoken to so harshly by Barnes. Never before had he been admonished by anyone. He glared angrily at his son, who stood with his head down.

"The boy had too much to drink," he offered.

"That's no damn excuse to destroy property, and to this extent? You know I have to do something, Mitch. This ain't no cookie jar theft!" chided Barnes, and his eyes settled on Baby Mitch. "What do you have to say for yourself, son?"

"I didn't mean for it to go that far," he said in a low squeaky voice.

"Too far? Are you daft, boy? You think fire has a mind that can think which way it wants to go? All it does is burn every damn thing around it!"

"Uh, no, sir," he stuttered.

"Fire is a dangerous weapon! You could have kilt that family if they'd been home. You got money to pay for the damages, boy?"

"No, suh."

"You ain't got a pot to piss in or a window to throw it out, an' you destroying folks property—you really are stuck on stupid!"

"Yes, suh, er . . . I mean no, suh."

"This is a charge that carries up to five years in the State Penitentiary," said Barnes, and all the color drained from Baby Mitch's face. The Judge paused, and looked at Big Daddy, and then declared, "Eight months in County Juvenile."

He slammed the gavel down on the bench and added, "Mitch, I'm sure you'll find a way to help Preecher rebuild."

"Yes, Judge," said Big Daddy.

However, there was another outcome of the fire that night that was far more abhorrent than the loss of the Preecher property. Sheriff Alton Collier remained in Piney to file an official report on a fire so vast it devastated nearly a half-acre of land; as a result, he and Cecil Miller, the county Fire Marshal, met out on the Preecher farm to survey the damage.

"Well, let's get on with it," said Cecil Miller, a scrawny man who wore a neck brace and walked with a cane. He certainly wasn't a man who would be taken for the town Fire Marshal. More likely, he ought to have been sitting in a rocker on the porch of an old folks' home. Nevertheless, Cecil had been the Fire Marshal in Piney for more than thirty years and although physically weak, he was reliable, and more importantly, he was loyal to all things Klan.

Sheriff Collier followed Cecil to the still-smoldering rubble only a few yards away from the main house. Cecil stepped through a doorframe, which was the only thing left standing of what was once a thirty-five-foot by twenty-foot wood shack. The fire had scorched the doorframe and everything beyond, and the walls were reduced to ash that crumbled at the slightest touch. Wisps of smoke from still smoldering wood drifted up and dissolved into the chilly air.

The blaze had consumed everything, but Collier recognized a small teapot and a skillet among the debris. "This Preecher's storage shack?" he asked, looking around and nudging the burnt metal with the toe of his boot.

"Yeah, and he let his sharecroppers live here," said Cecil, moving farther in and stepping gingerly around shards of broken wood. His neck was hindered by the brace and his eyes darted from side-to-side. Suddenly, Cecil stopped in his tracks, his eyes pinned on an object. He poked at it with his cane. "Goddamn! Collier, over here!" he shouted.

Collier found his way over to where Cecil was standing.

"What?" he said and his eyes followed the tip of Cecil's cane to the charred remains of a body.

"Aw, shit! What the fuck?" exclaimed Collier.

"Looks like we got a body here," added Cecil.

"No shit, Cecil!"

Collier shook his head, snatched his hat off and wiped his sweaty forehead on his arm. "That fucking Baby Mitch done gone and kilt somebody."

"I best get Mitch down here so we can figure out what to do with this," said Cecil.

The following day, Big Daddy left early to meet the Police Chief and the Fire Marshal at the Preecher farm. His truck bounced along Macland Road to Eagle Leaf Road, where he came to a stop.

"Eagle Leaf," he muttered, and shook his head with disgust. Chicken Alley had been the name of this road ever since he'd been a boy, until the county decided to butt in with official names and road signs. "Assholes," he muttered.

When he turned onto Eagle Leaf, the pungent stench left by the fire irritated his nostrils, and he sneezed a few times and his eyes watered. He sneezed again and wiped his nose with a rag he took from the glove box. Big Daddy stayed on Eagle Leaf until it dead-ended at the Preecher property.

The property was closed off with chicken wire, but the gate stood open and Big Daddy drove straight through. The old truck lurched and bounced over gravel and uneven road, shaking him around in his seat.

"Shit," he said, thinking about his transmission. Just ahead, he could see the damage. The barn, house, and a shed, were all reduced to rubble. "Damn it, Baby Mitch," he muttered as he pulled up next to the Sheriff's truck. He thought for a moment about the bones they found, it was probably one of Preecher's Niggers; who else could it be? He decided not to ponder on it; he really didn't give a damn one way or the other.

He spied Sheriff Collier and Cecil Miller standing in front of Phil Gagnon's bulldozer. Phil had agreed to let them use the dozer to help clear the rubble. One of Preecher's Niggers sat at the controls. He was an old man who had worked the property for years and was probably dumb as a rag, same as all Niggers, in his opinion. He smirked, and stretched his neck against an annoying kink, then heaved a weary sigh; soon, he could put all this mess behind him.

Big Daddy shut off the ignition and pushed his truck door open. It stuck halfway and he shoved it with his foot, giving him a wider space to get out. As he lowered himself from his seat, shards of pain burned the back of his thighs. He grimaced and waited until the spasm passed.

"Mitch, you coming or what?" Collier called out.

"Yeah, yeah, keep your shirt on."

Big Daddy took another minute and then shoved the door closed. No way he would let them see his pain. He ambled over to where the men stood. All three exchanged handshakes.

"Everything good with Preecher?" asked Big Daddy. "Yeah, he's in for whatever we have to do. He even sent his boy Minter Saul to help," said Cecil, nodding at the black man sitting in the bulldozer.

"Just get it covered up," snapped Sheriff Collier, clearly aggravated at the whole thing. "I ain't got time for this shit. I need to get back to Cumming."

"You ain't the only one with things to do." Big Daddy fired back.

"Me too," added Cecil.

Minter Saul was hunkered down in the seat waiting on instructions; he watched the three white men fussing at one another, and then glanced at the bones lying in the dirt. He knew the remains weren't from the fire the boy set; these bones were much older and had most likely been in the ground for years. This information he planned to keep to himself, but once these crackers moved on with their business, he would come back and see what he could find out.

"The dozer will bury everything," Big Daddy declared with indifference. At that point, he looked up at Minter Saul, raised his arm, and motioned with a flat hand from left to right. "Everything, boy. Take it all down."

That afternoon, at Police Headquarters in Cumming, Sheriff Alton Collier filed his incident report on the fire at the Preecher farm as accidental, with no known casualties.

Minter Saul had worked the Preecher farm for some sixty years and pretty much knew every inch of the property. He trudged over uneven ground and patchy grass as he maneuvered his way down a slope. He glimpsed the old dog lifting its leg against a bush. Minter Saul didn't pay much mind to the old dog, a mangy stray that came and went as it pleased. Now, it followed closely behind him sniffing at his heels, but when he reached the plot of soil he had pushed over the bones with the dozer, the old dog was nowhere to be seen.

"Prolly off chasing squirrels."

"Here we are," he muttered, and groaning against the stiffness in his knees he knelt down. After the Sheriff and the other men left, Minter Saul had returned and dumped four large bags of fertilizer on the grave. A generous scent, earthy and sweet, a mixture of dirt and fresh manure wafted under his nose. It was a special mix he used for flower planting. In his opinion, everyone deserved a decent resting place. The white flowers he had put down were sparse, but he knew in time they would thicken and spread out real pretty on the stranger's grave.

Minter Saul didn't understand the visions he had until the day Flora, Ned's colored nanny, told him he had a gift. Some folks call it second sight, she'd said. At the time, he had no idea what that meant. But as he got older, he accepted this strangeness as part of him, like someone with a cleft lip or a jealous eye, and he always kept his ability a secret from Ned and everyone else.

Now, as he squatted next to the grave, he placed his hand on top of the mound and in seconds a vision jumped into his thoughts.

A station wagon sped across the Preecher farm, its tires gouging the soil and leaving deep furrows in its tracks. When it finally squealed to a halt, a pimply-faced boy jumped out holding a gun in his hand.

"Let's get that Nigger out," said the man as he left the drivers' seat.

They opened the rear door of the station wagon; a bloody heap lay piled on the floorboard. The boy blanched at the Negro's appearance and blurted, "His skin, it's hanging off in strings, ugh."

"Your grand-daddy's bullwhip son; it rips the skin clean off. Now, grab his legs and pull 'em 'round."

The two hauled the Negro onto the ground and stood over him. The man's face was mangled and blood oozed from between shredded strips of skin turning what was left of his face crimson. But in spite of his suffering, he stared with large menacing eyes at the white man standing over him.

"He ain't dead!" the boy squealed and backed away from the hideous sight.

"Good," said the man and spat in the dirt. "He's gonna know that killing Whites ain't tolerated in Piney."

A vicious kick from the man's boot jolted the Negro's head, and the boy pointed his gun. "You want me to shoot 'em?"

"No."

"What then?"

"We're gonna bury him alive right here and while he's breathing in dirt, he'll think about his boy's body spread out in the field for the buzzards. And no one will ever find either one of em."

When the vision passed, Minter Saul was lying outstretched on the ground, staring up at the sky. The old dog stood over him. He reached out and scratched the dog behind its ear and then pulled himself up from the ground. He still didn't know who the bones belonged to, but he did know who was responsible for burying the man, alive.

Chapter 5

1971

Seventeen-year-old Vicki Taggart and five other spiritless cheerleaders piled into the piss-yellow school bus with the Piney football team and their two miserable coaches. It would be an uncomfortable and depressing ride back home after another embarrassing defeat. A score of 0-16 sent the Villa Rica Cougars home with a win after they had smashed the Piney Bulldogs into football oblivion. The Cougars were a brutish bunch, throwing elbows at the Bulldog players whenever they could get away with it. As the Cougars climbed back into their two brand-new, sleek, air-conditioned buses they flipped the bird at the losing team. Vicki turned away when the Cougar quarterback grabbed his crotch and performed a raunchy air grind in her direction.

"Asshole."

She wasn't surprised they had lost; in fact, no one was. The Cougars were vicious players who towered over the Bulldogs like giant carnivores devouring their prey. They were better trained and had state-of-the-art athletic facilities and a brand-new stadium to practice in.

The Cougar uniforms were modeled after professional football teams. They played like cavemen and weren't satisfied until their opponents' blood fed the turf. The team also had a dozen pretty cheerleaders versus the six girls Piney had, two of whom couldn't perform lifts because Maxine Williams had a weight problem and Jennifer Lee had scoliosis. Jennifer's mother got a note from a doctor to get Jenny on the squad, which was the last thing Jenny had wanted, and it showed in her lackluster performance and poor attitude. Therefore, the Piney Princess Squad sucked big time and offered very little encouragement to the team.

Vicki sat in a window seat next to Jenny whose head was buried deep in a biology book that served as a cover for the "True Confessions" magazine she was devouring. Vicki pretended not to hear the gleeful sounds coming from behind the book. She relaxed in her seat, head settled back against the green vinyl headrest, listening to the engine cough and whine as it strained under Mr. Gus's big foot. It seemed like forever before he was finally able to coax the weary bus to a decent thirty-five miles per hour.

Vicki looked out the window at nothing but fields of wildflowers and straw-colored grass and a few cows grazing under a shady tree. This was her last game. No more boring practices and traveling to football games in this hot stinky bus and pretending to care about winning. Vicki had only joined the team to please Mama, who had never finished fifth grade, and thought being a cheerleader was the next best thing to being a movie star.

"It's all a part of being in high school," Mama had said. "Participating in stuff. Besides, you're so pretty. You should be a cheerleader."

After graduation, Vicki had decided to go to Horizon Business School in Cumming. She would take typing and shorthand, and with those skills she could easily get a job in an office and make up to six dollars an hour, but most importantly she would get out of Piney.

The bus passed another wheat field and her gaze captured the goldenrods swaying in the wind. Their bristles brushed against one another waving loosely at the passing bus. She smiled, for soon she would be traveling this same road in the truck Big Daddy had promised her after graduation.

The school bus lurched and backfired, farting a plume of black exhaust into the air. The fumes invaded the open windows and the girls pinched their noses with cries of "Ew!"

Now they passed the Crawley farm. In the distance, she saw more than a dozen colored workers bent over in the field, picking cotton. The bus was passing a long stretch of fence. Somewhere along here, she had met Ella. Ella's smooth brown skin and her wide smile flashed in Vicki's thoughts but were quickly blotted out by another face and her heart jumped when the image of Ella's brother James appeared.

With a feeling of foreboding she looked out over the pasture and envisioned the horse charging through the field, its hooves beating the ground kicking up dirt as it dragged James in its tracks. Spooked by these memories, she gasped more loudly than she realized, causing Jenny to look up from her magazine, annoyed, and ask, "What's the matter with you?"

"Nothing," she replied, and focused her eyes elsewhere.

Taking a deep breath, she quickly banished all thoughts of that awful day as the old bus shuddered and rumbled up the road.

The bus traveled another quarter mile when out of the blue Mr. Gus hit the brakes and everyone lurched forward in their seats. Just as quickly they all snapped backward with a chorus of "Whoa!" as the tires on the old bus squealed to a halt.

"Sorry, everybody," said Mr. Gus, who was not only the bus driver but also the tenth-grade gym teacher at Piney. "Dang cow!" he blurted, and everybody watched when he opened the door and got out. Laughter ensued as Mr. Gus waved his arms in a harried attempt to shoo the cow from the road. Even Mr. Matt chuckled before asking the kids to keep it down. After a few minutes the animal drifted from the road and found a plump patch of green grass to chew on and when Mr. Gus climbed back into the bus he was greeted by an unexpected round of applause. "Alright now, he said, settle down."

While Mr. Gus tried to restart the engine, Vicki felt an urge to look out the window, and there on the side of the road stood a colored boy holding a basket of eggs.

The boy's hair was copper-colored and his brown skin ruddy under the hot sun. At the sudden sight of him she felt the skin on her arms crawl as fear crept from hidden recesses into her thoughts. The window was pushed all the way up and she could see the boy clearly standing among the roadside weeds. Vicki's mind searched for reason. This was simply a kid from the cotton field selling eggs to passing cars. What other reason would he have to stand on the roadside in the heat of the day?

And then she looked at his clothes.

His shirt was just a rag that barely concealed his thin chest. His pants were covered with dried dirt and ripped all around his legs, and then she saw that he only had one leg. He was leaning down on a black stump caked with dirt and dried blood. His arms were withered brown strings, but his hands were strangely large and held onto the basket of eggs with a hard-knuckled grip.

The bus groaned and rattled as Mr. Gus fiddled with the gearshift. "Damn thing! Oh, excuse me, kids."

Vicki looked away from the window just as the engine wheezed, sputtered and jumped to life, but as the bus strained to move forward, she felt compelled to look again and when she turned her eyes back to the boy, he looked up and she saw them.

Tiger's eyes.

He looked right at her and he smiled. It was James and he was still twelve years old. A loud commotion at the front of the bus turned her attention to Mr. Gus, who was cussing and arguing with Coach Matt, and when Vicki turned back to the window, James was no longer on the side of the road. Her eyes scanned the field and saw only the Negro pickers, but no sign of James.

"I was mistaken," she muttered to herself, "It was probably another Negro boy."

"Goddammit! Fucking gear shift!" The words shook Vicki from her worries, and she glanced around at the other students. They were all snickering and laughing at Coach Gus who was hurling dirty words in every direction. His face was beet red with frustration, and as he grew angrier, he banged the steering wheel with his fist and then pumped the gas pedal as the engine squealed to catch hold.

"Take it easy, Gus," said Coach Matt, who, two seats back, was turning a sallow green with each lurch of the bus. Vicki hoped he wasn't going to throw up.

"I'm missing my brother's cookout because of this lousy heap," Gus shouted, still pumping the gas pedal and pulling on the gearshift. Vicki could hardly blame Coach Gus for being mad. Everyone knew that his brother Gator was known as the grill king of Piney. Folks came from the whole neighborhood to sink their teeth into Gator's butter-soft rack of baby-backs with his secret red-eye sauce.

Vicki too was anxious for them to get moving, her nerves were shaken after seeing the boy on the road with the egg basket. She turned her attention to Coach Matt who was trying to keep everyone calm. "Okay, you guys settle down now. Coach Gus has it under control."

But Gus was so caught up in missing his brother's cookout that he forgot his foot was mashing the gas pedal flat to the floor. So, when the engine finally roared the bus jolted and kicked into high gear, sending it rocketing forward at a speed of sixty-five. It lifted from the ground and sailed through the stop sign, smashing headfirst into the side of an oncoming Piggly Wiggly food truck. Everything inside the bus was a blur as Vicki and the other passengers lifted out of their seats with many of the kids flying through the open windows.

When Vicki opened her eyes, she was flat on her back in the middle of a beautiful field with the greenest grass she'd ever seen, and sprinkles of rain misted her skin. A flock of geese flying overhead were strangely silent and she watched as they disappeared behind the treetops. When she moved her head, a shard of pain pierced her forehead and her wrist throbbed, but she managed to sit up and look around.

James was standing directly in front of her.

"Do you want to see the Dippers now?" he asked.

He was the same as the day she'd met him with a smile as wide as a canyon and teeth as white as the stars he loved.

"Well, do you?" he repeated. He was anxious. His eyes, streaked with burnished gold—tiger's eyes.

"I can't. I'm grown up now. I'm going to business school in Cumming."

"But I'm alone."

Vicki glanced at her surroundings and found some familiarities. The chicken wire fence, the trench—this was the Crawley farm. But she had been riding in the school bus on the other side of the road. She looked to James for answers, but he was gone.

Suddenly, the air rippled and her surroundings changed, she was looking at the hindquarters of a mule. It trotted past, laden with household items. Skillets hung from its saddle clattering against one another in a silent duel. Other mules followed, their sunken chassis so weighted with chattel, their underbellies dragged the dirt.

The wagons were next. The soundless wheels churned along the parched road. One wagon moved so close to Vicki, she skirted backward to avoid being run over. Another heat ripple and there were people on the road, Negroes, traveling in solitude, wearing clothes from another time. The women trudged the road in loosely tied headscarves, the hems of their long skirts were dirty and mud-caked. The men wore work clothes and tattered straw hats. A cloud of dust hovered over their heads the grainy particles sticking to their dark skin.

Vicki looked closely at these people. Who were they?

Groups of Negro men, women, and children all walked in haste. And as they coached the mules forward, not a word passed between them. Vicki was puzzled as she got to her knees. She was only an arm's length away from the procession when she noticed the sun sinking behind the trees. She remembered the man with the black mustache. He'd had a rope. He'd lassoed James. These people were afraid. They were trying to get out before sunset. But surely, she reasoned, if they helped her they wouldn't get into trouble.

"Hello," she called out. "Would somebody please help me? My school bus crashed. It's over there," she nodded toward the crash site.

Her words seemed to hit an invisible barrier that echoed inside her ears. Onward the travelers walked, muted, with not one turn of a head, not one blink of an eye as they tramped in haunted silence.

"Why are you ignoring me?" she said, growing frustrated. "I promise; you won't get into trouble. My father is Mitch Taggart. He'll be grateful you saved me, and he'll give you extra time to leave."

Without warning, a little girl rushed forward. Tears squirted from her eyes and her mouth was twisted into an unhappy frown. A strange feeling of empathy touched Vicki's heart, and she reached for the child who was just a holler away. But instead of catching her, Vicki's hands passed through and dangled freely inside a ghostly specter. Her heart slammed inside her chest as fear rocketed her senses. She opened her mouth to scream but instead heard a child's voice saying: "He'll be grateful you saved me. And then, was this Nigger messing with you, girl?"

Vicki fainted.

The next time Vicki opened her eyes, she was in a hospital bed looking through a mask of rippling gauze. A block of steel was weighted on her forehead transmitting searing bolts of pain with every turn of her head.

"Oh, God that hurts!" she said touching what felt like a mummy hat sitting on her head. "What the hell is this thing on my head?"

"Bandages," said a voice from her bedside. "You have cuts and bruises to your scalp and a concussion."

"Everything is blurry."

"Your vision will clear little by little," added the voice.

Her eyes slid upward, searching for the source. She blinked repeatedly to see who was there.

"You were in a wreck. You banged your head pretty severely and your wrist is broken."

Gradually, an older man in a white coat came into focus. "You're my doctor?"

"I'm Dr. Rowe. You came in yesterday after a school bus accident."

The memory of the bus crash came rushing back. She sat up much too quickly and was immediately rewarded with two high-velocity bolts of pain ripping through her forehead and causing her to cringe back into the pillow. "Ow, ow!"

"Take it easy. No sudden movements."

"Can't you give me something for this pain?"

"We did, but you need to relax, Vicki."

"What happened?"

"They brought you here after the accident." Dr. Rowe removed a stethoscope from his pocket, leaned in, and pressed it against Vicki's chest.

Her eyes traveled up the front of his white coat and settled on a web of nose hairs. "Ew," she muttered.

"Excuse me?"

"Nothing. When can I go home, are my parents here?"

"Probably today. But you're going to have a whopping headache for the next couple days. You were lucky, though."

"You call this luck? My head feels like it's about to crack open and my wrist hurts really bad."

The doctor put his stethoscope in his pocket and stepped back from the bed.

"The two coaches on the bus were killed and several of your classmates have far worse injuries."

Vicki's mouth fell open and shame drained the color from her face.

"Oh my God, that's awful!"

She touched her head where the pain still throbbed and the doctor, seeing her grimace said, "I'll write a prescription for pain medicine."

"Thank you," she said, meekly.

All at once, the door sprang open and Vicki saw her parents in the doorway.

"Where's my baby girl?" Big Daddy hollered, much too loudly for a hospital. He waddled into the room, sucking up all the air and sensibility. He pushed past the doctor and went straight to his daughter.

"Big Daddy!"

Two ham-hock paws clamped her face as he pulled Vicki forward and planted a wet kiss on her bandaged forehead.

"Ow, ow, that hurts!" she squealed.

"You okay, Sweet Pea?"

"Yeah," she said, pulling his hands from her face.

"Thank you, Lord Jesus," said Mama, her hands clasped against her chest, worried eyes lifted to the ceiling.

"You look much better today," said Big Daddy. "When we seen you last night you was out cold and a broke heap. They done good fixing you up."

"They did, yes, Lord, they sure did," Mama agreed.

"You done here, Doc?"

"Yes, Mr. Taggart you can take her home."

Chapter 6

After the funerals of Coach Gus and Coach Matt, the school held a memorial service in the Piney High School gymnasium, which was attended by the entire school. John Hurley was a quarterback with the football team. He was standing near the food table with his friends, but he couldn't keep from glancing across the gym at the girl he had carried from the crash. Her name was Vicki Taggart, one of the team cheerleaders.

The impact of the crash had ejected some kids through the open windows of the bus, others had cracked bones against the seats, but Hurley was one of the lucky ones with only minor injuries, so he was able to help at the crash site. They found Vicki unconscious in a field, and Hurley carried her to his father's car. He recalled her being as light as a feather when he lifted her from the ground; her red hair was matted with blood. Once safely in the car, his father had driven Vicki and two other injured students to the hospital while he continued to help with the search.

Hurley had planned a hospital visit, but she had been released before he got the chance. Besides that, things had been hectic with work at his dad's construction company and he was late filling out his application to the Police Academy. His life was pretty busy these days, and he didn't know if it was a good idea to get into something with a girl. But there was something about Vicki Taggart that peaked his interest.

"What the fuck, Hurley? You in La-La Land again?"

Pulled back to reality by his teammate Chucky Biggers, Hurley responded, "Naw, just stuff on my mind."

"You mean stuff like Vicki Taggart, who you been staring at since we got here?"

"Shut up."

"You should go talk to her before her crazy-ass daddy shows up."

Hurley knew Mitch Taggart; everyone in Piney knew him. Vicki's father was a big, fat, loudmouth bigot who had a bad opinion about everything and everyone. Beyond that, Taggart hated Hurley's dad because John Hurley, Sr. hired Negro workers. Still, he thought, this was an opportunity he couldn't ignore. So, he walked across the gymnasium.

"Hey," Hurley said to Vicki. He felt his cheeks flush when she looked at him.

"Hey to you, too." Her eyes flashed recognition and she said, "I heard you carried me from the crash. Thank you."

Pleased that she knew he'd helped her, his smile grew broader. "I was happy to help out and I'm glad you're okay."

"I was lucky," she said, repeating the doctor's words, "But it's so sad about the coaches."

"Yeah," he agreed. "We all miss them."

He stepped closer asking, "Do you want some punch?"

"No, I'm about to go. My daddy has a meeting later."

"Already? A group of us are gonna hang out for a bit."

"I have to ride back with my parents," she frowned.

"That's a bummer."

"Yeah. But if you hadn't taken so long to come over here, we'd have more time to talk," said Vicki.

"Oh, damn! You saw me?"

"Yes, John Hurley. You've been stalking me at every Bulldog game."

"Stalking! Oh wow, now I'm embarrassed," he said, his cheeks burning.

"It's okay. I've been stalking you, too."

"I never noticed that."

"That's because I'm a lot sneakier."

Hurley laughed. "So how about we go out?"

"You mean me with you?" she teased.

"Sure, why not? I'm kinda cute." Dimples pleated each cheek when he grinned.

"Yes, you are, Hurley, but in a funny-looking kinda way."

"Oh wow, are you gonna make this hard for me?" he asked, and poked out his bottom lip.

"I would, but why make you suffer any longer?"

"That's my point!"

"I'm really not supposed to date yet, but…"

"But what?"

"I'll be eighteen in another month and I'm graduating this year, so, I give myself permission to go out with you."

"Can I call you at home?"

"Better not. Let's just meet."

"How about Saturday at six? I'll pick you up in front of the diner."

"It's a date."

Twenty minutes later, Vicki climbed into the back seat of Big Daddy's truck with a self-satisfied smile that caught Mama's attention.

"Was that John Hurley's boy I seen you talking to?"

"Uh-huh. He wants to take me out."

"You don't wanna get in with them people, honey."

"Oh, Mama!"

"Don't you 'Oh Mama' me, girl. That family ain't like us."

"Ya'll need to quit living in the past," she said, examining her fingernails.

"You need to heed me, Vicki. No good comes from messing with those Hurleys."

"Never mind all that. I have a question."

"What?"

"How long ago was it that Negroes was run outta Piney?"

"You see Negroes everywhere you look in this town."

"Working, yes, but not living here."

"Why are you asking me that?"

"I had a real strange dream about it."

"Folks usually dream about things they're involved in," said Mama turning around and eyeballing Vicki. "You ain't ever been in nothing with a colored boy, have you?"

"No, Mama, it was just a dream."

The conversation ended when Big Daddy pulled the truck door open and took some time climbing into the seat. "Okay, enough of that," he said, breathing hard. "Let's go home."

"Did you have fun, Big Daddy?" Vicki teased.

"Hell no!"

"But why not? Most of your friends were there."

"It was a memorial. Besides, they all full of shit," he said as he backed the truck out, hit the gas, and sped down the road.

Meeting Hurley in front of the diner had become a weekly routine, and the lies Vicki told were flimsy. "Going to Mattie's," she'd holler, just before the door slammed behind her.

Vicki sat in the passenger's seat of Hurley's 1962 Chevy pickup facing Smileys Fun Time Fair, which was spread out over Cumberland field, just outside of Piney.

The fair included half-a-dozen rides and several games with prizes for the winners. The only animals were some baby goats and one ornery llama with a tendency to spit. Smiley's traveled to all of the small Southern towns and arrived in Piney every year in late April.

Melted ice cream ran down the sides of her cone and dripped onto her hand. Hurley watched in amusement as she licked it clean. "I love vanilla."

"Strawberry is what turns me on," Hurley said, as he quickly finished his own cone.

"Turns you on, how?"

"After you finish that ice-cream, I'll show you," he said, and his eyebrow arched into a seductive gaze.

"You're funny."

Since the bus crash, Vicki found herself spending a lot of time with Hurley. He was easy to talk to and didn't mind listening to her dreams of getting out of Piney. He was smart, funny, and not bad to look at, with his athletic physique and brooding eyes. A healed-over cut on his upper lip only added to his Southern-boy charm.

Vicki often steered their conversation to the bus wreck, a topic she couldn't seem to get off her mind. She hadn't told anyone, but she found herself thinking about the Negro travelers from her dream, and more often than not, the boy, James. She'd even thought she'd seen him around town when she rode with Big Daddy in his truck. If a colored boy was standing in the field or walking on the road, she was certain it was James. But a closer look always revealed it wasn't him at all.

"I swear, Hurley, they were coming up the road."

"Here we go again," Hurley rolled his eyes. "Didn't you say this was a dream?"

"I know, but it seemed so real," she licked ice cream from her lips.

"You were passed out."

"Not the whole time. I was awake at first. I know I was."

"Your head was bleeding, and your wrist was broken. I was very careful when I lifted you. You didn't wake up, which was a good thing with the injuries you had."

"I know what I saw."

Changing the subject, Hurley looked at the sky. "Pretty day today."

"I know what you're doing Hurley and it won't make me stop thinking about what I saw."

"I see," he said, sighed and shook his head.

With all the ice cream gone, Vicki attacked the cone itself, crunching with the ferocity of a rabbit loose in a carrot patch.

"How old did you say you are?"

"You know I'm eighteen."

"You eat that cone like you're eight."

"I like to enjoy every bit of my ice cream, so what of it?"

"You know," he said, his voice low and spooky. "There are ghosts in Piney."

Vicki stopped in mid-chew. "What the hell are you talking about?"

"You mean to tell me you've lived in Forsyth County all your life, and you don't know about the ghosts?"

"I guess not."

"They say that the coloreds killed by the Klan years ago come back."

Unwilling to share information about Klan in her own family, Vicki hesitated, instead asking, "What do you mean, come back?"

"Some people say they've seen them wandering the fields."

"Ghosts?" Her eyes widened.

"That's right; you'll see them floating in the air with blood red eyes. He crept slowly toward her, his fingers clawed, and in a spot-on Count Dracula voice, blah, blah, I vant to suck your blood."

Vicki slapped his hands away. "That's a vampire, not a ghost."

Yeah, but you should've seen your face!" He chuckled.

"That's not funny!"

"Okay, okay, sorry," he said, snickering into his fist.

"I'm telling you. I saw a long line of ghosts walking up the road."

"I wasn't serious. It's just a made-up story Vicki."

"I saw them. I swear." She responded in earnest.

"You had a dream." He shot back, emphasizing the word dream.

"But it seemed so real."

Hurley breathed an exasperated sigh. "Why don't you ask Minter Saul?"

"Who?"

"Minter Saul. He's the colored man who inherited Ned Preecher's place. They say he saw a Negro man standing in the field one day, and when he got close, the man just up and disappeared."

"How come I never heard about this before?"

"You know my father hires Negro help; sometimes, I have lunch with them and I get to hear the stories they tell. Minter Saul has been in Piney the longest; he's worked for the Preecher family all his life. I bet he could tell you something about ghosts around here."

"I don't have anything to say to that old Nigger."

"You sound just like your daddy."

"Yup, and I ain't ashamed of it, neither. If it wasn't for us Taggarts making sure coloreds didn't move in, this town would be overrun with them."

Hurley shook his head. He leaned over and tugged Vicki's ponytail. "Vicki, sometimes, I just don't know what to do with you."

Squeals and laughter turned their attention to the Ferris wheel.

Vicki brightened, saying, "How about taking me on that?"

"Yeah, let's go have some fun," he agreed.

Two hours later, Hurley carried a large stuffed elephant on his shoulders, and Vicki's arms were filled with the small prizes he'd won for her.

"How did you get so good at playing them games?"

"Practice. I worked at a carnival when I was fifteen and learned every trick to winning."

"Lucky for me."

"Yup, lucky for you and me." He winked. Hurley chucked the elephant into the front seat, scooped the other prizes out of Vicki's arms and tossed them in next to the elephant. He reached over and slid the key into the ignition, turned it once, and the truck filled with the twang of country music.

Hurley took Vicki in his arms and planted a warm kiss on her lips, tasting cotton candy. "Mmm, sweet," he said, and nuzzled her neck.

When he opened the back door, she climbed in and pulled him in beside her. Hurley was excited. He wanted their first time together to be special. He pushed her hair back and found her lips; they were soft and tender like petals on a newly opened rose. Slowly, he kissed her, adding gentle pressure until he felt her respond. He was reminded how inexperienced she was when he kissed her eyelids, and she giggled. But when Hurley parted her lips with his tongue and inserted the tip of his, she tensed.

"It's okay," he whispered, "Relax."

She rested her head on his shoulder, and he waited. When she lifted her head up, he found her lips again. More of his tongue entered, and she slowly moved her own tongue against his in a perfect waltz. He felt himself grow excited against her thigh, and his lips touched her ear.

"Do you want to?"

"Uh-huh."

"Are you sure?"

"I'm sure."

His hand was under her skirt and he slid her panties down. Her body went rigid, so he stopped and looked into her eyes. "You okay?"

"I think so," she said, not sounding as confident as usual.

"You sure you want to do this? I don't want you to, unless you want to."

"I want to. But this is my first time."

"I kinda thought so," he said, and kissed her again.

"Will it hurt?"

"I can make it easier."

"How?"

"Just trust me."

Hurley slid down her body and lifted up her skirt; his lips brushed her stomach, and his tongue found her belly button and twirled slowly around the pink curl. She giggled.

"Your ticklish spot, duly noted." And then he slid further down.

Vicki's eyes followed a moth trapped in the rear window. It batted against the glass in a frenzy to escape, she wanted to help the poor thing, but then she saw the top of Hurley's head between her legs and the moth was on its own. At first, she felt embarrassed to be so exposed in front of him and squeezed her eyes tight to block out the vision of him down there. But when his lips fondled her pubic hair, her eyes fluttered open with surprise and she moaned softly when his tongue parted her tender folds. With the tip of his tongue he explored her hidden pearl sliding his tongue over and around it until he felt it stiffen and pulse. The sensation teased her body with arousal, a feeling so sensual Vicki could barely stand it and she twisted her hips to get away, but Hurley's strong hands gripped her firmly in place as his tongue continued to seduce her throbbing jewel. When a final surge sent delicious waves of heat churning throughout her core, Vicki's body rocked with bliss, rendering her breathless, and her body bucked uncontrollably under his hands, until she collapsed, as limp as a rag doll.

Hurley looked up, "Was that okay?" he asked and inched his way into her arms.

Several minutes had passed when Hurley moved his hips against the softness of her body. Vicki opened her eyes and saw him sliding down between her legs. A fleshy softness touched her, and she imagined a kitten lapping milk from a bowl. Hurley was enjoying her like he did the strawberry cone, and once more a salacious surge aroused her. This time, he was on top and she felt him grow hard against her leg and she arched her body toward him. He touched her delicately until he found her opening. He pushed slowly and was immediately rewarded by a warm sticky tightness that felt so erotic he could barely hold back, and when he felt a hindrance, he pushed against it until he heard Vicki gasp and he paused asking, "Am I hurting you?"

A soft moan was her only answer, and after a few seconds, he was moving his hips in a steady rhythm, his manhood swelling with pleasure and when he reached a crescendo that jolted his body like an electric shock, he collapsed on top of her, his face buried in the delicate curve of her shoulder.

The singer on the radio contributed a slow country ballad, crooning, almost yodeling about a long-lost love, and sending a foreboding message that Hurley failed to hear.

Chapter 7

For many folks living in rural communities, owning a pickup was a necessary commodity. Trucks also served as a hideaway on wheels, a private space to talk, listen to music, and to make out. Curled up together in the back seat of his truck, Vicki was the happiest she'd ever been. With Hurley, she could forget about her fears and feel safe from the daunting memories that haunted her. He was becoming the one good thing that had come out of the bus wreck. She was in love with him and love always made things better. She watched him closely, his dark brown eyes were mischievous and his constant need of a haircut matched his lighthearted demeanor. The radio was on, and they listened as a couple bantered back and forth in a funny skit that amused Hurley. Her head rested in his lap and she watched his Adam's apple bob up and down when he laughed at the corny jokes. The sun had already departed, and Vicki looked out the window at silver gems twinkling on a black marquee.

"You know anything about stars?"

"Like what?"

"I don't know; anything."

"I remember from school the Milky Way, the Big Dipper, and the Little Dipper."

"You know about the Dippers?" she asked, suddenly wondering if he knew as much as James did. She was a little disappointed when he replied, "Not really."

"I knew this boy once, who knew all about the stars."

"Who?"

"Oh, just someone I met one time."

He smiled, rubbed her knee, and stuck the tip of his tongue into her ear.

She squirmed and hit him on the shoulder. "He wanted to be an astronaut."

"An astronaut?"

"Yeah, but he died."

"Oh, that's too bad."

"He never would have been an astronaut, no way."

"Why?"

"He was colored."

A singer with a throaty baritone sang about catching his girl with another man and Hurley patted Vicki's knee in time to the beat.

Without warning, Vicki bolted upright. Her arm went around Hurley's neck as she clutched him in a headlock. "You ain't going nowhere, mister," she said, tightening her grip.

Hurley wrested her arm loose and held her close. He nuzzled her neck. "Girl, you trying to choke me to death?"

"I don't want you to leave," she said, through pouty lips.

"I don't wanna leave either, but my training starts in two days, and I have to drive to Albany tonight in order to check in tomorrow."

"Why can't you train in Cumming?"

"Vicki, I've already explained all this. They don't have any more openings in that class. I gotta go to Albany before it's too late."

"I don't see why you want to be in the police department anyway."

"Because it's a good career for me. I can move up, maybe be a Sheriff one day. Maybe, right here in Piney."

"Piney has Sheriff Collier."

"Collier is based in Cumming. Piney hasn't had it's own Sheriff in a long time the town is growing and needs its own Sheriff to handle crime."

"Niggers trying to move in; that's the only crime I see."

"Vicki, you need to stop saying things like that. Negroes have a right to live anywhere they want."

"Big Daddy would shoot you dead if he heard you say that."

"He's crazy."

"That's just why he don't like you, Hurley, and if you keep thinking thataway he ain't never gonna agree for us to get married."

"Get married? Who said anything about marriage?"

Vicki sat up. "Have we been seeing each other all the time, or am I hallucinating?"

"No, of course not."

"Ain't we boyfriend and girlfriend?"

"Well, yeah, I guess."

"You guess?"

"Look, Vicki. I have a lot to do before I'm ready to settle down."

"I gave you my virginity!" she said, her face flushed with anger.

"But that don't mean we're getting married any time soon."

"So, we are gonna get married?" she asked hopefully.

"Well, I don't know. Aren't you going to business school?"

"Yes, that's my plan, but that don't stop us from getting married, too."

"Vicki, I think you're getting too far ahead of yourself. We've only been dating a few months."

"Six!" she said.

"Okay, six months. That's still not a lot of time."

Vicki's eyes filled with tears and her bottom lip quivered. These were emotions Hurley had never witnessed before.

"C'mon now, Vicki; don't cry. Right now, you're going to take that secretary course and get the job you've been talking about, and I'm going to the Police Academy," he said, cupping her chin with two strong fingers and turning her tear-streaked face in his direction. "When I'm finished and working, we can talk about this again and see how we both feel."

Vicki pushed his hand away and turned toward the window, saying, "Take me home."

The windows inside the house were dark when Hurley pulled up and cut the engine. Only the chirps of the night crawlers welcomed her home.

They sat next to each other in awkward silence. "Looks like everyone's asleep," he said, breaking the silence. "How are you getting in?"

"Around the back. I have a key."

"You want me to walk you back there?"

"No." She avoided his eyes.

"Listen," he said, touching her shoulder, "You go ahead to business school and finish those classes so you can get that job you want."

"I know."

Hurley leaned over for a kiss, but Vicki scooted across the seat and opened the door. Before he could say anything more, she was out of the truck and walking around the front of it. Spotlighted by the headlights, she offered no cheery goodbye. She continued down the path leading to the back of the house.

Hurley slumped in the seat, unsure of what to do. Should he go after her? But, knowing Vicki, it could turn into an argument and wake up the whole house. This was not the send-off he'd envisioned. Of course, he had thought of marrying Vicki, one day. But it wasn't something he wanted to have on his plate right now.

His career was what he wanted to focus on; everything else would have to come later. However, watching her go, he could only imagine how bad she felt.

He shook his head and hit the steering wheel with his fist; he should have explained things better. He watched her wade through the knee-high weeds that squired her along the path.

As Vicki stepped through the grass, the crickets, emboldened by her presence, warbled nosily. On she walked, never once looking back before disappearing behind the house. Hurley sat for a moment, hoping she would come back. When she didn't he flashed his headlights before pulling away.

Vicki stood with her back pressed against the house, tears in her eyes as she watched his lights flash and the truck make its way up the road.

"Asshole," she muttered, and tiptoed up the back steps. Standing in the darkness, she fished around in her bag for her key as her thoughts replayed their conversation in the truck. "Damn it. Where is it?"

She glanced at the sky. Gray clouds passed in front of the moon casting dark shadows across the yard. Her fingers touched the grooves of her key and closed around the keychain. She lifted the key to the lock when something more daunting than the nightshade pulled her under its coarse wing. So sudden was the attack that any utterance she attempted was petrified in place. Fear snatched her senses, flooding her body with adrenaline. She wanted to run, but she was caught in something terrifying. Her heart thundered like the hooves of a galloping steed.

Vicki clawed at the rough material scratching her face. The smell of dirt and something more pungent enveloped her, and she recognized the sickly-sweet stench of manure. Her head was in a manure bag. She flailed against a steel barrier, and quickly realized that it wasn't a barrier and it wasn't steel. It was a man's arm—she could smell his sweat. She was locked in his ironclad grip.

He was large, his body so firm and tight she felt no malleable surface. Her assailant held her hands tightly behind her back. She feared being suffocated and huffed against the bag, sucking it into her mouth. The scratchy fabric stuck to her tongue, coating it with particles of dung. Her attempts to cough the fabric out only pulled it further in, and she knew she was in danger of choking. She breathed deeply through her nose, ingesting the pungency of animal waste.

His arm was a clenched muscle on her neck, and he pulled her backward down the steps. Her shoes popped off when her heels hit the ground, and then he dragged her through gravel, the sharp rocks cutting into her feet. One of her hands became free and she punched at his arm, but when she felt his grip tighten, she stopped. He pulled her up some steps; they were metal, short, only four of them. It was familiar. He was taking her into the Air Streamer.

Inside the trailer, he threw Vicki to the floor. She heard the door close, the lock turn. She heard him breathing, moving around, opening and closing drawers and cabinets. Then she heard the familiar sound of tape being stretched out. He wrapped it around her neck fastening the burlap sack on her head. She heard more rummaging, and then he cut a small hole in the bag near her mouth. He wanted her to breathe. She took that opportunity to speak to him.

"I'm Mitch Taggart's daughter, Vicki Taggart."

Without a word, he wrapped more tape around her wrists and pulled her arms up over her head and fastened them to the leg of something behind her, a table or a desk.

"Please, let me go, please."

Next, he cut her dress away from her body, ripped her bra off, and then did the same with her underwear. She lay naked on the hard wood floor. She heard him removing his clothes—his pants rustling and the loud clink of a belt buckle being unfastened, and then a thud as the heavy buckle hit the floor. She cried out and pulled her knees up and tried to twist away, but he pinned her down, pushing her legs apart with his own knee. She could feel the thickness and the hairiness of his knee as it moved in between her legs and rubbed against her thighs. He groped her until he found what he wanted. When she screamed, he slapped her face so hard she tasted blood on her lips. Then, she went to someplace dark.

When coolness touched her face and water dripped into her mouth; she moved her head and pushed her tongue out for more. A trickle of water ran down her neck and her eyes shot open, but all she saw was the stitched pattern of the burlap. The odor of dung was still there, but that was okay; it meant she was alive.

When she groaned in pain, she heard him move toward her. She felt him kneel down beside her, and then he applied something wet and slippery between her legs. It smelled like something from a garage; lube grease. In minutes he was assaulting her again. She needed to vomit, but she held it back, afraid she would choke. She coughed and some of the vomit came up, and she spit it out into the bag. For the next several hours Vicki was abused and after a while, she no longer felt any pain. She was numb.

The burlap sack was now a sodden mask stuck to her face by sweat and vomit. He was very still, but she knew he was right next to her; she could smell his stench and hear his ragged breathing. The waiting was as frightening as the assault and she whimpered like a sad puppy. That was when she heard him chuckle, a silly, girly giggle, high and childish. He was enjoying the show.

Angered, she bucked like a wild horse under the restraints and spat, "Fuck you!"

Vicki kicked out with both feet and to her surprise she struck him. She heard him grunt and fall backward. The effort took her breath away, and she heaved desperately for air inside the sack. Finding one more ounce of courage, she screamed for help and then something hard slammed into her face.

Chapter 8

Vicki awoke to searing pain hammering her forehead. Her jaw ached; it was unhinged, hanging limp like a broken puppet, blood and saliva dribbling from her open mouth. But when she moved, she found that one of her arms was free. He had untied one of her hands. She sat very still listening to the silence in the room. Not yet certain she was alone; she nevertheless took a chance and untied her other hand. Quickly, she unraveled the tape around her neck and pulled the burlap sack from her head.

At last free from that horrid hood, she took a deep breath inhaling the foul odor of sweat and vomit that clogged the room. Suddenly, she began to cough and gag on the scum coating her tongue and throat. Her eyes watered and her throat constricted and she retched up mucus and blood. Her nude body trembled with fear, and even while she felt he was gone, she was compelled to look under the desk and peer into the dark corners of the trailer. She saw the Klan robes hanging from hooks, dozens of them. Big Daddy's gun rack was on another wall, every gun gleaming and war ready. Staring down at her from the wall was a portrait of the Confederate General Nathan Bedford Forrest, the first Grand Wizard of the Klan. The General's dead eyes had witnessed everything.

She looked down at her body. Her thighs were smeared with lube grease and covered with bruises and bodily fluid. Between her legs, the skin was scraped raw. She started to cry but then stopped, realizing she had to get out of there.

Leaning on the desk for support, Vicki propped her arm on a chair and pulled herself up. Her rear end was sticky; she had been lying in her own blood. When she moved her legs, spasms of pain shot through her private parts and her thighs burned like fire when they touched. She was as weak as a baby as she limped over to the window and looked out.

She saw her shoes lying at the bottom of the steps near the house. Tears jumped into her eyes, but she fought them back and limped around, looking for her clothes. Her dress was on the floor under the desk; she couldn't reach it, so she grabbed a gun from the rack and fished it out with the barrel. She leaned against the wall and stepped into her dress and then staggered to the door and opened it. The sun was coming up behind the cornfield; she shivered in the crisp morning air. She had been with her rapist for the entire night.

The cornfield was still; it would not come alive for another hour or so.

With legs as flaccid as strands of soggy spaghetti, Vicki stepped onto the top step. She gripped the handrail and slowly placed one foot down but was quickly challenged by a shard of pain that shot through her pelvis, convulsing her body like a calf under a cattle prod. Vicki cried out, but quickly pulled the sound back in, scanning the yard through giant orbs of fear. She bit down on her lip so hard that blood oozed. She took the next three steps down, suffering silently through each agonizing movement.

Then, she was standing on the ground. Two blackbirds cawed from the roof of the Air Streamer and a fat bumblebee hovered over her head then sped off. She staggered slowly past the clothesline. Another blackbird sat on the rope watching her, squawking loudly as she passed. Vicki hobbled to the back steps and carefully lowered herself down. She looked back at the Air Streamer. As a kid, she'd always wanted to go inside, but Mama said it was full of Big Daddy's business and not for children. Over the years, she had lost her desire to enter the trailer. To her, it had become an aged leviathan from another time. Now, the trailer door stood open. A trail of blood followed her down the steps and across the yard. Thick clots of blood clung to the back of her legs like leeches.

Her broken jaw sagged and leaked bloody saliva; any attempt to speak caused searing pain. She stood and leaned against the railing, tears streaming down her face. Unable to make it up the stairs, she looked around and there next to the stairs was the rake Big Daddy had gotten back from Clement. She lifted it by the handle, and with all the strength she had left, hit the back door again and again until she heard the lock turn and Mama was there, rushing down the steps.

"Breathe, Vicki! Breathe!" The nurse was a small woman wearing a crisp white uniform and a pair of white shoes. Her nurse's hat looked like a bird with outstretched wings. "It's okay, Vicki, just breathe into this paper bag."

But Vicki slapped the bag away, gripped the armchair with white knuckles and threw up on the nurse's shoes.

"Oh, goodness!"

In her present state, the bright lights, scattered voices, and the medicinal essence of the emergency room appeared like another vicious assault, and her eyes darted the room like a caught animal. She cringed at every touch and rejected the nurses and their attempts to treat her.

"Where does it hurt, hon?"

They had to know she couldn't answer. Her jaw was hanging down and slung to the right side of her face. Drool leaked over her bottom lip onto her hospital gown.

Vicki squinted at the nurse through black-and-blue-rimmed eyes so swollen she could barely see. The only sound she could make was a grunt in answer to the nurse's questions.

"Are you still nauseated, hon?" A second nurse placed a plastic basin on Vicki's lap only moments before her stomach heaved another round.

Under the harsh lights of the exam room, Vicki peered at the doctor through hazy vision. Her adrenaline pumping a mile a minute she resisted all attempts to help her, batting at the medical staff with clenched fists until a sedative pulled her into unconscious sleep.

Directly outside the emergency room, Big Daddy could hear his daughter's misery. "What the fuck is going on in there?" he shouted at Mama.

Mama trembled, her face void of color, her hands clasped against her breast. "Oh God, please!" she begged, looking up at the ceiling.

"Woman, go sit yourself down somewhere!"

Mama found a seat on a plastic waiting chair. He waddled behind her and stood, hands planted on his wide hips. "Just tell me again what happened."

"I heard banging on the back door. I found her on the back steps beaten and bloody."

"What did she say?"

"She couldn't talk, just pointed at the trailer."

"What the hell was she doing in my trailer? You give her a key?"

"No, Mitchell. She ain't never showed no interest in that trailer, not since she was little."

"She probably went in there to screw that Hurley kid."

"What?"

"You the only stupid one, Bertie. She's been sneaking around with him for months." Big Daddy turned away from his wife and paced the floor.

All of a sudden the doors to the Emergency Room swung open and a doctor appeared. With a cigarette fixed to the corner of his mouth he leafed through several pages of notes on a clipboard. He squinted against the fumes curling into his eyes then took a deep drag, cigarette smoke sailed over his curved lips into the waiting room.

"Excuse me, Mr. and Mrs. Taggart? Your daughter—Vicki, is it? Well, Vicki has been raped."

Mama stood up so quickly the plastic chair tipped over and Big Daddy grabbed her arm before she fell over with it. "Hold on now!" he hollered, when he caught her. Turning back to the doctor he said, "Who are you and what the hell are you talking about?"

"I'm Dr. Berger, the ER physician. Mr. Taggart, I'm sorry to tell you that she's been extremely violated. We're going to perform surgery to close the ruptures, in her, well … her vagina."

Mama screamed as Big Daddy held on to her.

"Also, her jaw is broken. That will have to be wired."

"Oh, my God!" cried, Mama.

Dr. Berger, suddenly sympathetic, said, "Uh, sir, I can come back if your wife needs your attention."

Angered by Dr. Berger's seemingly casual demeanor Big Daddy's mouth clenched in anger and he said, "Yeah, you come back." And he watched Dr. Berger push through the Emergency Room doors. He heaved an exasperated sigh and guided Mama to a chair, then pulled another one next to her and sat down. "Okay, just calm yourself down."

"I knew something was bound to happen!"

"What in the world are you going on about?"

Mama wrung her hands. She looked at Big Daddy through tears of panic and worry. "Our family, the things we done. It's the law of retribution. An eye for an eye."

Big Daddy ignored Mama's foretelling, saying, "Bertie, will you shut the hell up with that mess!

"Her injuries are so bad, Mitch. She'll never get over this."

"I'll call Alton Collier; see what he can find out."

Mama took Big Daddy's hand, even when he tried to pull away she gripped it. "Mitch, did you do anything?"

Her eyes searched his face for an inkling of untruth.

"What the hell you talking about?"

"I know how you are Mitch!"

Angered, he snatched his hand away and pointed at the Emergency Room. "Do you think I would let someone do that to my daughter?"

Mama paused and rethinking her suspicion she said, "No, no; of course, you wouldn't."

"Then don't ask me bullshit like that!"

He got up and paced in front of her, the wheels in his head turning. "We need to keep this as quiet as possible. Folks don't need to know Taggart business."

Mama looked him in the eye, something she rarely did. "This is the start of something bad, Mitch. I can feel it in my bones."

Chapter 9

Big Daddy sat on the porch sipping from a tall glass of lemonade the old rocker creaked under his weight as he rocked back and forth while awaiting the arrival of Sheriff Alton Collier. It had been over four months since Vicki was attacked, and Big Daddy wanted to know where Collier was with the investigation.

He raised his glass to his lips and emptied it in one thirsty gulp, burped and called his wife. "Bertie!"

The screen door creaked and Mama stepped out, wiping her hands on a towel.

"What we eating?"

"I got stewed chicken and potatoes with green beans."

"Enough for Collier?"

"If he stays; he don't never stay."

"What's Vicki doing?"

"In her room, resting."

"Collier will be here around noon. He's gonna have questions."

"She ain't up to it. I can tell you that right now."

"It's been past four months; her jaw is healed. She has to talk to Collier!"

"She's ashamed, Mitch." Mama lifted the pitcher of lemonade. "You want some more?"

He nodded. She refilled his glass and set the pitcher down.

"All right, let me know if he's stayin'." The screen door clapped shut behind her.

By noontime, the Georgia sun had transfused a steady stream of heat, sending all living things scurrying to find shelter. Big Daddy was no different. He had avoided stepping down from the shady porch; instead, he rocked while fanning himself with an old farming leaflet. He looked out at the flag pole and the rebel flag hanging as limp as a rag, its colors faded beyond recognition. He studied the flag from his rocker and shook his head. He would get a new flag once all this mess with Vicki was over and done. He hoped that would be soon. He was ready to get on with things. He rocked, fanned, and sipped his lemonade as he peered up the road for the dust cloud that would be Collier's truck.

Just then, he caught movement out of the corner of his eye and his head turned back to the flagpole. A mangy dog sniffed the dirt around the pole.

"Where the hell did you come from?"

The dog was mud-gray with black spots. The torso was elongated, the ribs visible through its skin, the same as the wild dogs he'd seen in the backwoods. These dogs usually hunted in packs and stayed far away from people, so why the hell was this one in his yard?

There was something strange about it. The face, for one thing, wasn't so much a dog's face. The snout was oddly long and rounded at the end, he didn't see a nose, and the ears stood up like it was listening to something. The eyes were set low like two pieces of black coal stuck right into the skin. He knew it was looking at him, even as it proceeded to lift its leg and urinate all over the flagpole. That was when Big Daddy pulled himself out of his chair and wobbled to the edge of the porch.

"Get the hell away from there!"

The dog continued urinating, its eyes glued to Big Daddy.

"You son of a bitch!"

He grabbed the railing for support and hobbled down the steps, threatening the dog with each painful movement, but the animal never flinched. Its ears flickered as it continued to empty its bladder in a seemingly endless stream of urine. When Big Daddy's feet hit the ground and he lumbered forward, the animal lowered its leg and sat down.

"Damn you!" he yelled, shaking a fist.

Big Daddy struggled against his weight, but managed to bend over and snag a rock. He pitched it at the dog. The rock landed at the animal's feet. It looked at the rock and back at Big Daddy.

"Get on away from here!"

Big Daddy lurched from side-to-side as he moved closer, but then he stopped suddenly, when he realized this was a wild animal and he had no gun.

"Bertie!"

He looked back at the screen door. He had put too much distance between himself and the house for her to hear him. When he turned back, the dog hadn't moved.

"Git!"

He raised his arms over his head shaking them wildly hoping to scare the animal off. But instead of running away the dog turned around and squatted and defecated against the flagpole. The stench slapped him in the face burning his nostrils and his eyes watered.

When he wiped his eyes with his hands they were bloody. Shocked, he blurted, "What the hell is this?" Confused and scared he blinked several times, and when he looked at his hands again there was no blood.

"What the hell . . . ."

Fear shook him so violently he staggered back and almost fell down. That was when the dog began to wail. The sound was feral, a broken aria of beastly origins that pierced his eardrums. So high was the pitch that it sent Big Daddy into convulsions. His body lunged forward and then snapped backward, and warm piss trickled down his leg. He fell to his knees. Drool dribbled over his lips and he vomited on the ground.

"Stop!" he shouted through ragged breath, and was relieved when the entire ungodly episode ceased.

There was another sound, different, and he looked up. It was the blaring of a horn. A dust cloud lifted along the road. It was Alton Collier's truck. Big Daddy stumbled to his feet and planting them firmly on the ground he stood straight up. His chest heaved. He was sweating like a pig. He felt sick. His ears were clogged, so he jiggled a finger and popped them open, and looked around the yard. The animal was nowhere to be seen.

Sheriff Collier's truck rumbled across the gravel driveway and stopped next to the patchy grass. Big Daddy prepared himself to greet Collier but then looked down at himself. "Shit." His pants were wet. He hoped Collier wouldn't notice that he had pissed himself. Resignedly, he stepped toward the truck just as the Sheriff climbed out and walked across the front lawn.

"What the hell you doing standing out in this heat, Mitch?" He snatched a handkerchief from his pocket and mopped his brow with it. He'd already rolled the sleeves of his white shirt up around his elbows and removed his tie. "You okay? You look a bit peaked."

"Did you see that dog?"

"What dog?"

"A spotted gray dog with a long snout."

"Where?"

"It was in my yard, pissing on the pole. Wouldn't leave."

"Why didn't you shoot it?"

"I didn't have my gun with me, or I would have."

"I guess it run off, then."

Warily, Big Daddy scanned the yard.

"Yeah."

The Sheriff looked around too, then shrugged and walked up to the house. "You got something cold to drink?"

"Up on the porch."

Big Daddy followed Collier back to the porch. He didn't want to think too hard on what he saw. It had just been an old, mangy dog. All that other stuff that happened was most likely his diabetes acting up. Made him imagine more than was real. Just a wild dog—that was all it was. He would tell Bertie to set him up to see the Doc.

Still, he would come back out tomorrow to see what damage the thing had done, and this time, he would bring his gun.

Sheriff Collier sat in Big Daddy's rocker, picked up the full glass of lemonade, and took a big gulp; he licked his lips and said, "So, she don't have no idea who done it?"

Big Daddy sat in Mama's smaller rocker; the straw pinched his meaty thighs.

"She said, he got her from behind, put a sack over her head, and drug her into the Air Streamer."

Sheriff Collier rocked back and forth, taking small sips of lemonade. "I gotta tell you, Mitch, it's been over four months now that she ain't cooperated with the investigation we got going."

"She don't wanna talk about it."

"I can understand that, but with no new leads, the investigation has stalled."

"Gotta be somebody who knows my property, knows about the trailer back there," added Mitch. "What about the Men's Association, some of them are new in town?"

"They all got alibi's tighter than a tick's asshole."

"What about that Hurley kid she was messing with?" Big Daddy filled his glass from the pitcher.

"He was on his way to the Police Academy in Albany," said Collier, "Was stopped for gas at the time it happened. The gas attendant can attest to it."

The Sheriff leaned back in his rocker and took one more sip before setting the glass on the table.

"Something else I need to tell you, Mitch."

"What's that?"

"I resigned as Sheriff. Moving up north with the family."

Big Daddy's face darkened and his eyes flashed resentment. "What in hell, Collier?"

"Missy has family in New Jersey, and she wants to be near her mother now that she's up in years. He leaned forward in the rocker. I put in for a position with the Jersey City Police Department and I got an offer letter. I took the job."

"I don't believe what I'm hearing!"

"I know, but things are changing in Piney, and there's something going on, too."

"What you talking about?"

"You know how I planted a whole acre of tobacco sprigs?"

"Yeah, last spring."

"Since then, all that's come up is some kind of black stuff, thick and runny and black as tar."

"The whole field?"

"Yeah. I had Doc out to take a look because he knows a lot about planting, and he said he ain't never seen nothing like it before."

Mitch glanced at his own yard of patchy weeds, but his eyes quickly shifted to the flagpole.

"The worse thing is the smell." Collier screwed up his nose.

"Stink?"

"Like a field of shit. We can't even sit out on the porch; it's so bad."

"Did you plow over it?"

"I borrowed Nate's plow and paid his son to push a load of topsoil over it. He done that two weeks ago, which seemed to help. But then, Mitch, I swear, I was out there yesterday and that thick shit is coming through the new dirt stinking even stronger than before. Not only that, I found Bessie dead in the barn two days ago."

"Your cow?"

"I had her since she was a calf. Best durn milk cow in the county."

"What happened?"

"Don't know. She was just lying on her side, dead. Missy is so upset. She loved that cow; she weren't but a few years old."

"That's a damn shame."

"We gotta go, Mitch. I got a bad feeling."

The rocker groaned in protest when Big Daddy pitched it forward. "You're Klan, Collier, you can't run away from that."

"I ain't running. I got my beliefs, that won't change."

"I can't believe I'm hearing this bullshit," Mitch said, shaking his head.

"I got a chance to start over someplace else."

"Feels to me like you running out."

"I knew you'd feel that way, but I gotta think about my family. Listen, Mitch, I'll do whatever I can to help with finding out who hurt Vicki before I leave town," said the Sheriff, stretching his arm across the table for a handshake. "No hard feelings?"

"Fuck off, Collier," Big Daddy said, icily.

Collier withdrew his hand. "I hate you feel that way. We go way back."

"Things are bad here. We need a Sheriff like you more than ever."

"I gotta be straight with you, Mitch; the Government don't like the way the counties have been running themselves. More Sheriffs will be appointed and the laws are going to be fully enforced, especially when it comes to integration. I done a lot of things for the Klan, but a Sheriff like me has to know when to move on before it's too late."

Collier rocked forward and then stood up. He extended his hand again to Mitch. Big Daddy looked up at Collier, eyes full of disappointment, but this time shook his hand.

"I got about four weeks left. Let me know if Vicki is up to it, and I'll come out to see her before we leave town. I can pass whatever information she gives me on to the investigation team we got."

Collier trudged through the weeds on his way back to his truck. The sun beat down on top of his head searing into his bald spot and he wished he'd worn his hat. He had known Mitch wouldn't be agreeable to his leaving. He didn't feel like he was running out, as Mitch implied; he had done more than his share for the Klan. Put his own job in jeopardy to help keep Niggers out of the County. Yep, he muttered, he had no regrets, had served the Klan well.

He felt lucky that he had another chance, a new job, away from this place. Collier's musing turned to Mitch and he shook his head with disgust. The man could barely walk straight anymore and he couldn't even hold his bladder, pissed all in his trousers.

Collier climbed into his Ford pickup grimacing against the hot seat, he felt like a slab of bacon in a frying pan, he should've parked in the shade.

He looked back at the porch; Mitch was still sitting in his rocker staring straight ahead at the flagpole. Collier wasn't worried; the Klan in Forsyth County hadn't been active for years. As Sheriff, he had protected them and had been instrumental in covering up the killings of hundreds of Negroes in the county. He had done his duty. If it weren't for him and his loyalty, they would all be in jail.

"Damn seat!" He shoved a rag under his ass to block the burn.

The inside of the truck was an oven, and beads of sweat popped up on Collier's forehead. He pushed the key in, stepped on the brake, when he turned the key the engine roared and he glanced back at the porch again, this time, Mitch was gone. He probably wobbled his fat ass back into the house. Collier smiled to himself; he had so much on the Taggart family he could easily make a deal. But no, he'd rather just leave town and let sleeping dogs lie.

He huffed a sigh of relief as he pulled away from the Taggart property. He was glad that was over with; now, he could concentrate on his future. As he drove along, he glanced over at Mitch's so-called cornfield. It stretched along the road on the left the unmoving weeds stood stern and solid and it reminded him of the walls surrounding a correctional facility. Only, this was living vegetation. Insects buzzed over patches of wildflowers growing alongside withered cornhusks. The Sheriff snickered and shook his head; in all the years he had passed that lot, not once had it yielded any corn that he remembered. It had been good for only one thing, something he quickly pushed out of his mind.

When he turned his eyes back to the road he was startled, his foot slammed the break rocketing him into the steering wheel.

"Shit!" he blurted, as he jerked forward and then back against the seat. He looked through the windshield.

An animal was sitting in the middle of the road.

"What in blazes?"

It stared at him through eyes so black he couldn't make out pupils. The snout was oddly long and he couldn't tell what kind of animal it was. He rolled the window down and leaned out.

"Git!" Collier shook his fist, attempting to scare it off. "Git outta the road!"

Collier bore down on the horn. The sudden noise sent startled birds flying from the cornfield, but the animal didn't budge.

"Oh, you just gonna sit there?" he hollered. "I guess I gotta run your ass over!"

His foot touched the gas, and the truck moved slowly forward. He eased the truck closer hoping it would run off, but it sat as still as a statue.

"Goddammit!"

He was close enough now to get a good look at it, and he doubted that this was even a wild dog. For one thing, the eyes were planted like tree knots stuck to its head; it was strange and frightening to look at.

But what alarmed him most was the snout, which reminded him of a river crocodile he'd seen in a TV show. He remembered that it was found somewhere in India. Was this one of those? If so, what was it doing in Piney?

No. This can't be a croc.

This thing had the body of a dog or a hyena or some land animal. Collier hadn't felt fear until the bottom half of the snout snapped open, revealing a line of razor-sharp teeth sitting in points all along the bottom and top of its mouth. The two front teeth were longer and hung down over the bottom lip.

"What the hell?"

It stood up and lifted its head, its ears stood alert and Collier knew it was sizing him up. Fear prickled the hair on his neck and his heart thumped rapidly. He thought about what Mitch had said about a dog in his front yard, and he wondered if this was what he'd seen.

"You're not gonna move? Okay, I'll just go around you."

The Sheriff put the truck in reverse and backed up enough to go around; he pushed the gearshift into drive and drove to the right.

But suddenly, it moved over just enough to block the road.

"Shit!"

In reverse again, he backed up, then drove to the left. The animal drifted back across and sat in front of the truck.

"Fuck!" he yelled, and took a breath. "I didn't want to do this, dog, or whatever the hell you are, but it looks like you're gonna make me run you over for real."

Collier backed up several feet and now the animal was directly in front of the truck. He slammed his foot on the gas, the truck shot forward, running straight over the animal. He was jolted from his seat on impact, but quickly gained control and slowed to a stop.

He scoffed, "Ha! Now see what you made me do?"

He twisted the rearview mirror left and right, looking for a dead animal in the road, but there was nothing in the mirror. Alarmed, he rolled the window down and leaned out looking up and down the road. But it was nowhere to be seen.

"Where is it?" he exclaimed, as he rolled the window up and punched the lock down.

A sinister growl sent shivers through his body and he turned to see the animal standing in the passenger's seat beside him. It's mouth hung open and filmy strands of slime oozed down and puddled on the seat. The animal watched him through two lifeless cavities except for hundreds of small insects crawling in and out of the holes. A quick shake of its head splayed him with drool and then it mewled a low riveting cry that burned inside his ears.

"Oh, God!"

The Sheriff leaned away from the thing, and his hand fumbled over the doorsill searching for the latch, but his sweaty fingers weren't able to grasp the lock and pull it up. He wailed with panic and as he recoiled in terror and shoved his shoulder into the door in a hopeless attempt to force it open his thoughts went to his gun holstered on the back seat.

All at once, the animal evacuated its bowels in the passenger's seat and Collier gagged against the stench. It took a step closer; the snout was so large its ragged breathing lifted the hair from his brow. Collier could see the reptile tongue lashing about, he tried to turn away, but it lunged forward biting into his face. It latched onto his nose wrenching it clean off. Collier screamed and his hands flew up blocking the gaping hole while the animal chewed the soft tissue and swallowed it. It nuzzled its long snout between Collier's hands snagging his cheek and ripping it. Collier screamed as he battered and punched at the beast and tried to shove it from on top of him. But the animal had grown twice in size and he was trapped under its unyielding weight.

Collier didn't die until it bit into his jugular and his blood spurted like a broken water spigot. After that, the only sound inside the truck was the crunching of bone and gnawing of gristle as the creature proceeded to devour Sheriff Alton Collier piece by piece.

Chapter 10

The following day, Big Daddy inspected the ground around the flagpole. He looked around for animal droppings but found none; in fact, there was no sign of the ground being disturbed at all. He slung his rifle over his shoulder and touched the .45 in his belt. He knew he had seen some kind of dog, speckled with a long snout but he was puzzled there wasn't any animal shit on the ground. Big Daddy kicked a small pile of dirt with the toe of his boot and looked around the yard again. His eyes settled on Doc Jenkins's truck parked in the driveway. Doc had driven out to see Vicki and give her an exam. Four months had passed since she'd gotten out of the hospital, five since the attack and she was finally moving around the house. She had refused to talk to Collier yesterday. He couldn't force her to speak to the man; besides, Collier was leaving the county. What good would it do? He had his own suspicion about who was behind his daughter's rape and that was something he'd already dealt with. He shrugged, and continued looking around for evidence of the animal. Bertie said Vicki was talking about going to that secretary school again. He was glad the girl was coming around. It kept him from having to listen to Bertie crying and talking about sin. She was getting to be too much with that mess.

He had just turned back toward the porch when he heard it, a blood-curdling scream that sent his heart straight up to his throat. It was coming from the house. He waddled as quickly as his bent legs could carry him, hobbling up the steps as the screaming turned into long hard sobs and he heard Vicki crying out. "No, oh no, this can't be!"

"Its okay, honey; calm down." It was Bertie's voice.

The screen door screeched open and Doc Jenkins stepped out holding a glass of lemonade. His face was flushed, his mouth puckered.

"What's going on, Doc?"

"She's gonna have a baby, Mitch."

"Dammit!" Big Daddy collapsed into his rocker sinking the seat cushion. Doc Jenkins sat down in Mama's rocker.

"Can she abort it?"

"She's too far along," said Doc. "She had to know. She's five months. Probably didn't want to believe it." He shook his head.

"Tell me this, Doc; is it the rapist's baby?"

"As far as I can tell, yes. Five months is right on the nose of the attack, unless she was with someone else around that time." The doctor stood. He took one more sip and set the glass on the table.

"I gotta go, Mitch. Lots to do in town today. I'll come out again if you need me."

Doc started down the steps, stopped, and looked back. "Oh, say, I seen a truck parked up the road a ways. Looked like the Sheriff's pickup. He break down or something?"

"Not that I know."

"I didn't stop. It was just sitting on the side of the road. No one inside that I could tell."

"He was out here yesterday. I'll drive out and take a look."

Big Daddy didn't bother to go inside to see about Vicki. If she was pregnant, there wasn't nothing he could do about it. He just hoped the child wouldn't be a whore like its mother. However, he did wonder about the Hurley kid. He'd heard that he was in the Police Academy but why, in all this time, hadn't he tried to see Vicki. He pursed his lips and sent a stream of spit into the yard, muttering, "Just like I figured; Nigger lovers ain't worth shit."

Vicki was curled up hugging her pillow and watching Mama out of eyes weak from crying. Mama's hands were involved with busy work but her face revealed her worry. She had been shocked by Doc Jenkins diagnosis; a baby had been the furthest thing from her mind.

"Can I get you something to drink, honey?" Mama tried to sound cheerful, but Vicki knew when Mama was covering her pain. "I Just made a fresh pitcher of lemonade."

Doc Jenkins had delivered the news in his old-timey, disapproving demeanor, his voice casting judgment while shaking his head. "Um, young lady, I think you know; you're with child."

The doc left a list of instructions for Vicki to follow, and hurriedly packed his bag and left. As soon as the door closed, Vicki had cried and wept uncontrollably in her mother's arms. Her body depleted, she felt like a wet rag wrung dry.

"Don't fret; things will be okay," soothed Mama.

Vicki's tears had left her eyes feeling taut and dry and while she felt miserable she had no more tears left to shed. She remained quiet while looking around her room. It was the cleanest she'd ever seen it, thanks to Mama trying to help in the way she knew best. Her cheerleader uniform hung on the door and Vicki vowed to stuff it in the trashcan; in her mind that girl no longer existed. Her hand moved to her slightly protruding belly. She had ignored all the early signs, her missing periods, the vomiting, but now, her fear had been confirmed—the rapist had left a constant reminder of her torture.

To make things even worst she'd spent all those months waiting for Hurley to come to her, and in all that time, she refused to think of anything else but him. Where was he? He had to know what happened. Never had she imagined he would abandon her, but evidently, he had. Her heart ached from Hurley's betrayal, from his deliberate spurn, and now she hated him; she hated everyone and everything, especially this thing growing inside of her.

Big Daddy's pickup was sitting in the driveway. He hobbled across the weeds not bothering to tell Bertie where he was going. At the truck, he pulled the door open and sucked in his breath, summoning what strength he had to climb in. When he finally sank back into the driver's seat, he pushed his gut out of the way and turned the key.

Just like Doc said, the Sheriff's truck was on the side of the road. Big Daddy drove to a spot behind it and parked, then worked his gut loose and climbed out of his vehicle. When his feet hit the ground he winced in pain but hobbled forward looking around for any sign of the Sheriff.

"Collier!" he called out.

Big Daddy made his way to Collier's pickup and tried the door handle. It was locked. The window was filthy. He wiped it with his sleeve and peered inside. The bile that rose in his throat was so sudden; he spit up all over the door. He fell back against the side of the truck, fighting to keep his legs from buckling. His head swam and vertigo played with his balance. The pulse in his forehead pounded so hard it terrified him.

"Please, Lord, don't give me a stroke out here."

Determined not to fall over, he held on tightly to the ledge of the truck bed. If he fell to the ground, he didn't know if he could get up by himself. The gruesome sight inside the Sheriff's vehicle was stuck in his mind: pieces of torn flesh and blood everywhere, and then he saw the Sheriff's ripped shirt and his badge lying on the seat and he knew it was Collier.

Big Daddy gripped the ledge and pulled himself along the side. He had to get back to his pickup. When he reached the rear of Collier's truck, he prepared to let go. He straightened his weak legs and willed them to move in a steady path.

That's when he saw it sitting on the side of the road.

It was no more than twenty feet away, its black eyes locked on him. He was sure it was the animal from yesterday; only, now it didn't look anything like a dog. It had morphed into something more hideous. It had grown larger and coarse hair bristled along its back. The muzzle was huge, and its eyes were pitch-black holes hollowed in its head.

The animal was eating something, and its long tongue slid around each sharp tooth, lapping velvet globs of what looked like blood. Once again, Big Daddy found himself defenseless. His gun lay on the back seat of his pickup, and he was terrified as he stepped against a pounding heartbeat. His only hope was to keep moving and get to his truck. He let go of the ledge just as his frail bladder spurted and he staggered through a shower of piss. When he made it past the animal, only then did he realize he had been holding his breath. He let it out and wheezed a cluster of ragged phlegm that he spat into the dirt.

Big Daddy tugged the door open and tried to pull himself onto the seat, but his sweaty palms slipped from the steering wheel. Tears sprouted as he tried again and again to pull his girth into the truck.

"Take it easy," he whispered. "You can do this." He stopped struggling and took a few deep breaths, grabbed the steering wheel with one hand and the seat with the other, and hauled himself in. He pulled the door closed and started the engine.

That was when the animal stood up and the engine died.

A strong wind suddenly picked up, whipping the blanched cornstalks left and right, twisting them into a mini-tornado. Broken branches and husks rained down on the truck as Big Daddy tried in vain to crank the engine. Dark clouds appeared out of nowhere and he watched the day turn into night and then back into day again. Steely rain pummeled the truck so vigorously he feared that at any moment, the windshield would shatter. The onslaught seemed endless, but when the whirlwind finally ceased his watch showed only minutes had passed and when he looked out the window the animal was nowhere in sight.

His trembling hand reached for the ignition key but dropped when he saw the cornfield rustle with movement. His breath caught in his throat when a Negro man stepped out of the cornfield nude from the waist up. A noose was knotted around his neck and his head sloped to one side. His dead eyes were trained on Big Daddy, and then, without warning, his mouth fell open releasing a blizzard of horse flies that swarmed and flew straight at the windshield. Big Daddy screamed and covered his face as the flies struck, leaving pus-filled welts on the glass. When he uncovered his eyes and looked back at the cornfield the man was gone and the truck suddenly sprang to life, the engine roared and Big Daddy knew that he was being let go—for now.

When Big Daddy made it back to the house, he went straight to his bedroom and locked the door, refusing to talk to anyone. That night, Mama found herself sleeping on the sofa, and the next morning when Big Daddy still didn't come out of the room, she called Doc Jenkins.

The arrival of Doc Jenkins brought Big Daddy to the living room. He sat down on the sofa so the Doc could examine him. Mama brought out a pitcher of lemonade and two glasses. She filled one and handed it to Big Daddy; he drank it down in one thirsty gulp.

"None for me, Bertie," said the Doc.

Big Daddy was unusually quiet during the exam as the Doc pressed his stethoscope to his heart and listened for a few seconds. Doc Jenkins sat back and pulled the stethoscope from his ears saying, "So, how do you feel, Mitch?"

"I'm okay; just a bit shaky that's all."

"Your heart beat has picked up some, but that could be from stress. You got anything more than usual going on?"

"No."

"You need to come in for some blood work, and a physical."

"I'll see that he does that," Mama said.

The Doc wrapped his stethoscope around his hand and stuffed it in his bag.

"I don't know if you heard, but they found Sheriff Collier dead this morning."

"Oh, my Lord!" Mama blurted.

"Everyone's in shock about it," said Doc.

"They think a coyote got in his truck, tore him up."

"Sweet Jesus," Mama gasped with horror.

"I ain't seen Collier in a while," said Big Daddy. The lie rolled off his tongue so easily that Mama looked at him, puzzled, as did Doc Jenkins.

"Apparently, it was an animal attack, so ya'll be careful out here." The Doc stood up and Mama walked him to the door.

"He's okay Bertie. You make that appointment soon," he said, patting her shoulder, "Oh, and about Collier don't fret what Mitch says, it's all quite a shock."

After Doc Jenkins left, Mama turned back to Big Daddy. "Why did you say you didn't see the Sheriff?" she asked, picking up the glasses.

Big Daddy's eyes narrowed with anger. "Don't you ever question what I do!"

Surprised by his response, Mama nodded, and left the room.

Big Daddy never told Mama or anyone else about what he'd seen. But she knew her husband, and his behavior told her that something bad had occurred.

With each day that passed, Big Daddy became more anxious and jittery. He took to staying inside the house, moving from window to window, checking the locks. One day, when Mama opened the kitchen window for some much-needed fresh air, he nearly took her head off. "Shut that damn window!" he screamed.

Big Daddy became obsessed with houseflies and stalked them relentlessly. Once spied, he collided with tables and knocked over lamps to reach a single interloper. He savagely attacked those caught with a plastic fly swatter and used it to pummel the insect into dust. Another change Mama noticed was his interest in religion. In all the years they were together she had never seen him crack any book, but since the Sheriff's death, she found him sitting on the side of the bed, poring through his mother's old Bible. She dared not question him about it, but secretly hoped it would make him a better person. However, her hopes went unrealized because any further change was not for the better.

Trudy Taggart was a cute baby with big brown eyes and a thatch of dark brown hair that hung in ringlets around her chubby face. However, when Vicki looked at her, she didn't see anything of herself or Hurley, and she assumed the worst—the rapist fathered this baby. As a result, instead of the usual joy a new baby brings, Trudy's presence had the opposite effect, especially from Vicki, who showed little interest in providing for her child, and Trudy lay in the crib, uncomforted and ignored.

Mama felt a similar way about Trudy, who seemed more like a stranger in the house than her grandchild. However, she knew it wasn't the baby's fault for the way she came into the world, and she pushed Vicki to be a mother to the child.

The baby's cries carried down the hallway to the kitchen where Mama was peeling potatoes for dinner. "Oh Lord, please don't wake Big Daddy," she muttered, as she pushed back the chair and stood up. Her slippers flapped down the hall to Vicki's room. When Mama stepped inside, she scrunched her nose against the odor. "Good Lord, Vicki, this room stinks. Why don't you change this baby?" She went to the crib where Trudy lay in a soiled diaper, her little face red from her strained cries. Vicki sat at her mirrored dresser seemingly undisturbed by the racket.

"I was just about to, but I'm gonna be late for work. Would you do it?" She swept her hair up into a French twist.

"You still have a baby to look after; don't expect me to take care of her for you," Mama grabbed a diaper from the dresser.

"That's what Grandmas do, ain't it?" Vicki quipped, as her mother pulled the soiled diaper from Trudy's bottom and replaced it with a clean one.

"I had my share of babies with you and your brother." Mama lifted Trudy from the crib, patting her back until her cries slowed to a sorrowful whimper.

Vicki scoffed over her shoulder and said, "You wanted me to keep her!"

"What do you mean by that?"

"I was gonna take her to that orphanage over in Cumming, but no, you wouldn't hear of it, so now, Vicki waved her hand at the baby, there she is."

"You can be so evil sometimes. I feel sorry for this baby."

"You need to feel sorry for me and the hell I went through!" Vicki complained, and turned back to the mirror.

"I can't do this with you now, Vicki. I got too much on me with your father's sickness."

Vicki shrugged and lined her lips with a lip pencil.

"Since you seem to be too busy to care for your own baby, I'm going to ask Pastor Thomas if Teeny can help look after Trudy during the day."

Vicki looked at her mother in the mirror. "You mean that girl that lives with them, the slow one?"

"She's slow, but Teeny is very sweet. She helped me with Trudy yesterday."

"Do what you want, Mama. I don't care as long as I don't have to miss work."

Vicki's disdain for her daughter didn't change, so it was ten-year-old Teeny who spent most of the time with the Trudy. At ten, Teeny was tall, nearly 5'8" and chubby, with light brown hair that her foster mother cut into pageboy style. While Teeny was some help, Mama had to give her constant direction that soon became a chore in itself. At the end of each week, Mama paid Teeny three dollars and she skipped home, with a smile and a wave. "See you tomorrow."

When Trudy grew older, the two caused a ruckus running around the house playing games, and after a while, Big Daddy didn't like all that noise, or Teeny.

"What's that retard doing here again?" Big Daddy said, not looking at Teeny who was sitting across from him at the kitchen table with Trudy.

"Vicki is working today."

"I don't like looking at that girl."

"Teeny, take Trudy out on the back porch for a while."

"And keep that door shut, don't let the flies in!" Big Daddy went down the hall and Mama flinched when the bedroom door slammed shut.

At five years old, Trudy started school and her shoddy clothes and tangled hair quickly labeled her as needy to the teachers. On more than one occasion, Trudy brought home a note from her teacher, asking that her mother wash Trudy's hair. Trudy gave the note to Mama Bertie.

"Damn it! Vicki needs to do this; come here, Trudy," and she stood quietly as Mama Bertie tried to pull a brush through her tangled locks. At the same time, Vicki came in the back door, reeking from alcohol. She staggered to the sink and filled a cup with water and slurped it down before hurrying to her room.

Frustrated when the brush caught, Mama shouted, "Vicki! You need to wash this child's hair some time!"

"No, Mama Bertie; Vicki's mad," warned Trudy, her eyes wide with fear.

But it was too late. Vicki stormed up the hallway, her bloodshot eyes blazed and she gripped Trudy's arm and snatched her away from Mama.

"Dammit, Mama, all you gotta do is put some water on it!" And she hauled the frightened child to bathroom.

"No, Vicki!" Trudy cried, as Vicki turned on the water in the sink and shoved her head underneath the faucet. The running water soaked Trudy's head and face, and she twisted away splashing water on Vicki.

"Come here!" Vicki ordered, and when Trudy inched closer, Vicki snatched her up, spun her around, and wacked her hard on her bottom until Trudy screamed in pain.

"Now, you stand still, you hear me?" And Vicki pushed her head back under the water faucet.

Overwrought by the child's screams, Mama hurried to the bathroom. "What're you doing?"

"You said wash her hair; that's what I'm doing!" Vicki shouted, and kicked the door shut in Mama's face.

Chapter 11

By the time Trudy was seven years old, she was use to taking care of herself. She woke up early every morning and found something to wear to school. This morning, she pulled on a pair of shorts and found a shirt in a pile of clothes on the floor. Getting down on all fours she pulled a paper bag from under the bed. Inside the bag were a brand-new toothbrush and a tube of toothpaste, a pink brush, and a pack of hair clips. She knew that if Vicki found the bag, she would be punished for taking handouts, and the bag and everything in it would end up in the trash. With the bag in hand, Trudy tiptoed across the hall to the bathroom. She squeezed the toothpaste onto the brush, "Yummy," she said, tasting peppermint, and she vigorously brushed her teeth. Next came the brush with the pretty pink handle, and she pulled the soft bristles through her long dusty strands and used the clips to hold it down. Satisfied, she smiled at her reflection and said, "Thank you, Mrs. Culpepper."

When Trudy went down the hall, she looked into the living room. Vicki was sprawled across the sofa asleep, with a liquor bottle in her lap, and Mama Bertie was sleeping in Big Daddy's armchair. Trudy left through the front door and walked the half-mile to school.

Mrs. Culpepper was Trudy's favorite teacher and from her seat in the back of the room, she gazed adoringly at the young woman as she moved around the classroom smiling and gesturing as she talked. Mrs. Culpepper said something funny, and all the kids laughed including Trudy. Yesterday, when Trudy found the brown bag in her desk, she knew it was from Mrs. Culpepper because when she looked up, Mrs. Culpepper winked. Getting a secret gift from her teacher made Trudy feel special. From the very first day of school, Mrs. Culpepper always spoke kindly, but sometimes she asked questions about Vicki that made Trudy nervous.

"Trudy, have you been giving your mother the notes I send home?"

Trudy dropped her head, her cheeks burned. "Yes, ma'am."

"Do you know why she hasn't contacted me?"

"No, ma'am."

"Does your mother go to work in the daytime?"

"Yes, Vicki goes to work."

Puzzled, Mrs. Culpepper asked, "Is that your mother's name, Vicki?"

"Yes, ma'am."

"Why do you call her by her name?"

"She told me to."

Mrs. Culpepper sighed and leaned back in her chair. She took only a few seconds to think about the situation, and then, taking Trudy's hand said, "Lots of farm families are having hard times these days. Kids have to be patient with their parents until things get better. Okay?"

Not really understanding what Mrs. Culpepper was talking about, Trudy simply nodded saying, "Yes, ma'am."

In the meantime, at least once a week, Mrs. Culpepper continued to slip small items into Trudy's desk. Once, Trudy found a bag of pretzel snacks, and another time, a new pencil and eraser. Mrs. Culpepper's kind words also encouraged Trudy to do her best in school. Every day, she woke up extra early and after fixing herself a bowl of cereal, ran out the front door and down the road to the school where she sat on the steps until the janitor unlocked the doors. Trudy had perfect attendance and always raised her hand even when some other kids snickered and called her teacher's pet.

But then, one morning, as Trudy and the other kids were taking their seats, Mrs. Culpepper said, "Children, I have an announcement. I will be leaving school for a while."

Disappointed groans echoed throughout the room, until Mrs. Culpepper smiled adding, "My husband and I are having a baby."

The classroom erupted with cries of shock and surprise.

"Is it a boy or a girl?" asked Mary Johnson, followed by Teddy Druell, "I bet it's a boy; boys are better!"

"They are not," said Mary.

"Are too," shouted Teddy.

"Okay, children, calm down; we don't know yet whether it's a boy or a girl, but we will be happy with either one."

"When will you come back?" asked Robbie Atkinson.

"I'm really not sure when I'll return," said Mrs. Culpepper. While the other kids asked more questions, Trudy stared at Mrs. Culpepper and her eyes filled with tears. The rest of the day was a blur, and by the end of that week, Mrs. Culpepper was gone, leaving Trudy heartbroken.

Mr. Eugene Fox had spent four years in the Army before he turned to teaching as a profession. He was a strict taskmaster who marched into the classroom everyday with ramrod straight posture and a somber face. His presence instantly silenced the room of third graders as they sat in fear of being singled out. Unfortunately for Trudy, Mr. Fox had noticed her grubby appearance from his very first day of school and today he decided to address the class about hygiene, using her as an example.

"Trudy Taggart, come up here," he barked.

Fifteen sets of eyes turned toward Trudy. Her face grew hot with embarrassment and she scrunched low in her seat, trying to hide behind Steven Fuller's, big head.

"Trudy!"

Terrified and shaking, Trudy rose from her seat and stepped into the aisle. Muffled laughter followed her as she moved toward the front of the room, and she became acutely aware of the holes in her sweater, her wrinkled pants and her run-over shoes.

Mr. Fox sat stiffly, scribbling in a notebook. She had never been this close to him before now, and she could find not one glint of kindness in his face. Everything about Mr. Fox was scary. His mouth was a hard line sliced into the skin under a long sharp nose. His black pupils didn't focus on any one thing because his eyeballs continually twitched like jumpy little fleas behind his round-rimmed spectacles.

Trudy stood nervously in front of his desk, unaware of the reason she was being singled out. Behind her, she heard her classmates whispering, but all she could do was stand there and wait for him to look up from his desk. Finally, Mr. Fox looked up. Trudy saw his eyes travel over her hair and clothes; he looked at her ragged sweater and back at her hair again. He sneered and turned his nose up like he smelled something foul. Mr. Fox stood up; he was tall, towering over Trudy like the Frankenstein monster, and she felt herself tremble.

"Look down," he ordered.

Trudy looked at the floor. Mr. Fox took a pencil from his desk and ran it through her hair, parting it with the tip, inspecting her scalp. Trudy fought against the tears standing in her eyes. Mr. Fox threw the pencil into the trashcan. He plucked a tissue from a box on his desk to clean his hands, and threw that into the trash as well.

"When was the last time your mother washed your hair?" Trudy's cheeks burned with shame.

"Dirty hair and dirty bodies will not be tolerated in this class. Germs lead to disgusting odors and deadly disease. If your family is on Welfare, a bar of soap is still affordable, no more than ten cents in the bargain store."

Then his eyes shifted to the rest of the class.

"All students must bathe on a regular basis. Inform your parents." He looked down at Trudy and said, "Return to your seat."

Trudy's eyes followed the floor back to her desk where she lowered her head and hid beneath her arms.

Mr. Fox hushed the whispering in the room and directed the class to open their readers. Trudy sat up, wiped her dripping eyes on her sweater, and opened her book.

With that one horrible encounter, Mr. Fox had managed to crush any friendships Trudy had in her class. Before then, most of the kids wore hand-me-down clothes and paid little attention to her appearance, but his awful words had branded her dirty, and therefore, unworthy. On the playground, Trudy was horrified when she was left out of team games. Marvin Wilson said she smelled, and when Tina Bellson pointed at her, and yelled, "Trudy's got the cooties!" Everyone ran away. One day, in the girl's bathroom she heard the girls laughing at her clothes and she hid in shame inside a stall until a teacher made her come out and return to class. The only thing she could count on was the meanness her classmates inflicted every day. She never expected kindness from any of them—until one day; she received her one and only friendship ever, from a girl named Sue Ellen.

Sue Ellen was new in school, and even though she was the most beautiful girl Trudy had ever seen, no one would talk to her either. One day at lunch, Sue Ellen pulled her orange apart and gave Trudy half. It was the most delicious orange Trudy ever had, not that she tasted an awful lot. The school cafeteria only gave oranges to the free-lunch kids on holidays. Any other time, an orange cost ten cents, and Vicki said they couldn't afford it. But after that, Sue Ellen brought an extra orange every day. Trudy couldn't believe another kid could be so kind.

Sue Ellen's mom liked to embroider, and she wore a different dress every day, each with a bodice of intricately embroidered pink flowers. "Pink is my favorite color," said Sue Ellen. The flowers looked beautiful against the golden-brown color of her skin. Often, Sue Ellen would wear matching ribbons in her thick, black, braided hair. Trudy admired her dresses so much that sometimes she reached out to touch the embroidered flowers, but then quickly pulled her hand back. She didn't want to get the dress dirty.

Trudy and Sue Ellen ate lunch together every day. At recess, they ran to the swings taking turns pushing each other high to the sky. Being friends with Sue Ellen brought back the joy that Trudy had lost with Mrs. Culpepper's departure. One day, when the school bell rang and the children piled through the front door, Sue Ellen came running up to Trudy. She could hardly contain her excitement saying, "Trudy, I have a surprise!" Her smile was wide, her teeth bright white, and she took Trudy's hand.

Some boys walking by scowled and spit at their feet, but Sue Ellen seemed as unfazed as Trudy was, and they ignored the boys. Outside, Sue Ellen's mother stood across the street next to a car that reminded Trudy of a ladybug, but Sue Ellen said it was called a Beetle.

"Hello, Trudy, I'm Mrs. Cornish. I've heard a lot about you from Sue Ellen. I'm so happy she has a friend in school."

Sue Ellen's mother was dark brown with beautiful dark eyes full of kindness. She had small eyeglasses hanging from a chain around her neck and she smiled at Trudy with a gladness that she had never seen before.

"How was school today, girls?"

Trudy was stunned. Vicki never asked about her day.

"Mommy! Give it to her!" Sue Ellen shouted, with excitement. "Give it!"

Mrs. Cornish smiled and took a package from the car seat, handing it to Trudy. "I embroidered this for you last night," she said. "I hope it fits. Sue Ellen thinks you two are the same size and looking at you, I think she's right."

"It's just like my dress!" Sue Ellen hopped up and down clapping her hands with glee.

Inside the package was the dress, blue with pink and white roses embroidered on the bodice. Trudy looked at Mrs. Cornish with disbelief. "Is this for me? This can't be for me. I never had anything so beautiful."

"Of course, silly," Sue Ellen said, "Now we can be like sisters. Can you come to my house to play?"

At that moment, Trudy would have loved nothing more than to be the sister of Sue Ellen and play at her house, until she heard Mrs. Cornish say.

"I'll have to ask Trudy's mom first, Sue Ellen." Trudy's joy melted away when Vicki's voice boomed in her ears, *"Bring your ass straight home from school. I gotta work tonight!"*

"I can't. She blurted. I have to go home. Thank you for the dress."

Trudy clutched the package close to her heart and hurried home.

"Wear it tomorrow!" Sue Ellen called out.

The next morning, Trudy pulled the dress over her head and tiptoed past the sofa where Vicki lay sleeping. She hurried through the front door, pulling it closed behind her. As was her usual habit, she jumped from the porch and landed flat on the ground, then sidestepped the tall weeds and ran past the flagpole down the road to school. When she arrived, she was elated to see that Sue Ellen had on a pink dress just like hers.

At recess, Bobby McElroy was swinging by one hand from the monkey bars, staring hard at Trudy. He blurted out, "You look pretty, Trudy."

"Shut up, Bobby."

Sue Ellen snickered, pointing at Trudy, "You're turning red in the face." She giggled, and whispered into Trudy's ear, "He likes you."

The two girls ran to the swings, twittering like baby birds.

After school, Sue Ellen's mom was once again parked across the street.

"Look, Mama, Trudy has the dress on."

"I see," said Mrs. Cornish. Trudy liked the way her eyes crinkled when she smiled. "You girls look very nice. Since tomorrow is Saturday, I'm taking Sue Ellen to the movies. Would you like to come with us? You can sleep over."

"Say yes, Trudy!" Sue Ellen jumped up and down and grabbed Trudy in a tight hug.

"Well, I don't . . . ."

"I'll ask your mom. How's that?" said Mrs. Cornish.

"She's not home," Trudy, said quickly, followed by a silent prayer. Please don't ask about Vicki.

Mrs. Cornish looked at Trudy, quizzically. "Okay, maybe another time. Why don't you get in the car and I'll drive you home?"

Trudy knew that Vicki had picked up an extra shift at work today and Mama Bertie was visiting Aunt June. Big Daddy stayed locked in his room.

"Okay."

Sue Ellen and Trudy scrambled into the back seat, fawning over Trudy's new dress. She was relieved that a meeting between Vicki and Mrs. Cornish wouldn't happen. Vicki had given her strict instructions to never, ever, tell her business to anyone, and never bring strangers to the house.

When Sue Ellen's mother pulled up in front of the Taggart house, Trudy's heart slammed against her chest and heat surged up her neck flaming her cheeks. Vicki's truck was crouched in the driveway like a giant black spider.

Mrs. Cornish shut down the engine and as her eyes scanned the property her compassion for her daughter's friend tugged at her heart. A picket fence had fallen down and prickly weeds sprouted between the weathered planks. What once was a small garden now held a horde of waist-high weeds and dead bushes. The house itself was sad. Mrs. Cornish looked at the sloping gutters and the overly patched roof. Two worn rockers sat on a run-down porch. In the center of the yard a withered flag hung limp on a pole. She breathed in a sigh of regret that she hoped the girls didn't notice. Brightening, she said, "Here we are."

But Trudy's fearful eyes were glued on Vicki's truck.

"Is that your Mama's truck?" asked Sue Ellen.

Trudy nodded.

"Yay! Your mom's home! Mama, will you ask her if she can go to the movies with us?"

Not wanting to leave the safety of the car, Trudy sat unmoving as tears sprinkled her cheeks.

"What's the matter?" asked Sue Ellen.

"Vicki's home."

"You call your Mama Vicki. How come?"

"I don't know," she said, and shrugged.

Mrs. Cornish opened the car door and got out. "You stay in the car, Sue Ellen, and I'll be right back." Her smile never wavered when she opened the door for Trudy. Trudy slid off the seat and stood next to her friend's mother who took her hand and together they walked across the yard.

When they stepped onto the porch and Trudy looked at the screen door, she began to tremble. Mrs. Cornish noticed her distress and knelt down in front of Trudy; she gently patted the tiny roses on her dress.

"Look, honey," she said. "This may not be a good time. Maybe we can try for next weekend. I'm just going to leave now and . . . ."

The voice she heard next was raspy and coarse and spat foulness from the doorway. "What the fuck is going on out here?"

Vicki appeared in a brume of stale booze, peering through the screen with bloodshot eyes. "Who the hell is that parked out front?"

She peeled off her false eyelashes and flicked them from her fingers and like moths caught in lamplight; they flitted away. In the other hand, she held a plastic cup with a cigarette perched between two fingers.

Vicki swayed on wobbly legs and her drunken glare fixed on Trudy, but then, as if seeing her for the first time, she looked at Mrs. Cornish.

She pushed the screen door open and stepped out, asking, "Who the hell are you?" Without waiting for a response, she turned to Trudy. "What did I tell you about bringing people to the house?" Her free hand shot out and connected with her daughter's face, a blow so violent Mrs. Cornish cringed. Trudy tumbled backward down the stairs, landing in the dirt.

"Get up here!"

Trudy scrambled to her feet, hurried up the steps, and ducked around Vicki into the house. Vicki turned and followed Trudy inside.

Mrs. Cornish was shocked and stood frozen on the porch. She was torn on whether she should leave or try to help Trudy. She reached for the door handle, and when she pulled it open the door screeched loudly and she stepped inside.

Hearing the door open, Vicki spun around shaking her stringy hair out of her eyes and angrily confronted the woman.

"What the hell do you think you're doing?" she barked, and inhaled deeply from a freshly lit cigarette.

"Oh, my! I'm so sorry. This isn't Trudy's fault."

"You need to get the hell outta my house!" Vicki warned.

"I just wanted to explain. I'm Mae Cornish. We just moved here, and Trudy and Sue Ellen, that's my daughter, are friends in school; she liked the dresses I made for Sue Ellen, so I made her one and . . . ."

"Dresses, what the hell are you talking about? Trudy! Get over here!"

Vicki sipped from the cup and took a long drag from her cigarette. She pursed her lips and spewed the smoke into the woman's face. Mrs. Cornish coughed and stepped back as Trudy crawled from under a table, standing slightly out of reach of her mother's hand.

"I said get over here!"

Cautiously, Trudy inched closer.

"You made her a dress?"

"Yes, just so they could be alike." She laughed, nervously.

"Be alike?"

"Well, not exactly alike, but, you know, how girls like to dress the same sometimes, when they're friends."

"You think she needs clothes? She don't need no clothes from you."

"Oh no! I never thought that. It was simply a gift."

"Don't make me have to move, Trudy!"

Trudy stepped forward. Vicki squinted at her through a haze of smoke, and then snatched her arm pulling her closer.

"Is this the dress?" She fingered the little roses on the neckline and then released Trudy's arm.

"Yes, I like to embroider when I'm not working, and, well, Trudy liked the dresses I did for Sue Ellen, so, I thought it would be nice to make her one."

"So you work?" Vicki sneered, her cigarette bouncing on her lower lip.

"Um, I just got a new job at the water company in Cumming," she explained, "I've been there a few weeks and it's been hard fitting in. I was so happy when Sue Ellen found a friend at school."

Vicki ignored the woman's attempt at civil conversation; she sucked on her cigarette, her eyes crawled over the Negro woman with disgust. The burning smoke ensnared Mrs. Cornish in a shroud of tobacco and she leaned away from the sickly stench.

"Did you just get home from work?" She asked, hoping to gain a mutual understanding between two working mothers. Mrs. Cornish realized her mistake when she saw Vicki stiffen and her eyes constrict with anger.

Her voice was deadly when she said, "Why you asking my business?"

"Oh! I'm sorry. I didn't mean anything."

But it was too late; Vicki's face was full of hate when she snapped, "I don't give a shit what your black Nigger ass does for the fucking water company!"

And as Vicki stepped threateningly toward her, poking the air with her cigarette held fingers, her mouth twisted into an ugly smile. "She don't need any fucking handouts from the likes of you!" Without warning, Vicki turned to Trudy who was standing beside her and grabbed the neckline of her beautiful dress and savagely ripped it all the way down the front.

"Get out of it!" Vicki's eyes bulged like insect orbs under lurid blue eye shadow.

As quickly as she could, Trudy pulled her arms out of the sleeves and let the dress drop to the floor. She stepped away from it and stood statue-still in her dingy underpants.

Vicki poured the contents of her cup onto the dress and threw her lit cigarette on top. A small flame erupted, and Mrs. Cornish watched as the tiny white and pink roses coiled into the flames and Trudy's eyes filled with tears.

"Get some water and put that shit out," Vicki barked at Trudy. She turned back to Mrs. Cornish. Don't you ever think you can come in my house or give my kid anything! I get her what she needs! Now get outta my house, Nigger!"

Mrs. Cornish's whole body was trembling and her face was wet with spittle from Vicki's verbal attack. She didn't think she could be any more humiliated until she backed up and tripped over the doorsill, landing flat on her rear end. Vicki's taunting laughter pushed her to scurry away on her back like a crab, scooting across the porch down the steps and finally onto the dirt, where she rolled over on her hands and knees and staggered to her feet. With tears streaming, she backed away from the house when she heard Vicki holler, "I thought that bitch would never leave!" The door slammed so hard the house shook on its foundation.

Chapter 12

Minter Saul walked under a dark sky sprinkled with shimmering stars. He stepped over scores of withered shrubs as he followed a path he had made on previous visits. It was a quarter-mile walk through what had once been a vibrant cotton field but now tenacious weeds and prickly brush bullyragged the field and robust wildflowers grew into small trees. All around him, phantom apparitions appeared, pulling the memory of cotton from lifeless stalks and shoving fluffy wisps of nothing into ragged sacks. Minter Saul had grown used to these hauntings, in as much as they were used to him, and neither seemed bothered by the other's presence.

He saw a flash of white and knew he had reached the spot. He hunkered down next to the small memorial bush he had planted for his parents, Atticus and Patch. The white Begonias had grown a foot high and were still blooming nearly two months later. He would replace them soon with white Marigolds, which were more suitable for the hot summer months ahead.

His eyes caught movement, and he watched the specter of a Negro gardener raking the earth next to the flowers. Minter Saul nodded in gratitude and the man vanished.

He had set up the memorial years ago and looked forward to his weekly visits. White flowers had been Patch's favorite. They shimmered like a beacon and brightened the barren field. Another ghostly visitor appeared, this time a Negro woman in a flowing dress. Minter Saul hoped it was Patch, but upon closer observation, he saw that it wasn't. The woman smiled at him and stepped forward onto a breeze with the ease of stepping into a streetcar, and then she was gone.

He had always known that Piney was a town of earthbound spirits. Ghosts of murdered Negroes—most of who were buried in the Taggart cornfield—had appeared to him since he was a little boy. At any given time, he would see these apparitions working the field, not knowing their jobs were long over.

As a boy, the sightings had frightened him, but as he grew older, he reasoned that they were simply looking in on him, maybe because they knew that loneliness was his only companion.

Minter Saul sat back on his haunches. He touched the petals of the Begonias and considered his current situation. Lately, he was having trouble recalling his movements, mainly the when and where of things. Was it yesterday, or days ago? Maybe even months had passed, he wasn't sure.

When was it that Baby Mitch had shot him?

After he'd inherited the Preecher property, he'd expected some trouble. No way in the world a white man would leave all his property to a Nigger. So said the courthouse lawyers, until they'd read Preecher's Will. That day, he'd walked out with the deed to the house and property.

If any Whites were set to give him trouble it would be the Taggarts, and sure enough, Baby Mitch was constantly lurking around. Minter Saul did recall being in his house sipping from a tin can of black coffee, the old dog glued to his heels like a shadow. He had sensed someone lurking around outside and his gaze settled on Ned's gun hanging over the mantle, a standard Pattern-Rim 400 rifle. He remembered when Ned had ordered it from one of them catalogue books. It had been like Christmas day when the mail truck delivered the gun. Ned had spent hours outside shooting at any ill-fated animal that crossed his path.

When Minter Saul was certain that someone was trespassing, he had taken the gun down and slipped out the side door.

He pointed the barrel of the gun directly at Baby Mitch's ear. "Stand up, boy." He wanted so badly to pull the trigger. "You on my property."

Baby Mitch let his own rifle drop to his side. "This ain't your property, Nigger, and you know it! I don't know how you done it, but ain't no way Preecher left all this land and his house to you."

"I got me a Will says so."

"Will or no Will; this is supposed to be Taggart property."

"Looks like Preecher changed his mind, don't it?"

"I think you killed Preecher—did you, Nigger? Did you kill 'em?"

"Get off my property, cracker, before I blow your head clean off."

"You talk mighty big for an old man."

"This here gun doing the talking, boy. You trespassing."

Baby Mitch backed up. "You ain't gonna live long. Then we'll get what's coming to us."

"Oh! You gonna get what's coming. That you will, boy. Oh, that you will!"

Baby Mitch spat at Minter Saul's feet, turned and walked toward his truck, but as soon as Minter Saul lowered his rifle the boy spun around and cranked a chamber.

A fireball, that's what it felt like, a metal ball of fire that burned into his flesh. It was a pain that Minter Saul would never forget. He remembered lying flat on his back in the field and how angry he'd been at being shot by this dang-blasted crazy son of a gun.

Old dog must have been close because his wailing could wake up the dead. Baby Mitch had pumped two more chambers and when he'd heard the old dog yelp, he knew he got him too.

The boy came in for a closer look, and Minter Saul observed his gangly legs twitching nervously as he'd paced back and forth. He watched a grin spread across his pimply face and Minter Saul recalled the grinning cat in a fairy tale book he had seen one time. After that, everything had gone dark, and as hard as he tried, that was all Minter Saul could recollect from that night.

Chapter 13

"Mama, ain't we got any more coffee?"

Vicki tipped the Maxwell House jar, spilling a slim amount of brown grains into her cup. On the stove, a burst of steam whistled from the kettle and Mama flipped off the flame.

"In the cupboard," she responded. "You want some grits?" She whisked two eggs into a fluffy mound as bacon sizzled on the grill.

"I don't have time," Vicki said.

"By the way, what the hell was that colored woman doing at the house the other day? When June drove me home I seen her getting in her car. If Big Daddy had come out . . . ."

"Well, he didn't come out, Mama. He never comes out, so don't worry about it. I took care of it and Trudy knows she better not bring anyone here again."

"You working late?"

"Yeah."

"You know Trudy needs help with her homework at night."

"You can help her."

"I ain't her mother; you are."

Vicki sipped her coffee, ignoring Mama.

"If you left that alcohol alone, you could help her." But Mama knew her words fell on deaf ears. Vicki had changed since Trudy's birth eight years ago, and not in a good way. Her once smart and vibrant girl had chosen a path of misery and anger, and it took very little to set her off. Mama had been told more than once to mind her fucking business.

The screen door creaked and Baby Mitch strolled into the kitchen.

"Well, look what the dog drug in," Vicki quipped.

"It's about time you came around to visit your family," said Mama.

"Where's Big Daddy?"

"He's still 'sleep, I guess."

"Is he sick again?"

"I don't know what's wrong with that man," Mama said.

Baby Mitch's eyes darted around the kitchen like a weasel caught in a cage.

Mama knew that look. "What you up to, boy?"

"I need to talk to you," he said, looking at Vicki.

"Me?" Vicki pointed at her chest, feigning disbelief.

"C'mon girl, I ain't got all day. Let's talk in the living room."

"You better go ahead, Vicki," Mama said, sarcastically. "See what new scheme he come up with now."

Vicki got up from the table and followed him into the living room. Baby Mitch grabbed her arm saying, "Sit down."

She snatched away from him. "Get your hands off me! Don't ever touch me!" she warned.

Baby Mitch snickered, "You crazy, girl."

"I don't have any money."

"It ain't like that."

"What's it like, then?"

"The Preecher place."

"What about it?"

"It's mine, uh, I mean, ours."

"I thought that colored man inherited it. The one that worked for Preecher."

"Minter Saul? Naw," he said, shaking his head.

"He done something; no way Preecher would leave all that property to him."

"Done what?"

"He probably killed Preecher and his wife."

Vicki laughed. "Really? So you think that a Nigger here in Piney murdered his white boss along with his wife, and inherited all his property? You're as simple as Teeny."

She started to leave, but he stepped in front of her, and she backed up.

"Vicki, listen to me. Come sit down." He motioned toward the sofa, but she didn't move.

"You better be quick," she said, folding her arms in front of her.

"Okay, okay." He lifted his hands in surrender. "I think he killed them. But even if he didn't, he don't deserve that property and I'm planning on making things right."

"Meaning what?"

"Meaning, that place is as good as ours."

"How you figure that?"

"Because it's gonna be available. I've been talking to the county executor, and it will be up for sale for next to nothing if the owner abandons it."

Vicki looked at her brother with suspicion. "Did you do something, Baby Mitch?"

"Hell no!"

"I don't want to get mixed up in none of your schemes."

"Do you want to keep living in this dump?" he nodded at the worn furnishings.

His words gave her pause and she looked around the room. Nothing had changed in the twenty-six years she'd lived there.

"And what about the trailer?" he said. "Big Daddy will never get rid of it and you know that thing gives you the willies."

She turned away from him. He had pushed a button and she didn't want him to know it. But he was right. Her life was like an endless horror film playing over and over on a busted projector. It was bad enough she had to look at Trudy every day. Vicki avoided the back yard. Just seeing the trailer caused her heart to race, so now she parked her truck out front. All of that, plus the visions of James pushed her to drink even more.

"What the hell you need me for?" she said, facing him again.

"When we get the Preecher house, we could sell it and split the profits. You could buy your own place."

"You could do that without me," she said.

"They ain't gonna let me get a loan with my arrest record. But you would have no problem at the bank. Think about it, little sis," he said, grinning through butter colored buckteeth.

Vicki was unwilling to let him know her thoughts on the subject, so she stayed quiet. As bad as she wanted to move, she knew never to trust her brother. But this sounded like something that could change her life for the better.

She followed Baby Mitch as he sauntered back into the kitchen and snagged a piece of bacon from Mama's plate. "Mama, we got business tonight. Do you think Big Daddy's up to it?"

"I don't know. He don't talk to me."

"Well, me, Clement, and Wilber will be in the yard tonight."

"Y'all don't need to be doing that no more, Baby Mitch."

Ignoring his mother, he left by the screen door, shoving it so hard it banged against the house. "Take it easy on the damn door!" Mama hollered, her face taut with anger. "Damn that boy. I don't know why he's still doing that business. When God was giving out good sense, he was too dumb to get in line."

Vicki finished her coffee and placed the cup in the sink.

"Whatever he's doing won't turn out good." Mama warned.

"There could be a chance for me to move out, get my own place," Vicki said.

Mama brightened. "A new home for you and Trudy could be just what you need."

"Not Trudy. Just me."

Mama flinched, her jaw tightened, but she said nothing.

"I gotta go. I'm late, messing with that fool."

"You gonna check on Trudy before you leave?"

"She's fine. I heard her in the bathroom."

Vicki walked through the living room and out the front door.

"Vicki?" a small voice called from the hallway.

"She's already gone, Trudy," said Mama.

Vicki slid in behind the wheel of the truck. She fished around in her purse, found a pint of whiskey, unscrewed the top, and took two sips. The first swallow of whiskey went down rough and she coughed and frowned against the bitterness. Another sip, then another, and she burped, giggled, and smacked her lips.

Back in her purse again, she found a tube of lipstick, tilted the rearview mirror in her direction, and carefully filled in her lips with creamy red. However, her eyes caught another reflection in the mirror; startled, she dropped the tube and turned around. James stood beside the truck leaning down on a bloody stump, one arm propped on a stick. His eyes flickered bronze with a gold glint, but the rest of his face was torn and ripped to the bone. And when the decayed corners of his mouth lifted into a smile, her heart rocketed with fear. She wanted to look away, but was transfixed on the grinning corpse. Her mind expelled a memory of standing in the weeds at the Crawley farm. She heard a voice inside her head and she sank down to the floor of the truck in an attempt to hide. But the voice was asking, "Was this Nigger messing with you?"

"No, No, he wasn't. He wasn't!" she screamed over and over.

Suddenly, another voice called out to her. "Vicki, what's wrong? Are you all right?"

Mama had come off the porch and was standing at the driver window, her face strained with concern. "What's the matter?"

Vicki lowered her hands from her eyes and looked up from the floor. She climbed into the seat.

"What happened?" Mama was asking, her voice shaken.

Vicki looked at her, then at the empty yard. She blotted her tears on her palms and said, icily, "Nothing, Mama."

"But I heard you scream."

"Nothing!" Vicki shoved the key in the ignition and mashed the gas. The engine roared and the spinning tires riddled Mama's legs with gravel as the truck shot forward.

The truck tore through the front lawn, narrowly missing the flagpole. Down the road, she sped, the cornfield on her left. On her right, Negro farmhands pulled cotton as they toiled under the scorching sun. Her hand trembled as she shook a cigarette out of the pack. On the dashboard, the lighter popped and she held it to the cigarette until the tip blazed red-hot. Vicki cranked the window down and let the humid air moisten her face.

"I'm going crazy."

Chapter 14

Whenever Minter Saul passed the huge Magnolia tree where he and Ned played as boys a memory appeared in his thoughts and he heard Ned's voice. Damn, Saul! Your hands are blacker than the rest of you. He held his own white hands next to Saul's in comparison.

The two eleven-year-old boys sat together under that great Magnolia, pulling honeysuckle flowers from the vines that blanketed the trunk of the tree. They pinched the ends of the stems and pulled the thread-size stalk for the reward of a tiny drop of honey on their tongues. Two best friends, licking honey from the flowers. The only difference between the two was the color of their skin. Minter Saul thought he had no better friend then Ned Preecher.

When he looked at his hands now, he mused over Ned's childish observation. His hands always were the darkest part of him, and now, as an old man, they were blacker still, burnt from years of pulling cotton under the blazing Georgia sun.

Ned's Daddy, Sherman Preecher, used Negroes to build a fine house, barn, and cultivate a lucrative cotton plantation. In later years he also planted sugar cane that provided a profitable harvest. Laborers were Negroes who remained in the South after emancipation, working for meager wages. None of them were able to read or write, and

Sherman coerced them into signing work contracts that bound them to a lifetime of indentured slavery. To Sherman and his like, this wasn't as beneficial as the free labor slaves had provided, but Sherman found a way to make additional profits from them anyway. He rented Negro workers to other plantations and was not only paid by the renter, but he also charged the Negroes for use of his rundown shacks and a small mound of dirt they could use to grow crops from which he garnered half the profit.

Minter Saul's parents Atticus and Patch, descendants of slaves, had lived on the Preecher plantation for most of their lives.

Atticus was a dark-colored Negro, six feet tall with a slight frame. He was a hard worker who never complained, mainly because as a young man, he was beaten into submission. His wife Patch was the color of churned butter with a patch of brown freckles. Little Saul would count her freckles each time he sat on her lap—twelve little dots across the bridge of her nose.

Atticus and Patch worked on a plantation far away in the town of Cumming, Georgia. Cumming was the County Seat and home to many large plantations. Saul's parents worked for Earl Davis, the County Clerk who didn't care for Nigger kids running around his property. Sherman had talked Atticus and Patch into going to Cumming without their son Saul, in exchange for a piece of his property they could call their own when they settled down.

But seven-year-old Saul didn't understand why they were going away, and he fell into a crying fit when they left him behind. To take his mind off his worries, Sherman handed him a burlap bag and started him in the cotton field.

Minter Saul would never forget the last time he saw Atticus and Patch. It was Easter Sunday more than forty years ago at the Church Revival the Preechers held on their property. People from all over came to the Preecher farm for a day of praise and worship, after which free food and drinks were provided along with hayrides and horseshoes. Most Negroes got a half-day off from work to attend the Revival, and Minter Saul was excited to see his parents again. He still recalled sitting on his Daddy's lap, leaning his head on his chest and feeling the soft vibrations coming from his gravelly voice.

"How you doing, son?"

"Fine, Daddy."

"You getting so big," Atticus said, smiling proudly.

Patch was happy, too, and as she moved around the table making plates of food for them, Saul could not stop looking at her. She was tall and willowy and she moved like fountain grass caught up in a summer breeze. When she sat next to him, he went through his ritual of counting her freckles.

"One, two, three, four, five, six, seven, eight, nine, ten eleven, twelve! You have twelve dots on your nose, Mama."

"So you is learning yo numbas; that's good, son."

Minter Saul remembered how she pulled him between her breasts and kissed his face in every single spot. She smiled and laughed, and even shed some tears at how much he'd grown since the last time. He and Daddy arm-wrestled on the picnic table, and Daddy always let him win, fussing over how strong his son was getting. Saul had noticed that his mother's stomach was growing big and she said she was having a baby soon. She pressed his hand to her growing belly, embarrassed, he snatched it back, and Patch chuckled.

"You gonna have a brother or a sister, son."

He beamed and blurted, "I will?"

"That's right. You ain't gonna be alone in the world when we ain't here.

"Yes, Mama."

"You gonna be the big brother."

"I hope it's a boy!"

"I don't know. But whatever God sees fit to send us, you look out for him, or her, you hear me?"

"I will!" he smiled, brightly.

Before sundown, the Negro workers began boarding wagons for the trip back to their work plantations. Atticus and Patch each held Saul for as long as possible, saying they would see him next Easter. But Saul was only seven, and tears bubbled up in his eyes and spilled over like a waterfall. His small hands hooked into Patch's long skirt and he clung to the folds for dear life, refusing to release her. Finally, Atticus had to pry his little fingers loose and Minter Saul remembered seeing tears streaking his father's dark skin.

Seeing their son so distraught, Patch told Atticus it was time they stayed back with Saul, especially with her baby due soon. But when they told Mister Sherman of their decision, he was not happy. He was making good money renting them to Earl Davis and he didn't want to give that up, just yet. "Tell you what, he said, you go one more year and I'll have Miss Rachel, teach Saul to read. How's that?"

Patch knew how important reading was for Negroes, and it was something she wanted badly for Saul. They both agreed to one more year with the promise that Patch could keep the new baby with her.

On that, Patch knelt down and hugged Saul close, kissing his wet eyelids. "Just one more year," she promised.

Miss Rachel, carrying a bowl of potato salad, said, "Tell your Mama and Daddy goodbye, Saul. They got work waiting."

"I don't wanna say goodbye," Saul cried, into his mother's bosom. But Patch kissed his tears away and whispered in his ear, "Every goodbye ain't gone."

That was the last time he saw Patch and Atticus.

As a child, Minter Saul hadn't really understood what it meant when Sherman told him that his parents were never coming back. He had heard the Negro workers whispering that Patch died having a baby and Atticus fell from a roof, but he didn't believe any of them. On Easter day, he waited next to the road as wagon after wagon of Negro workers arrived for the Revival. When the very last wagon rumbled past, Minter Saul knew in his heart they weren't coming, but he pushed those thoughts aside sat down in the weeds and watched the horizon.

When dusk claimed the daylight and the crickets began to chirp, he waited. Even as the workers piled into the wagons for the trip back to their plantations, he waited. By the time darkness shrouded the landscape, his salty tears had cemented his eyelids closed and he fell into a dreamless sleep.

A Negro worker who knew Atticus and Patch plucked him out of the roadside weeds and brought him back to the farmhouse.

"You gonna be all right, little fella," he said.

Chapter 15

"Get him outta there!" Baby Mitch shouted from the truck. Clement and Wilbur let down the tailgate and yanked the Negro man by his feet. The dead man's face was covered with blood and his head lagged on a broken neck. He was nude except for his underpants and his hands were tied behind his back. They dragged the man down on the ground, hauled him to the edge of the cornfield, and hoisted him up.

"This Nigger's light as a feather," said Wilbur.

"He's a young one, that's why," replied Clement.

Baby Mitch chimed in, "Get 'em while they young, I always say."

The darkness of the kitchen shrouded Mama as she stood quietly at the open window. The new screen Big Daddy had installed kept the bugs out and let the night breeze seep in, along with voices in the yard. She had been awakened by her son's truck pulling in, and carefully eased out of bed so not to wake Big Daddy. It was after midnight, and she had hoped the "meeting," as he called it, had been called off. But here he was, doing what he'd grown up doing, only this time without his father.

Now, she stood barefoot in her nightclothes peeking through the window. She knew that Baby Mitch was emboldened by her husband's illness. She shook her head and rubbed her temples; a headache was threatening, and she wondered if there was any aspirin left. He was her son, even if he didn't have good sense.

Most everything Baby Mitch did turned into trouble. How many times had they bailed him out to keep the Taggart name from being dragged through the mud? Now, without Big Daddy to rein him in, she feared what would become of her reckless boy. After all, she had brought him into the world and she loved him in spite of everything.

In the yard, Baby Mitch lit a cigarette while he waited on Clement and Wilbur; it was a long time before the two men stomped back out, covered in dirt and weeds.

"Whew, it's a wild mess in there," complained Clement.

"Did you get it done?"

"Yeah."

"Six feet down?"

"More like four."

"Shit! I told you six."

"Next time you dig the hole if you want six," Clement threw down the shovel and ambled over to his truck.

"Okay. Let's give it a rest for a while. I think we done good," said Baby Mitch, adding, "At least we got one in."

"These Niggers will soon enough get the message to get the fuck out of Piney," said Wilbur as he brushed weeds from his trousers.

"It's just like back in the day," Baby Mitch grinned. "Old General Bedford Forrest would be proud."

"Yeah," Wilbur chuckled, "Don't let the sun catch your ass in Piney, Nigger."

"We need to put those signs back up on the roads," said Clement. "Save us all this hole-digging."

Baby Mitch brushed his stringy hair back from his forehead. "Wish we could, but it's against the law. It has to be a quiet message."

"What about that new Sheriff?"

"Hurley? Don't worry about that fool. He used to date my sister."

Mama let go of the curtain. She took a cup from the dish rack and filled it with water. In the cupboard, she found a small bottle of aspirin. She shook two into her hand and tossed them back, followed by the water. Then, she rinsed the cup and set it back in the rack. Still at the sink, she stood in the darkness, pondering over her son's behavior. She needed to talk to him, convince him to stop before he got caught. Would he listen to her? Not likely. She thought about Vicki and Trudy and finally Big Daddy. Everyone was going through some mess and she wondered when it would all end. So many useless years with nothing to show, and now she was tired. She listened as the trucks pulled out of the yard. The linoleum was cool under her bare feet as she tiptoed back to the bedroom.

The next morning, sitting alone in the kitchen, Mama stared into her cup and observed specks of coffee granules floating on the surface. She had managed to skim most of them with her finger, depositing the tiny specks into a napkin. The others, oh well, she thought, what harm could they do? She took another sip of the hot liquid. The aspirin bottle sat next to her cup. Two more aspirins this morning hadn't calmed the pulse in her head and she massaged her temples with her fingers. A tapping sound caused her to look up from her cup. It was Teeny smiling at her through the screen.

"Miss Bertie, can Trudy play today?"

Mama sighed, and got up from the table. "Teeny, what are you doing here?"

"I wanna play with Trudy."

At twenty, Teeny was a grown woman but mentally just twelve years old. Pastor Thomas and his wife Elizabeth refused to send Teeny to a special school because they didn't trust that she would be safe, and therefore, Trudy was the only friend she had.

"Trudy's at school."

"She is?"

"Yes. You need to go on home. I'll let Pastor Thomas know when you can come over, okay?"

"Can I play with her ball?"

"No, Teeny, you go ahead now." Mama closed the door and pulled the curtain over. She sat back down with her coffee and her headache and listened to Teeny clump down the back steps.

However, Teeny didn't leave; instead, she crouched to pet Trudy's orange cat and then sat down on the ground and pulled it into her lap.

When Baby Mitch strode around the side of the house, the cat, a former torture victim of his, jumped from her lap and skidded away.

"Hey, Teeny, why're you sitting on the ground?"

"I wanna play with Trudy."

"Get up off the ground, girl," he said, and reached his hands out.

Teeny took Baby Mitch's hands. He pulled her up a bit too hard, and she bumped his chest.

"Damn, girl, you really have grown up." He stroked her long hair and eyeballed her full breasts.

"I know," Teeny said, giggling.

"How old are you now?"

"Pastor Thomas said I will be twenty-one before we know it."

"Twenty-one, huh? Do you have a boyfriend?"

"No, no," she said assuredly, and shook her head.

"I bet you would be a good girlfriend."

"Pastor Thomas said no boys for me."

"Oh, what does he know?" He moved closer and leaned in for a kiss.

Teeny didn't understand what was happening and let him kiss her, but was quickly disgusted by his body stench and roving hands. Growing more aggressive, he put his hand under her skirt and his thick tongue lapped at her like a thirsty dog. Teeny tried to squirm out of his grip.

"Stop it," she said, growing fearful.

"Come on, Teeny, let me be your boyfriend," he tightened his grip.

"I wanna go home now."

Baby Mitch pulled her toward the Air Streamer. "Let me show you something," he coaxed. Frightened, Teeny snatched away and backed up so quickly she tripped and fell hitting the back of her head on the cement steps.

Baby Mitch saw Teeny strike her head, her body quivered and twitched on the ground before going limp. Blood seeped, fanning out from under her head, and panic slithered through his addled brain. "Oh shit!" Suddenly, his practiced bravado was cast off like a mask and his cowardice emerged in a flurry of tears and he screamed, "Mama!"

Inside the house, Mama looked up when she heard her son yelling. She opened the door, stepped onto the porch and saw Teeny lying at the bottom of the steps.

She gasped and her hands flew to her mouth. She looked at her son standing over Teeny he was pale and scared and she knew she had to remain calm. The last thing she needed was Mitch coming outside with his insane ranting.

"What the hell happened?" her accusing eyes drilled into him.

"It was an accident, Mama, I didn't do nothing. I came by to see Big Daddy. She was in the yard chasing that orange cat. It ran in front of her, and she tripped over it and fell."

"Then why is she lying on her back like that?" she asked, angrily.

"I don't know!" he paced the yard, hugging his boney frame. "Mama, you know that Pastor Thomas ain't gonna believe it was an accident. They'll throw me in jail this time. Real jail!"

Mama moved down the steps, knelt next to Teeny, and placed two fingers on her neck. Unable to locate a pulse, her eyes shifted to her son.

"Get her in the cornfield."

Chapter 16

Vicki plopped a mound of lumpy oatmeal in a bowl and slid it in front of Trudy.

"Eat it while it's still hot and I got some chores for you."

"When is Teeny comin' back?" Trudy's eyes settled on Mama Bertie for an answer.

Unable to maintain Trudy's questioning gaze Mama peered into her cup.

"How the hell do I know?" barked Vicki. "I'm glad she's not here; she keeps you from doing your work."

"Why don't you do something with Trudy's hair?" Mama said, changing the subject. "It's a damn nest."

Trudy's hand moved to her head patting her hair down. "Did Pastor Thomas take Teeny somewhere?"

"I think they went to Cumming to visit other churches." Mama lied.

"When is she coming back?" asked Trudy.

"We don't know! Are you deaf?" snapped Vicki. "Stop asking so many damn questions!"

Mama observed Vicki's own hair. It was swept up like a funnel cloud and held in place with butterfly clips. Her cobalt blue eyelids were bright canopies over her green eyes and the apple red lipstick was the perfect bulls-eye. "You auditioning for a circus clown?" Mama said, with a disapproving shake of her head.

Ignoring her mother, Vicki grabbed the kettle and poured more hot water into her cup; she spooned in some coffee granules and took a few sips as she looked up at the clock. "Dammit. I'm late." She put the cup down and hurriedly snatched her keys from the table.

"I hope you ain't at that bottle again."

"Don't start with me, Mama. I ain't in the mood."

She glowered at Trudy. "You get that rug cleaned today."

"Yes, ma'am."

"That burn ain't coming out," scoffed Mama. "It's through to the damn floor."

"She can clean around it."

Annoyed, Mama sipped her coffee.

"If Teeny don't come back, can I play with the boy?" asked Trudy.

Vicki stopped in her tracks, her body tense. "What boy?"

"I saw a colored boy in the yard; he told me his name was James."

Vicki's face went stark white with shock, but then, anger blazed her cheeks.

"Trudy, if you want another whipping like the last one, just keep telling lies!"

"It's not a lie, I saw him!"

Vicki ignored the tears welling in Trudy's eyes. "I gotta go, I'll deal with you later," she threatened.

Mama's eyes swept over her daughter and she shook her head. The waitress uniform she wore encased her body like sausage skin. Her cleavage burst over two open buttons, exposing her creamy breasts like vanilla cupcakes in a frilly brassiere.

"You know that dress is too tight."

"The tighter the dress, the better the tips," Vicki quipped, and walked through the living room. When she shoved the screen door open, it cracked against the house. Mama's head jerked, her eyes taut with anger. "Ya'll just determined to break these doors clean off the hinges!"

Vicki stepped out onto the porch and looked cautiously around the yard, seeing no one, she hurried down the steps to her truck and got in. Glancing back at the house, she saw Trudy watching her through the screen and quickly looked away. She had been shocked to hear that Trudy had seen James. She didn't want to believe it, but then, she said his name, James. What the hell was going on, she wondered, why was he appearing to Trudy? The fear that was her constant companion whispered bizarre answers in her ear, but not wanting to hear, she opened her purse and unscrewed the cap on a pint of whiskey and took two belts, and a third just in case. She checked the rearview and backed down the driveway.

Mama Bertie came up behind Trudy and together they watched Vicki drive off. She rubbed her hand over her granddaughter's tangled mop.

"I might as well try to wash this mess. Your Mama sure ain't gonna do it."

Vicki was only part of the way to town when her truck began to lose power. "Dammit," she uttered, as she coasted to the side of the road across from the cornfield. Each time she turned the key and mashed the gas pedal, the engine whined and choked until all she could get was an exasperating clunk.

She got out of the truck and went around to the front, popped the hood and propped it open, she tinkered with the water hose and looked at the battery, but really had no idea what she was doing. When she heard rustling coming from across the road, she turned and saw a Negro step out of the cornfield. Terror gripped her senses. It was James, and he was coming toward the truck.

"Oh, God!" she cried, as her heart raced. She wanted to run but her legs felt paralyzed and it took everything she had to will herself to get to the door and climb inside the truck.

He was closer now. She hurriedly screwed up all the windows and slumped down in the seat. Now, he was standing just outside the window. She covered her eyes against the grisly sight she knew she would see.

"Go away!" she cried. "Please, go away!"

At the same time, she heard tapping. He was tapping on the window. She forced herself to look, and when she did, it wasn't James, but an old man. His face was as dark as burnt wood and deep lines creased his brow. He had tired eyes, but they brightened when he looked at her.

"You need help, Miss?"

He said his name was Minter Saul, and he was the new owner of Ned Preecher's property. The old man walked around and looked under the hood. Out of the truck now, Vicki stood back and watched him through wary eyes. His head was bent low and she heard hissing and clanking as he worked. Then, he stood back wiping his large hands on a rag he pulled from his pocket.

"You got some alternator problems, Miss," he said. "Nothing that can't be fixed. It will cost you a pretty penny if you take it to Mister

Thornley's garage. You should take it over to Chester Cabbage. He'll fix it for half the price Thornley charges. Climb in and crank her up. Let's see what we got."

Vicki inserted the key into the ignition. The engine coughed and wheezed and the truck shuddered and started up. She brightened as the engine settled into a satisfied drone. "Thanks," she said.

"Happy to help. Good I come along."

"You never asked my name."

"Vicki Taggart," he said.

"You know me?"

"Everyone knows the Taggarts."

"So, you know my father?"

"Sure do; I know about your daddy, Mitch Taggart, your granddaddy, Cyrus, all the way back to your great-granddaddy, Beasley Taggart—all loyal Klan members."

Embarrassed at the old man's knowledge, Vicki cut her eyes away, but then, she suddenly felt emboldened by her family history and she spoke her mind.

"No hard feelings. It's just the way things ought to be between Negroes and Whites. Ya'll should understand that by now, and keep with your own kind."

Minter Saul stepped back from the truck. "No need to worry, Miss Vicki; things have a way of getting right." He touched his hat.

Vicki shrugged off his comment and pushed the gearshift into drive. "Well, goodbye Minter Saul and thanks for the help."

She pulled the truck onto the road, considered offering him a ride but then thought better of it. She hit the gas leaving him standing in the road.

Minter Saul watched the truck's rear lights flash. "Every goodbye ain't gone," he muttered.

Chapter 17

Nobody notices a church mouse, that's why it gets the cheese.

Mama took a sip from her coffee mug and sat the cup on the table. She thought about her mother's words, urging her to keep still whenever her father was in the house. Over the years, Mama had trained herself not to think about her mother Daisy, with the sad brown eyes and stringy hair. But sometimes, she couldn't hold back memories of Daisy's gentleness and love.

Whenever she conjured the image of her mother's battered face, she became five-year-old Bertie, sitting in the darkness of her room, knees pulled up to her chest, as quiet as a church mouse. Although just a memory, she could still hear the sickening sound of daddy's belt as it struck Daisy's bare skin. When Daisy's muffled cries slipped through the thin bedroom wall, Bertie covered her ears and wished her Mama could be quiet, like a church mouse.

Now Mama sipped her coffee, listening to the soft swish, swish, swish of the scrubber Trudy pulled back and forth across the ragged carpet. She could see Trudy's rear end from where she sat, as the girl crouched on her knees in the living room. What a useless task. That carpet was over thirty years old and threadbare in most places.

The house had gone to seed over the years because Mitch refused to spend a penny for fixing up. He had been more concerned with the meetings inside the Air Streamer and the weekly rituals they held in the yard.

These days, with Big Daddy down sick, they were struggling to make ends meet. It was all poke and grit, a saying her Mama Daisy used during lean times when there was nothing in the house to eat. "You can poke out your mouth and grit your teeth, little Bertie," she said, "But ain't nothing in the cupboard today."

Mama and Big Daddy lived on their monthly benefit checks from Swain Slaughterhouse, and they got a little from Social Security, too. Vicki gave money sometimes, but not often enough.

Mama had started working at Swain Slaughterhouse when she was fourteen years old. That very first week, she'd met Mitch Taggart. Three months later, she was showing with Baby Mitch in her belly. Her daddy came up to the company and spoke to Mitch in private. The next thing she knew, they were getting married. She had just turned fifteen; he was thirty-two.

At Swain, Mitch was a foreman. His men would slit the throats of the pigs and cows and then hang them upside down on the hooks to drain before they hit the conveyor belt. The blood-soaked belt moved slowly along to a line of girls, her included, who would hose the dead animals down and slice them into quarters with a meat cleaver.

She sipped her coffee, remembering how she had thought marrying Mitchell Taggart was such a prize, but it wasn't long before she realized he didn't love her at all. The only intimacies they shared were when he climbed on top of her each night. Otherwise, he was cold and distant. Her pregnancy was not easy. Her legs had swelled to the size of tree stumps, and she stayed nauseated for the whole nine months.

Mitch ignored her misery saying, "If you wanna get a house, you best keep working."

And so she did, every day, and she continued to work even after she became pregnant again with Vicki.

They lived in his parents' attic. It was large enough for all of them to sleep, but the rest of the house they shared. She fed the kids in his mother's kitchen and her mother-in-law, Sadie Taggart, watched her like a hawk.

"You gonna waste all that oatmeal? Put it up for later; this ain't no fancy restaurant." Sadie hadn't been pleased with her son's pick for a wife, and she showed it every chance she got. "You need to scrub them kids better, they filthy. Put them in the big washtub out back and use the lye soap. That will clean them up good." Her father-in-law Cyrus was quiet and said very little.

The only thing that got Bertie through each miserable day in that house was the thought that one day she and Mitch would have their own brand-new house. She dreamed of decorating with new carpets, the ones that looked Chinese with the bright colored swirls and symbols, and fancy furniture with a U-shaped sofa, and drapes that you could close for privacy and pull open for light, just like in the Good Housekeeping magazine.

"You need to stop wasting good money on magazines, girl!" Sadie would say. She called Bertie a doll head, full of saw dust, always dreaming.

Sometimes, when Bertie went with Mitch to town, she stopped in Piccolos' Furniture Store while waiting on him. She'd walk around savoring the smell of the imitation mahogany and eyeing the Oriental-style tables with gold-painted dragons holding up the glass. She'd imagine them in her living room; they would match her dream carpet perfectly. Back in the truck, she would tell Mitch about what she saw.

"We ain't havin' no chink-made furniture."

Bertie would take a deep breath, fold her arms, and sit back in the seat. She knew not to press it. Chinese furniture wasn't worth a slap in the mouth. She would simply look through the magazines for another idea.

But five years went by, and they were still living in the attic. And in spite of both their salaries, the money didn't seem to be there at month's end, and she didn't know why. Then, without warning, Tangeline Moore, a long-time secretary, left Swain. The word was she had moved to Atlanta for work, but Bertie found out she left because she was pregnant, and when she checked further, she discovered that Mitch was sending Tangeline money. He never told her anything about Tangeline, or a baby, and she knew better than to ask.

One morning, Sadie called up to the attic for Mitch to come down and see about his daddy.

"I can't wake him!"

Mitch sat perched on the mattress next to Cyrus, tears streaming down his face, shaking his daddy and crying for him to wake up. Sadie had sent for the doctor, and when he entered the bedroom and looked at Cyrus, he immediately concluded the old man was dead. After the funeral, Bertie and Mitch moved downstairs and Sadie moved into the attic.

A year later Sadie Taggart died and Bertie had the run of the house. She bought brand-new wallpaper from the money she saved and put it up in the kitchen. It was a lovely scene of bluebirds perched on tree limbs with pink buds and a brilliant sunset in the background. It was the beginning of what she had always wanted—a place that she could make her own. But the new wallpaper turned out to be the extent of her renovation effort.

"Stop wasting money!" Mitch barked at her. "My Mama's furnishings are just fine."

Now, thirty years later, Mama looked around the timeworn kitchen. A thick layer of cooking grease crusted the wallpaper concealing the bluebirds beneath black grime. In all these years, not one other thing in the house had changed. They even slept in Cyrus and Sadie's old bed and used their furniture. In fact, some of Sadie's clothes were still hanging in the wardrobe and whenever Mama opened the doors, the faint aroma of vapor rub and violet toilet water stirred her dismal memories.

Mama's sigh came from a dark place, so desolate it frightened her, and she clasped her hands and uttered a quick prayer hoping to boost her spirits. She moved to the screen door and peered out into the yard. A feeling of foreboding prevented her from stepping outside, but being indoors didn't quell her fear any less. This was Sadie Taggart's house; all her things were still here, Mama and her family where merely tenants.

Across the yard, the Air Streamer stood vacant. It frightened Mama, sometimes appearing in her nightmares as the entrance to hell.

Nobody notices a church mouse.

Mama recalled when the trailer first arrived; she'd been stirred from her chair by the sound of an engine straining and rocks crunching under its wheels. She'd hurried to the window and watched as Tate's field tractor hauled the Air Streamer by two heavy chains.

As the trailer rolled by, hope had surged and she'd envisioned family trips. Mitch had waved the trailer into the yard and Tate maneuvered it into the spot where it sat for three decades. Mitch never offered an explanation for the trailer and she didn't ask for one. Almost immediately, other men had arrived and gone inside where they'd remained for hours.

Mama wasn't stupid. She knew what Klan meetings looked like; he was holding them in the Air Streamer. Mitch was in charge and they were carrying on the legacy of his Klan ancestors. No. The trailer was never intended for the family.

Over the years, Mama got use to those weekly meetings and as small children, Baby Mitch and Vicki slept through the brutality outside their windows, while Mama sat quietly in the living room. Big Daddy had told her to never interfere when he was holding a meeting. Nobody notices a church mouse. So, she stayed still in the chair, leafing through Good Housekeeping magazine while humming a tune to muffle the sounds of murder.

Mama would remain in the chair until the rim of the rising sun cracked the sky with enough light for the men to get in their cars and creep away. Then, she would go into the kitchen put on a pot of coffee and fix something for her husband to eat.

She'd never felt any sort of way about what went on. She knew it was necessary for the safety of the county. She understood the Klan, and she knew what they stood for. She had seen these things all her life, and not just with Mitch. She'd been born in a town much smaller than Piney, and they'd held lynching's at the town fair every year.

It was a lively event for the people in her town, most of whom worked long hard hours for meager wages. Folks brought picnic baskets and sat on the grass while their kids played tag and bobbed for apples. Parents and children enjoyed the fun in anticipation of what would be the climax of the afternoon festivities, a grisly show the kids called loop the noose.

As the Sheriff's men pushed a Negro into the saddle, his hands fastened behind his back, the spring breeze played with the noose, swaying it back and forth like a child's swing. Soon enough, it would be transformed into an implement of brutal persecution inflicted by the hands of a youngster. A boy, with the permission of his parents, would scamper up the tree and shimmy out on the limb and loop the noose over the victim's head. Then, as quickly as possible, he would slide back down and run around to the back of the horse where the sting of his switch caused the animal to run forward. As the noose snapped tight, the man was snatched from the horse and the crowd went silent, transfixed by legs battling the air for a solid surface, eyeballs bulging beyond the rims, and the squeals of breath being choked into a thick drool oozed down his chin. When the body finally went limp, another horse was led to a tree limb and a different kid got a chance to play loop the noose with the next victim. The hanging ceremony could last for hours, depending on how many men were to be lynched that day.

As a child, Mama had seen countless public hangings. She had grown up playing under the feet of dead Negroes, their bodies swaying from the limbs of the large oak trees in a grove behind her own house. Her daddy and brothers used the bodies for target practice, shooting at them from the back porch. When the Undertaker finally showed up, he never asked why the bodies were riddled with bullet holes.

All of this was a way of life for Mama, no different than killing the coyotes that threatened the livestock.

She stepped out onto the porch. The sky was a dismal panorama over a bleak landscape. In the cornfield, the blanched cornhusks shuddered against the wind, a sure sign a storm was approaching. Best to bring the clothes in from the line, she reasoned. She looked back at Trudy still scrubbing that useless carpet. She would tell her to stop when she got back.

Mama hurried down the steps, scooped up the pail for the clothespins, and went to the line. The large sheets snapped against each strong gust, and Mama snatched the clothespins and draped sheets over her arm. She thought about Big Daddy, sitting in the bedroom, leafing through the Bible. She chuckled and muttered to herself, "I sure hope the Good Book don't catch on fire."

A brisk wind whipped her skirt up around her thighs and lifted her hair from her shoulders. She pushed her skirt down, saying, "Where in the world did this strong wind come from so fast?"

As soon as her words left her lips more gusts whipped in from all directions, sending sheets flying across the yard and snatching Big Daddy's shirts from the line. Mama balked, when the sheet on her arm lifted and sailed into the cornfield.

"Dang it!" she said, and that was when she saw him.

Mama wanted to run, but her legs wouldn't move. She wanted to scream, call out for Mitch, but her mouth had gone bone dry.

He leaned into the wind and his shirt billowed and flapped like a flag all around his bleak frame, and then, all at once the gust died down. Mama could see him clearly now—a colored boy with bright red hair. She sensed he was comfortable amidst the weed-ridden flora. The boy's garments were old, and encrusted with dirt, but it was his eyes that stunned her, pupils twitching with movements of a living entity, dark and glazed with gold flecks that flashed like lightning.

He limped on one leg; the other was severed with ragged skin that dripped blood from a torn stump. He looked at Mama with the presence of something that was not childlike; it was the face of something aged.

But the boy alone wasn't what caused the hair on her neck to prickle and rise; it was the dark shadow that stood behind him. Mama's skin crawled up her arms at the hundreds of flies in the form of a man.

They were black houseflies with shimmering wings that glinted as they twitched around the face, and then its eyes popped open glaring at her with evil intent, but suddenly, another voice broke the spell it had on her.

A sweet voice called to her. "Miss Mama Bertie."

Mama looked around and saw Teeny, standing at the edge of the cornfield just on the other side from where the boy stood. She was shocked as she looked at the girl and quickly reasoned that Trudy hadn't been dead when they carried her into the cornfield. But on second thought, she couldn't be alive, not after Baby Mitch had buried her. Yet, here she was, smiling and waving at Mama. Teeny's dress was dirt-ridden from the grave and her blond hair was dark with dirt and dried blood.

"Hi, Miss Mama Bertie."

Mama tried to speak, but she couldn't get any words to leave her mouth until finally she found enough saliva to moisten her parched tongue. "Teeny?"

"Come here, Miss Mama Bertie."

Mama was terrified. She didn't move. She looked back at the boy and the thing that stood behind him. His voice was gentle, soothing, the voice of a child when he said, "Go with Teeny if you want forgiveness, Miss Mama Bertie."

"Forgiveness?"

"Yes."

Mama stepped forward and staggered toward Teeny, but as she got closer Teeny backed into the cornfield.

"Wait, Teeny."

Now, Mama found herself inside the cornfield, and all around her, the hovering stalks bristled and shook their silky tassels in the breeze. A hamlet of toads croaked incessantly alongside an aria of chirping insects. Mama was astonished at the activity in the seemingly barren field.

Only a few feet away, Teeny beckoned Mama with a sweet smile. She felt compelled to follow the girl, but every time Mama was close enough to touch Teeny, the thick foliage closed in, preventing contact.

"C'mon, Miss Mama Bertie," Teeny sang out.

Without warning, Teeny took off running, her short legs moving through the wilderness with ease.

"Hurry up, Miss Mama Bertie."

Mama was stunned at Teeny's quickness, but she was also conflicted: should she follow Teeny, or turn back? The boy said forgiveness, and that was something she wanted badly. There were so many things she had done, had ignored, or helped to cover up, would she be forgiven for all of it? She heard Teeny's laughter and decided to push forward.

As she shoved the weeds aside, another thought emerged. Maybe she could make things right. She could bring Teeny back to Pastor Thomas, and Trudy would have her playmate again. Now, instead of being as quiet as a church mouse, she could do something good. Her heart leapt at the thought of redemption.

The shifting breeze was gone as Mama trudged through the cornfield in the blazing heat. Sweat poured from her body, drenching her housedress and slicking her hair back. She frowned at the denseness of the vines and creeping plants. She swatted at the insects that buzzed in her ears and nervously sidestepped a fat ground frog underfoot. It croaked when she stepped over it. It was a sound that vibrated in her ears like the call of a hundred frogs croaking all at once.

It croaked again and she felt fluid trickle down the side of her face. She touched her ear and saw blood on her fingers. Mama shook her head, something was moving inside her left ear. She pushed her pinky inside and yelped in pain when a black fly tumbled out unleashing fresh blood. Yet, she wasn't afraid. Her only concern was getting Teeny and bringing her home.

Mama moved away from the huge toad as quickly as she could, especially when she saw it growing to the size of a well-fed dog. She had to get away before it croaked again. This time, the sound might shatter her head open. She thought for a moment about what she was seeing; these things made no sense, but she had no choice but to keep going.

Mama pushed forward even as the path became increasingly difficult to navigate. The corn stalks were now hard and ridged and she used all her strength just to pull them apart and step through.

"Teeny!" she called out.

Her eyes caught flashes of Teeny's yellow sweater as the girl waggled ahead of her, parting the stalks with ease. Her giggles swirled in her wake and the tune "Bingo" rose from her lips, a musical path for Mama to follow.

"Teeny, stop! Wait for me!"

Mama rubbed the red welts and bug bites that pinched her arms and caught one last glimpse of Teeny disappearing into the brush. But now, a wall laden with vines so thick and hard blocked her path and she was unable to follow. Terror shook her senses when Mama noticed that the cornhusks were inching forward, surrounding her with masts so unyielding they blocked any means of escape.

Her eyes widened to the size of melons and she burst into tears and she screamed and screamed and called out to Teeny. "Teeny! I'm sorry, I'm so sorry!"

But Mama knew it wasn't just Teeny. It was all the others that she had ignored, like the boys and men whose bodies rotted, here, in the soil of the cornfield.

She felt movement under her feet and looked down and was horrified when she saw plant roots wriggling out of the earth and crawling toward her like hungry snakes. She stomped on them but her flimsy house shoes were useless and fell from her feet. As Mama fought to avoid the creeping roots, the cornstalks continued to close in. She lashed out, shoving them over, but they rose up more burley than before. In minutes, Mama was encased in a shroud of thick cornhusks, and like a Chinese finger trap the more she struggled, the tighter the sheaths constricted, until she was completely immobilized, the only part of her still visible was her head.

Terrified, she screamed out for her husband, "Mitch! Help me! Mitch!" Her breathing restricted by the tightening plants, she grew weaker by the minute and she gasped for air. Suddenly, the sharp ends of the creeping roots pierced her feet and she yelped in agony as the tenacious roots wriggled inside her legs sliding over bone and tissue and creeping up through her organs. On they traveled, like slithering parasites past her lungs and into her throat. Mama gagged on clots of blood, and broken flesh gurgled in her mouth, she spat blood but managed only two words: "I'm sorry."

Wrapped tightly in a hardened cerecloth, she was rendered mute when the weeds severed her tongue and then traveled up inside her head where they pierced her eyeballs and sprouted yellow flora on her face.

Mama was now a permanent part of the cornfield, her head a hideous bloom.

Chapter 18

Big Daddy traced the words in his mother's Bible with a nervous finger, reading aloud, "Isaiah 54:17: No weapon formed against thee shall prosper."

"Here it is, right here," he said, breathing a sigh of relief. "I'm protected."

He wiped sweat from his forehead and looked up at the overhead fan. The blades whirred slowly around a wobbly base that sloped down on a withered cord. "When you gonna fix the fan?" he recalled Bertie saying. "It's gonna drop and kill us one day." He smirked. Killed in bed by a fan would be a better ending than what he feared.

"No weapon formed against me shall prosper," he repeated and awkwardly crossed himself. He closed the Bible and held it close to his chest. "No weapon formed against me shall prosper."

All of this had started weeks ago when that hideous animal turned up in his yard and literally scared the piss out of him, but it was what he had seen in Collier's truck that sent him to the safety of his room. He closed the Bible and affectionately stroked the leather-bound cover.

"No weapon formed against me shall prosper."

He was hearing things, voices, right here in the room. Last night, he imagined something standing next to the bed, causing him to cower under the covers, his eyes jammed tight against visions of terror and shivering in a shower of sweat. He heard a whip snapping against skin and bloodcurdling shrieks. The suffering went on throughout the night preventing the sleep his tired body craved.

"I only used it one time!" he shouted.

His daddy and granddaddy had been ruthless with the whip. The things he had seen them do had been seared into his brain and stuck with him like a fat tick on a dog.

"No weapon formed against me shall prosper."

His eyes had popped open from a fitful attempt at sleep and he was suddenly shaken by a pitiful voice that seemed to be coming out of the ceiling fan. He looked up at the blades whirring around on a lopsided base and heard Bertie's voice—she was calling Teeny.

What on earth, he thought, sitting up in bed. It sounded as if Bertie was actually talking to the girl. "Come here," he heard her say. The rustling of leaves told him Bertie was in the cornfield. He heard her whimpering and crying out for help.

Sorry, Bertie, he thought, as her voice faded.

"No weapon formed against me shall prosper."

Big Daddy pushed the cover back and sat up. His feet hit the puckered linoleum and he groaned against a stabbing back pain but managed to stand. He moved to the corner end of his dresser and let loose a stream of piss into a bucket. Bertie's voice was gone now, the fan silent except for the annoying hum of the blades.

"Another nightmare," he muttered.

The fan droned in concert with the drumming of his piss hitting the metal bucket, but there was still something else. A tapping sound that reminded him of the woodpecker that hammered into a dead tree in his daddy's yard. He'd always wanted to shoot that bird, but by the time he'd gotten Cyrus's gun, it had flown off.

As the rattling of his pissing dwindled, the tapping continued and he realized it was someone at the bedroom door.

"No weapon formed against me shall prosper." He whispered.

"Granpa, it's me, Trudy." She tapped again, softly, in case he was sleeping.

"Sweet child," he muttered, but he wasn't going to answer. He heard the pads of her bare feet run back up the hallway.

"Damn fool, JT."

He thought about Vicki, his little sweet pea had changed so much over the years; she didn't take the Klan seriously. His first mistake was when she was caught talking to a Nigger boy. He wanted to take a switch to her right then and there, but Bertie had stopped him, saying she was only a child. Things were fine for a spell, until Vicki graduated high school. After that, he heard she was spending time with the Hurley boy and he was enraged; the Hurley's were a family of Nigger lovers, which, in his opinion, was just as bad as being a Nigger. He was done listening to Bertie and he reckoned someone else could make Vicki see reason.

It had been his idea for JT Smalls to talk to Vicki. JT had just started work at Frasier and Son's Garage and was a Klan member in the Athens Chapter. JT was a big guy who didn't talk much and was only a few years older than Vicki. When he explained to JT that Vicki was caught up with a Nigger lover, JT nodded his head with understanding. Big Daddy had hopes that JT could turn her interest and the two might start dating. However, Bertie didn't like JT; she said she didn't trust him, said he had a darkness about him that was worrisome to her, but Big Daddy paid her no mind; she worried about everything, so he didn't tell her about his conversation with JT.

In hindsight, Bertie had been right. When he saw how badly Vicki was beaten and found out that she had been raped, he jumped in his truck and drove to Athens, found JT, and put a bullet in the back of his head. Best not to mention any of that to Collier, he didn't need to know everything. The only person who did know was Baby Mitch who rode with him to Athens and knew how to keep his mouth shut.

Now, Vicki had a child she hated and a problem with the bottle, but at least she wasn't with that Hurley boy, he reasoned. He had left it up to Bertie to handle the aftermath of Vicki's attack; he had other things going on that he was trying to make sense of.

The room was stuffy and hot. His sweaty feet stuck to the linoleum as he limped back to the bed and sat down. He wasn't hungry, but quenched his thirst from a water jug he kept next to the bed. He gazed up at the ceiling; water stains were spreading. He needed to get more shingle tile from the Jew before the next big rain. He figured the humming sound he kept hearing was from the fan, but then he realized it wasn't. It was coming from the window. He stood up.

"No weapon formed against me shall prosper."

Big Daddy pushed the shabby curtains aside. A haze of dust floated in the sunlight and he sneezed loudly, twice. He wiped his nose on his wrist, and then pulled the blinds all the way up. The outside of the window was covered with a dark, sooty substance.

"What happened to the damn window?" he said.

Then he noticed an opening the size of a quarter in the center of the screen, and like a peeping Tom, pressed his eye to the window glass and looked through.

At first, he was looking at the front yard, but suddenly, the air rippled like a great heat mirage and it wasn't his yard anymore. It was the Crawley farm.

He saw himself sitting behind the wheel of his Fairlane Squire station wagon. Two men rode up on horseback. It was Owen and Ernest. It had been their turn on patrol. He watched himself open the car door and step out to meet the men.

"We got one, Mitch!" Ernest yelled.

"Good thing we got there," added Owen, "Your little girl was out there with 'em, and it looked like something was going on between the two."

"Where's he at? Can you get him to the cornfield?" Mitch asked.

"No need. The horses kicked and ran so hard he's scattered all over Crawley's," Owen chuckled.

"All right, then," Mitch said. "Less work for us to do."

But as the three prepared to leave an old truck roared through the field gouging up dirt and grass. It skidded to a halt, alarming the horses and causing them to rear up. A Negro man holding a shotgun jumped out.

"Where's my boy?" he shouted, his face full of rage.

"Who you think you talking to, Nigger?" Owen said, and spat a wad on the ground.

The man pointed the shotgun at Owen's face.

"Hold on now, Nigger," Ernest yelled.

In an instant, he swung the shotgun around and let loose a barrel into Ernest's chest, his body exploded from the blast and hit the ground with a grisly thud and his horse took off running.

"Oh shit!" Owen shouted. "Are you crazy?"

The man swung his shotgun and once again pointed the barrel at Owen's face. "I said, where's my boy?"

"Okay, now hold on." Owen lifted his hands in surrender.

Mitch's hands rose as well.

At that same time, the man saw the rope looped around the horn of Owen's saddle. The long end trailed behind his horse. Angry tears brimmed as he looked up at Owen.

"You dragged my boy?" he said in disbelief.

"Wait; hold on, Nigger, he was messin' . . . ."

The shotgun jerked twice. The first shot blew Owen's head from his shoulders and the second shot took out his chest. His horse whinnied in fear and reared up, it charged through the field with Owen's bloody remains still stuck to the saddle.

Then, the man swung his rifle on Mitch.

"Okay, hold on, boy," Mitch, said. "I just got here. I don't know what the hell is going on."

The man wiped the tears from his eyes, his finger resting on the trigger. Suddenly, a shot rang out and Mitch staggered backward but felt no pain. He saw the Negro man collapse to one knee, blood was pouring from his thigh and he fell over on his back. Mitch hurried over and kicked the shotgun away and then he looked around.

Thirteen-year-old Baby Mitch leaned out of the back window of the Ford Fairlane, Mitch's gun still smoking in his hand.

Mitch walked over and stood looking down at the man as he grimaced in pain on the ground.

"Bring me your granddaddy's whip, son," he said, and when Baby Mitch handed him the bullwhip, he lashed the man until the Negro's skin was flayed open. When he was done, he stood back huffing with exhaustion. His arm ached from yielding the whip and he wiped sweat from his brow. Baby Mitch stared at the Negro man's shredded body.

"He goin' in the cornfield, Big Daddy?"

"No. Let's put him on Preecher's side."

Mitch and his son loaded the Negro man into the rear of the Fairlane.

At the Preecher farm, they pushed him out onto the ground and when Big Daddy peered into what was left of the Negro's face he was startled to see the man's eyes glaring at him with hatred.

"Can I shoot him, Big Daddy?" the boy took aim.

"No, son."

"What we gonna do?"

"Get the shovel. We gonna bury him right here while he's still breathing, and before he takes his last breath, he'll think about his boy being dragged through the field and no one will ever find either one of 'em."

Mitch backed away from the window just as the hole closed over sealing the glass in blackness. "Fuck," he muttered, and wiped his beefy hands over his sweaty face. "What in hell conjured that up?" As he puzzled over what just occurred, he looked at the dark substance on the glass—it was moving. His curiosity brought him closer and he bent down, his eyes just inches away from the window when something fluttered. He jerked back as green and blue florescent wings came into focus. It was flies, millions of flies rippling on the glass.

"Jesus!" He blurted, but nonetheless reached out and touched the pane, confirming he was safe inside the room. He smirked. "You're out there and as long as I keep this window closed, you'll stay out there." Mitch pulled the blinds down and snatched the curtains closed.

"No weapon formed against me shall prosper."

Back on the bed, he breathed a sigh of relief and reached for the water jug. He raised it to his lips but abruptly pulled back and observed one small fly, its wings shimmering blue and green, hopping around the rim of the jug. The insect suddenly lifted off.

His eyes followed it upward where it joined a mass of quivering flies blanketing the ceiling. He watched in horror as the insects swarmed above his head and he quickly averted his eyes from the horde and squeezing his eyelids shut he repeated, "no weapon formed against me shall . . . ." Big Daddy's words were lost in the ungodly drone of fluttering wings -- and then he was shrouded in vermin.

Chapter 19

Hurley cruised along next to the cornfield; he was aggravated by the sky-high growth of useless weeds bordering the road.

He shook his head and grumbled, "When the hell are they gonna take all this mess down?" He turned his focus back on the road.

This morning, he had received a call from Vicki. She'd been upset. Her mother had gone missing and she wanted his help finding her. She had waited two days before contacting him and he figured things must be bad if she called him. He knew that he was the last person she wanted to see. Still, he was glad she called, and he would help her any way he could.

The previous Sheriff, Alton Collier, and his band of cretins had instilled suspicion in the community, and many hardworking people often never saw justice. With that being the case, Hurley was having a hard time gaining trust. He had a lot of work to do to change opinions, but he had faith that with time, people would see that he was an honest and fair Sheriff.

Hurley's hands were sweaty and his head ached with nervous anticipation as he neared the Taggart Place. He had not spoken to Vicki in years. The attack she'd suffered had been heinous, and at the time, he was immature and didn't know how to handle such a tragedy. He had put off going to see her, telling himself she needed time to recover. He had also used her family as an excuse. The two times he'd called, her mother had slammed the phone down as soon as she heard his voice. As the weeks turned into months and months into years, guilt weighed heavily on his shoulders and he could not find the courage to face her.

She had a child now. The town gossip said the baby was from the attack, but sometimes he wondered if the child could be his, which was another thing he pushed from his thoughts.

Hurley tried to convince himself that he and Vicki were finished, but still, he found himself driving by the Busy Bee Diner where she worked. The Diner had a large window and he could easily see inside. He watched Vicki taking orders from customers and was relieved because she seemed to be okay. He wanted to go inside, but what would he do next? Order coffee, a donut? What would he say? "Sorry I wasn't around for nine years?" So he kept driving.

Movement up ahead caught Hurley's attention, and he slowed. There was a child on the road, a little girl, and she seemed to be playing with someone in the cornfield. He watched as she tossed a ball into the cornfield and a moment later the ball sailed back out. It bounced and rolled on the ground. She scooped it up and quickly hit it over the high stalks and after a moment it again flew back out.

"I got it!" she hollered, in triumph.

Hurley pulled over and stepped out of the vehicle. "Hello."

The girl seemed unafraid and she proved it when dimples pleated her cheeks on each side of her smile. She had large brown eyes that were the same color as the tangled mane that hung down her back. Hurley noticed that her clothes were too small for a growing child and her shoes were run over.

"I'm Sheriff Hurley. What's your name?"

"Trudy."

"What are you doing out here alone, Trudy?"

"I'm not alone. I'm playing catch with my friend."

"Where's your friend?"

She pointed at the cornfield.

"I don't think that's a good place for your friend to be."

"He lives there."

"Is that so? Well, tell him to come out so I can meet him."

Trudy paused. She looked down, then back up at Hurley. "He won't."

"Why not?"

"He doesn't like grownups."

"What's your friend's name?"

"James."

Hurley called out, "Hey, James! I'm Sheriff Hurley. Will you come out so we can meet?" He winked at Trudy. "I promise not to hurt you."

Minutes passed without a sound from the cornfield.

"He's gone," she said.

"Where do you live, Trudy?"

She pointed at the house up ahead.

"The Taggart place?" he said, surprised. "Don't tell me you're Vicki's little girl?"

"Yes, suh."

"How old are you, Trudy?"

"Eight."

Hurley stood motionless as Trudy smiled up at him. He'd known that some time had passed since he'd seen Vicki, but hearing this child say she was eight years old crushed him to the core and his emotions bounced between guilt and regret like a Ping-Pong ball. What had paralyzed him so much that he had ignored the situation for so long? He shoved his hands in his pockets and looked up at the sky, his eyes burned with regret. But he composed himself and turned his attention back to Trudy. Her hair was the same color as his. Was it possible that she could be his daughter? And if she was, he had abandoned her too. She stood looking at him with a child's curiosity.

"Well, Trudy, he said. "I'm on my way to see your mother. Do you want a ride home?"

Her face lit up with excitement. "Yes, suh!"

Vicki stood barefoot on the tile floor and stared at herself in the bathroom mirror. A headache pulsed her temples. All she could remember from last night was drinking at Silkys Bar and the bartender telling her she had to leave, they were closing. She couldn't recall how she was able to drive home, but apparently she did, her truck was parked on the lawn out front. She had collapsed on the sofa still dressed in her waitress uniform, makeup smeared on the pillow, her hair standing on end, and her face swollen from another turbulent dream.

She heard Mama's voice in her head. "You look a hot mess!"

"Thanks, Mama," she mumbled.

Inside the medicine cabinet, she found the Witch-hazel and poured some of the acrid-smelling liquid onto a piece of toilet paper. She dabbed her swollen face with the astringent and closed the cabinet and looked in the mirror, "You do look a hot mess."

The tapping on the door was scant, reluctant. She knew who it was.

"Vicki," Trudy said, "Your friend, the Sheriff, is here to visit you."

"My friend?" she said, and smirked.

"Tell him to wait on the porch."

"Okay."

She hadn't wanted to call Hurley, not for anything in the world but two days had passed with no sign of Mama. Now Hurley was standing on her porch. Her head ached and she felt sick.

Vicki took a breath and then leaned close to the mirror, examining her bloodshot eyes. She had been crying in her sleep again. She opened the medicine cabinet and grabbed the bottle of aspirin and tossed two back, followed by a drink of water. Her hand rubbed her forehead, "I can't think about this now," she muttered and tried to banish all thoughts that led back to the reel of horror spinning in her head. But she knew that whatever happened in her dreams often reached into her waking hours trailing behind her like a lumbering beast. Vicki prayed for just an ounce of peace to get through the day, and when that failed, she reached for whatever liquor bottle she had in the cabinet. Right now, she would need some liquid courage to face Hurley. The pint of whiskey was new and she broke the seal.

Vicki unscrewed the cap and took two belts grimacing against the alcohol burn. She rubbed a dollop of toothpaste on her teeth with her finger and like she often did as a child put her lips on the faucet and filled her cheeks with cold water, then swished and spit.

"He can wait a few more minutes," Vicki said to her reflection, and she opened her makeup bag. Her whiskey-addled brain convinced her that makeup would hide her bedraggled face. The more she applied the less pain the world would see, so she began with her favorite—azure-blue eye shadow.

Vicki squatted in Mama's rocker glaring at Hurley who was perched on the edge of Big Daddy's chair to avoid the sunken seat pad. Uncomfortable under her gaze, he tugged at his collar. She looked at his tan uniform and starched trousers; the badge pinned on his shirt pocket was impressive. He had taken his hat off when he stepped up onto the porch and now he balanced it on one knee. His thick hair was mashed flat by his hat and he raked it up with his fingers. Her gaze went to the scar over his lip. She recalled the dozens of times she'd kissed it, but blinked the memory away and got to the point.

"Two days, Hurley. She's been gone two days."

"When was the last time you spoke to her?"

"I said two days. Are you deaf?" she snapped.

"I'm sorry, just trying to get all the information correct."

"On Monday before I left for work, we were in the kitchen. When I got home she was gone."

"What about Mr. Taggart? Has he seen her?"

"Big Daddy's sick. He don't even come out of the room no more."

"Sorry to hear that."

"Mama took to sleeping on the sofa so she wouldn't bother him."

Hurley scribbled in a note pad.

"Are you gonna find her?"

He paused, "Yes, of course."

"Like you found Teeny?" she said, icily.

Hurley stopped writing and looked at her, his eyes solemn. "I know it looks bad that we haven't located that girl. But I do believe she ran off. When someone doesn't want to be found it's a lot harder for law enforcement."

"Seems to me that Teeny doesn't have that much sense, but she could have gone off with someone."

"I'm looking into that possibility."

Hurley stood up, placed his hat on the table, walked to the edge of the porch and looked across the yard. "What about the cornfield? Would she go in there?"

He looked over his shoulder at her as she sipped from a cup of something he was sure wasn't lemonade. Hurley was disturbed by Vicki's appearance. When she'd first stepped out and he saw her, he was stunned and averted his eyes so she wouldn't notice. The dark-blue eyelids, false eyelashes and red lipstick rendered her almost unrecognizable.

"Nope, no way Mama would go in that jungle."

"I understand what you mean, but I think a search of the cornfield is needed," Hurley said.

"If you want to waste your time," she waved her hand indifferently. "But I'm telling you, Mama ain't in the cornfield."

"Let me handle this, okay?"

"Suit yourself." She stood up and immediately swayed off balance.

Hurley caught her and when he did, he smelled the whiskey. "You okay?"

"I'm fine!" she snatched her arm away.

"You know I'm here for you." As soon as the words left his mouth, he regretted them.

She balked. "You weren't here for me before. Why now?" She staggered away from him.

He looked at her with regret. "I wanted to . . . ."

"Go to hell, Hurley!" She teetered and grabbed the porch rail her face warped with anger. "Get off my porch until you have some news about Mama!"

Back in his cruiser, Hurley sat looking at the Taggart house, lamenting his reckless words.

"Damn it!" he muttered, shaking his head.

"Boo!" Trudy sang out as she popped up next to his window—grinning from ear to ear.

"Where'd you come from?" her sweet smile was infectious, and he smiled.

"I was hiding over there," she pointed at the cornfield.

"Did you go in the cornfield?"

"No."

"You think your grandma went in there?"

"Uh-huh," she nodded.

"What makes you think that?"

"James saw her."

"Your friend who plays with you?"

"Uh-huh."

"Can you show me?" he got out of the vehicle.

"Yes, but you can't go in."

Trudy led Hurley to a wall of cornstalks covered by scraggly weeds and dried husks that stretched the length of the Taggart property.

Up close, he was amazed at how strong the plants looked, almost like wooden planks surrounding the field. He reached out and tried to separate the stalks but the thick stems were stiff and immobile.

"See, they won't open for you."

"Who will they open for?"

"James and the others."

"What others?"

Trudy shrugged. "Are you gonna find Mama Bertie?"

"I hope so."

"I'm sad."

"Why are you sad, Trudy?"

"James said she couldn't come back and be with me anymore."

Hurley stooped down until he was eye-level with Trudy. "James sounds like he knows a lot. I really would like to meet him."

"You will," she said, smiling.

He stood up when he heard the screen door open and he saw Vicki step onto the porch. Her hands planted on her hips she glowered at Trudy and Hurley. Trudy's smile faded and she said, "I haveta go home," and ran back to the house.

She raced up the hill and stumbled up the porch steps. Hurley saw Vicki grab Trudy's arm and push her inside.

Inside the house, Vicki screamed at Trudy, "What did I tell you about talking to strangers?"

"But he's your friend."

"He's not my friend, and he's a stranger to you!"

"I'm sorry, Mommy."

"Don't call me that!"

Trudy shuddered and backed up.

"Did you tell him my business?"

"Uh...."

"What did you say?" She shouted.

"I only said I hope he finds Mama Bertie soon."

"Oh, I know you said more than that!" Vicki swayed and collapsed onto the sofa.

"You stay right there." Her finger poked the air.

"When I get up, you..." but then her eyelids heavy from lack of sleep dropped down and she began to snore. Trudy tip toed out of the room and ran out the back door.

As she stood on the back porch a voice whispered in her ear and her head turned toward the cornfield -- James peered at her through the enormous stalks.

"Hey," he called out, his arm waved back and forth over his head.

"C'mon and play."

Smiling happily, Trudy bounded down the steps and hurried to join him. When she reached his side, he took her by the hand and led her into the cornfield.

Chapter 20

The plastic hula doll jiggled wildly as Baby Mitch drove recklessly down the road bouncing over uneven ground and taking turns much too fast. He had won the little doll at Smiley's Carnival when he chucked six darts, hitting the mark each time. The doll was his first choice because she had nice pointy tits and a suction cup at the bottom that could stick to his dash. Unfortunately, in the summer heat the little doll's plastic head had melted inside the hot truck. However, even headless she was still a lively little thing, bobbing and swaying through each impure venture he set into motion.

Baby Mitch sang along with the radio; it was a country tune about a man who wanted a lady on his arm, a cook in the kitchen, and a slut in the bedroom. He laughed out loud and crooned, "A slut in the bedroom, I know that's right."

He flicked the hula doll with two fingers, sending her into a bobbing frenzy. When the song ended, he cut the radio off and thought about the Preecher house. He'd gone there yesterday, walked around inside, and went upstairs to the big bedroom. It would be nice having a real bedroom for him and Millie, and he would turn that office into a room for baby Jesse. He chuckled; he had named his son after the outlaw Jesse James. Now that was a name a kid could be proud of, not a stupid nickname he couldn't shake—Baby Mitch—he hated that name. He was almost thirty years old and everywhere he went people always called him Baby Mitch. But that would change when he got the Preecher house; then he would get the respect he deserved.

The first thing he wanted to do in the house was make more room, so he decided to get rid of all the books, the file cabinets, papers, and other junk kept in the office. A new coat of paint and a bed for Jesse would look just fine. He'd gone downstairs and looked in the kitchen, and walked out on the porch. He imagined the porch would be a good place for a marriage ceremony for him and Millie. Mama and Millie's kin could cook food in the kitchen for his guests.

Vicki had told him Mama was missing. What a crock. She had probably gone to Aunt June's house. She did that from time to time when she was fed up. These days, with Big Daddy acting a fool, she had plenty to be fed up about. He figured she would find some joy in preparing for his marriage ceremony, and he couldn't wait for her to get back so they could start planning.

Before leaving the house, he had bounded back up the steps and gathered up a bunch Preecher's papers from the desk, but only the ones that looked important. Now, they sat stacked on his passenger seat. He was headed over to see Vicki, get her to look through the stuff. He knew she wasn't sold on his plan, but he needed her good credit when the time came to go to the bank.

"Just be nice to her a little while longer," he muttered, "After that, she can go straight to hell."

All of sudden Baby Mitch's foot slammed the brake sending him rocketing into the steering wheel. "Shit!" He leaned back, rubbing the ache in his chest. "What the hell?"

He leaned forward and peered through the windshield at what looked like a dog standing in the road. But upon closer inspection he saw that the animal's body was too long for it to be a dog and it was low to the ground like a lizard. It was gray with dark spots and the snout was long and wide. The thing cocked its head and looked at Baby Mitch through black eyes that suddenly glowed red like the tip of an inhaled cigarette but then quickly turned black again.

"Shit!"

The lower half of the animal's mouth dropped down revealing a row of sharp teeth that were caked with something fleshy. When the creature continued to focus on him, he felt the hair on his arms prickle and his heart was thumping twice as fast.

"Here, boy."

The voice was familiar; it was a girl's voice and the animal's head turned toward the sound. The bushes rustled and something yellow hopped around behind the trees. When he looked back to the road, the animal was gone, he shuddered and a queasy feeling of nausea threatened. A grim secret tapped his muddled brain opening his thoughts to a myriad of repulsive acts he had undertaken and he recalled the sweater Teeny had been wearing, it was yellow. He had taken it off and wrapped her bloody head in it.

"This is bullshit," he said aloud, and quickly came up with a more acceptable explanation. "Coyotes," he decided. "Yep, that's what I saw, and they're some plumb ugly critters."

Baby Mitch turned to the little doll, "I bet there's a pack of 'em back in them bushes—but that voice?" He thought for a moment and then, "a kid," he decided, some kids fooling around." Puzzled, he scratched his head. "But way out here, with coyotes running around?"

Baby Mitch eased off the brake and coasted forward to the spot where the animal had been. He looked over into the clearing and his heart vaulted, sending his blood pressure sky-high.

Teeny stood watching him; her head was caked with dried blood and her face a shriveled prune. She looked at him through eyes brittle with mold and she was wearing the yellow sweater. Teeny waved at him, and like a wooden figure in a toy truck, Baby Mitch froze.

His heart pulsed violently as pain throbbed in his forehead and without warning blood gushed from his nose running over his lips and seeping down his neck. He quickly looked away from the horrid vision and ripped pieces from a paper napkin and stuffed each nostril, then opened his mouth to breathe.

"Okay, don't panic. Just drive!" he told himself and lifted his foot from the brake. The truck drifted past the bushes.

When he mashed the accelerator the truck leapt forward and he gripped the wheel with one hand, while trying to quell the bleeding with the other. Bouncing over rocks and uneven road, the little doll shimmied frantically.

"She wasn't dead," he said to the hula doll.

Chapter 21

"Vicki, get out here," Baby Mitch pounded on Vicki's bedroom door. "Vicki! Get the hell out here!"

Vicki cracked the door and peered at her brother through sleep-deprived eyes. "What the hell, Baby Mitch?"

He stared at his sister—her faced was creased from rough sleep, hair tousled and she reeked of booze.

"I'm sleeping! I worked late last night." Then she saw the blood on his shirt. "What happened to you?"

"I had a nosebleed, that's all."

"That was some nosebleed. Your shirt is soaked."

"Yeah, I know."

He looked down at his wet shirt and then quickly pulled it over his head and stood bare-chested in front of her.

"You look crazy."

He started to blurt out what he had seen on the road, the animal, and then Teeny, but he caught himself, instead saying, "I went to the Preecher place yesterday."

"What for?"

Vicki pushed past her brother and went into the kitchen; Baby Mitch trailed behind her dabbing his bloody nose with his shirt. At the sink, she filled a glass with water but before she touched her lips to the glass Baby Mitch plucked it from her hand and guzzled it down. Water drizzled on to his bare chest.

"You were thirsty, huh? She said.

"Yeah," he wiped his mouth on the back of his hand and leaned against the sink.

"Something happen?"

"Huh? Naw, nothing, just a nose bleed is all." He said, sheepishly.

Vicki filled another glass and took a sip. "So, why were you at Preecher's place?"

"Just to look around," he mumbled, while trying to appear as normal as possible.

"Uh huh," she muttered.

"That old black man let you look around his place?" she said, eyeing him suspiciously.

"He wasn't there."

"That's trespassing. You can't just go in somebody's house."

"It ain't his house. Besides, he's not coming back."

"You know that, how?"

"I just know."

She suddenly noticed the piles of papers stacked on the kitchen table. "What the hell is all of this?" She picked up a page and looked at it. "This is an invoice for Ned Preecher. What the hell, Baby Mitch? You stole a dead man's papers?"

"Borrowed Vicki, - - just so we can get an idea of his worth, you know?"

"No, I don't know!"

"I'll put everything back as soon as we . . . ."

"No!" she interrupted. "You need to take this stuff outta here right now."

"I just need you to take a look at it first."

The argument was cut short when a pitiful moan rumbled up the hallway – they froze and stared at each other.

"What the hell was that?" Said Baby Mitch.

"It's Big Daddy." Vicki put the paper down and hurried down the hall, stopping in front of Big Daddy's bedroom door. Baby Mitch was right behind her just as another moan crept from the room.

"Big Daddy, it's Vicki. What's wrong?"

Baby Mitch stepped around his sister and nudged her aside. "Big Daddy, it's Baby Mitch. Can I come in? I need to talk to you." He tried the doorknob. "It's locked."

Vicki looked at him. "He doesn't want you to come in, stupid."

"Shut up!"

The sudden thud that slammed into the door was so violent it sent them both scurrying back against the opposite wall.

Vicki looked at her brother whose face had gone stark white, the blood on his nose made him look like a demented clown. She smirked and pointed at his face, saying, "You need to clean your nose, Bozo." Her fingered scraped the bloody crust.

"Stop playing," he said, slapping her hand away. He nodded at Big Daddy's door. "What's going on in there?"

Vicki approached the door again, but Baby Mitch hung back against the wall.

"How could he do that, he's so weak," She said.

"You sure he's alone?"

"Yeah! He won't let anyone come in."

Baby Mitch stepped forward saying, "Well, I need to talk to him about important business."

"What makes you think he wants to talk to you?"

The bickering was interrupted by a small voice. "Granpa doesn't want to talk." Trudy was standing in the doorway of her room.

"What do you know about anything?" Vicki said, sharply.

"Well, hey there, little niece," Baby Mitch grinned and knelt down in front of the child. "Have you talked to Granpa lately?"

"No."

"Then how do you know he don't wanna talk to nobody?"

"James told me."

"Who the hell is James?" he asked, and looked up at Vicki.

Vicki's face blazed with anger and she yelled, "What did I tell you about lying?" She lunged at Trudy, who skirted past her and took off running down the hall, through the kitchen, and out the back door.

Baby Mitch, tickled by the whole thing, roared with laughter. "Run, Trudy, run!" he hollered, or the big bad witch will get you!"

An hour later, Vicki and Baby Mitch sat out front on the porch steps sharing a bottle of whiskey.

"Where did your kid run off to?"

Vicki shook her head saying, "I'm so sick of that kid lying to me."

"Kids lie all the time."

"The lies she tells are meant to hurt me."

"How does a kid, who barely talks, and is scared of her own shadow, hurt you?"

"She knows stuff."

"What stuff?"

Vicki took a sip of whiskey and handed the bottle to her brother. "I don't want to talk about it."

"Well," he sighed. "I guess we all have secrets." He swallowed from the bottle hoping to drown his vision of Teeny with alcohol.

"Yeah," Vicki replied, thinking he was alluding to her.

"You can always send her away. My friend Pete sent his son away when the kid started acting up." He took another swig of whiskey and gave the bottle back.

"Where?"

"I don't know. Foster care, adoption. Oh hell, just give her away. Who cares?" he joked.

Vicki lifted the bottle to her lips.

"C'mon, now. Don't tell me you haven't thought about it."

"Shut up," she said, and took another sip.

"Okay, but if you can't love a dog, give it away. That's what I always say."

"When did you ever say that?"

"Um, well . . . I just said it, didn't I?" he smirked, and took the bottle from Vicki.

Vicki watched her brother's antics through a whiskey-induced fog. "Hey," she said. "I got an idea. Go around the side and look in his window. Maybe you can see something."

"What're you talking about?"

"The bedroom window is right there," she pointed. "Go and look."

Baby Mitch didn't move at first, but with more coaxing from his sister, he stood up and stumbled down the steps. "Whoops," he said when he tripped.

"Go ahead!" Vicki barked.

"You know, you always were a bitch, Vicki."

He steadied his legs as he walked around the side of the house, then called out, "Did I tell you that you're a bitch?" he snickered.

"Oh, okay, here's the window," he said, his skinny frame swayed off balance as his hands formed pretend binoculars in front of his eyes. "I don't see nothin!"

"Go up to it! You can't see anything from way back there, stupid!"

"Bitch," Baby Mitch muttered and stepped closer to the screen. The window itself was sealed tight, the curtains inside drawn together.

"The curtains are closed. I can't see inside," he yelled, and staggered back around to the front of the house. Vicki stood on the steps, arms crossed, shaking her head with disappointment.

"No holes in the screen?" she asked.

"Nope."

"Something is going on in there."

"It's probably Big Daddy snoring. You know how loud he gets."

"But it sounded like he fell against the door."

Baby Mitch shrugged and scratched a tickle in his nose blood appeared on his finger. "Damn it, my nose is bleeding again. I gotta go."

"So, now you're just gonna up and leave after causing all this ruckus?"

"I need to get home and clean up." He dabbed at his blood-rimmed nostril and gestured at his bare chest – I need a shirt!"

"Come back inside and lie on the sofa until the blood stops," Vicki suggested.

Ignoring her offer, Baby Mitch backed away from the porch and zigzagged his way across the lawn to his truck. He looked back, saying, "If anything else happens with Big Daddy, call Doc Jenkins. Oh! Don't worry about Trudy neither, just like a fed cat, they always come back."

Baby Mitch yanked the door open and slid onto the seat and cranked the engine. He leaned through the window, yelling, "And make sure you look at Preecher's papers!"

Chapter 22

When Vicki's eyes opened her face was buried in one of Mama's sofa pillows. She sat up and used the end of her shirt to clean the drool from her chin. Sunset touched the window glass and an amber patina slid leisurely over the shoddy furniture, creating a burnished glow that instilled beauty where none existed. Vicki sighed, and her feet found the floor as daylight acquiesced to the somber shadows creeping along the four walls. In seconds, the room would be encased in darkness. She reached over and clicked on the lamp.

    A vague recollection of her brother with blood running from his nose chased away the cobwebs and she came fully awake. She guessed that more than two hours had passed since he got in his truck and zoomed off. After he left, Vicki had remained on the porch for a while before coming back inside.

    Now, the usual house creaks and leaky faucet drips were the only sounds she heard, and she got up and went directly to Big Daddy's room and listened at the door. All was quiet, but still she asked, "Big Daddy, are you okay?"

    With no response, she went back into the kitchen and stood at the back door, thinking about Trudy. The things Baby Mitch had said were meant as a joke, but confirmed to her that the family felt her resentment of Trudy. Her mood was jaded by bad memories and her mind still muddled by alcohol when she recalled Baby Mitch saying, "Give her away."

Vicki admitted to herself that in the first week of her baby's life, she wanted to give her away. But Mama wouldn't hear of it.

"Don't you even think such a thing," scolded Mama. "One day that girl will be all you have."

"Well, you take care of her!" she had said, and turned a deaf ear to all of Mama's reasoning. As Trudy got older, Vicki pushed her even further away, longing for the day she could finally be free of this child and hopefully the night terrors that came with Trudy's birth.

Vicki thought about Baby Mitch. What a jackass he was. He was only being nice because he wanted her help getting that old man's house. She wondered what he'd done to be so sure the house was available. Vicki was well aware that whatever he was doing, would be trouble. She would take Mama's advice for a change, and not get involved.

That morning, when Vicki saw Trudy standing in the hallway, she'd screamed at her in anger. Thinking back, she recalled the terror in her daughter's face when she looked up at her and Vicki saw a terrible monster reflected in Trudy's large eyes -- she was that monster. Trudy was so frightened she ran to a dead boy who was probably kinder to her than her mother ever was. Vicki's heart plummeted. In all these years, she had done nothing for this child but fill her with fear.

Now, standing at the window, tears were perched in her eyes as she watched the night sky. She recalled when Trudy had been a toddler trying to climb onto her lap. Vicki would quickly stand up allowing Trudy to tumble to the floor and then walk away, never once turning around, not even when Trudy cried, "Mommy, Mommy." Vicki had made sure to scold her when she used that word, and soon Trudy was calling her "Vicki."

"I just don't have it in me," Vicki cried, trying to reason to the empty kitchen. Her hands went to her face and her shoulders trembled as tears blurred her vision. And then she looked out into the darkness of the yard and with a heart filled with remorse she cried out "Trudy, oh Trudy, where are you?" And all of a sudden something surprising occurred to her. For the first time, her tears were not for her own self-pity, or in anguish, or anger, she was grieving for Trudy, for her missing daughter, and she was terrified that her child was gone forever.

Vicki wiped her face on the palms of her hands. In the silent house, a boozy headache brought her to the cabinet for the bottle of aspirin. The bottle was not in the cabinet but on the table where Mama left it. Vicki took two tablets followed by a few sips of water. She sat down at the table her achy head resting against her palm and then she noticed the stacks of papers Baby Mitch left behind.

"Idiot." she muttered.

Lifting the stack, she plucked out one folder and scanned the pages. "Well, look at this, she muttered, old Preecher wasn't the holy-and-sanctified man he pretended to be." She read further. "Looks like he was over-charging for everything he sold."

Vicki read page after page of illegal payments, and then stopped abruptly, her eyes pinned to a sheet of letterhead imprinted with the name Talbot.

She leaned back in the chair and took her time reading, trying to understand what the words meant. "I can't believe this," she said, sitting forward in the chair, eyes wide with incredulity. "The Preecher's sold a Negro baby."

Vicki's eyes were glued to the paper as she examined the information, when suddenly; she was startled by a burst of gut-wrenching sobs emanating from Big Daddy's room. She jumped up, tossed the file on the table, and hurried up the hall. Her first thought was she'd never heard Big Daddy cry before. But the voice was distinctly his and the sounds were coming from a deep dark place that gripped her in a wave of panic.

She leaned against the door, tried the knob. "Big Daddy, its Vicki. Are you hurt? Open the door."

His crying turned into long hard wails of anguish and despair, and she heard something that sounded like a Bible verse.

"Big Daddy, please open the door!"

Vicki leaned into the door with her shoulder, again and again she shoved against the thick wood but her only result was an aching shoulder.

Quite suddenly, the crying ceased and the hallway fell into an eerie silence that unnerved Vicki and she stepped back from the door saying, "I wish Mama was here." And then, she bumped into something behind her and fear quickened her heartbeat and her legs refused to move.

In an instant, her thoughts screamed, it's him! And she heard his laughter, his high, girlie giggle. Something slipped around her waist and the word "NO!" broke free from her lips and she waited for the burlap sack to enshroud her head in darkness, but instead; she felt strong hands on her shoulders, turning her around, shaking her.

"Vicki, it's me! It's Hurley."

Vicki felt her terror deflate like a broken balloon and she shouted, "Damn it, Hurley! You scared the hell outta me!" And she collapsed against his chest.

"I was just stopping by to check on you. The door was open. Are you okay?"

Her face buried in his shoulder, Vicki let her tears flow and Hurley instinctively wrapped his arms around her. "It's okay, he said,

I'm here now." Minutes passed before she let out a sigh and wiped her dreary eyes.

"What happened?"

"It's Big Daddy. He locked himself in the bedroom. I heard him crying. Hurley, Big Daddy never cries!"

Hurley approached the door and tried the doorknob. "Mr. Taggart; its Sheriff Hurley."

Silence.

"Mr. Taggart, if you don't answer I'm gonna have to break the door and come in."

Silence.

"Can you hear me, Mr. Taggart?"

Still nothing.

"Okay, I'm coming in."

"NO!"

Hurley looked over at Vicki.

She rushed to the door. "Big Daddy, open the door."

"No! Go away."

"That doesn't sound like your father," Hurley said.

"He's not himself."

"Mr. Taggart, is there anything we can get you?"

"Go away!"

"You've been in there for too long; time to come out now," said Vicki.

She glanced at Hurley. He nodded and backed up, preparing to kick in the door.

"Go and find your daughter!"

Hurley stiffened, locking eyes with Vicki. "What's he's talking about? Where's Trudy?"

Alarmed, Vicki looked away, but when Hurley crossed the hall to Trudy's room, she cried out, "Hurley, wait!" But he was already inside the room. Hurley looked around at the mess the child lived in. Piles of dirty clothes and broken toys were strewn around an unmade bed.

"Where is she Vicki?" His eyes were wide with alarm.

"She ran off."

"When?"

"This morning."

Hurley paced the room. "Your mama's missing, Teeny's missing, and you don't think to keep your daughter close?"

Vicki turned away from him. "I wasn't thinking straight. I had a few drinks, and I yelled at her for lying to me."

Holding back his anger, Hurley pushed past Vicki and hurried out the back door. Standing on the porch, he scanned the darkness, seeing only the distant glint of fireflies hovering in the cornfield. The door creaked when Vicki stepped outside and stood beside him.

He looked at her troubled face and stowed his anger; he knew that in her current state, she could easily explode and order him off her property. "Do you know where she would go?" he asked.

Vicki looked down. "No."

"What about friends? Does she have friends around here?"

Vicki shrugged. "I don't know."

"You don't know? Damn, Vicki, she's your daughter!"

"I work to take care of her, ain't that enough?"

"No, it's not! What the hell is going on out here?"

"She's not missing. She goes off all the time."

"Is she with that kid, James?" asked Hurley.

Vicki tensed when she heard him say the boy's name.

"Trudy told me she had a friend named James."

Saying nothing, Vicki leaned against the railing.

"What do you know about this boy?"

Hurt by his accusing tone, Vicki's grief suddenly turned to anger and her eyes flashed rage. "You son of a bitch! You have the nerve to question me? You left me, and after the attack you didn't even have the courage to come and find out how I was. How dare you judge me?"

"Is she mine?" he asked, suddenly.

Stunned by the question, she felt her face flush. "You ask me that now because she's gone, and you want to blame me? Well, the answer to that is, I don't know!"

Her fragile senses broken, she sobbed, and Hurley, clearly distressed, pushed his emotions aside and put his arm around her shoulder. She tried to push him away, but he held on until she fell against him. Then, he picked her up and carried her inside to the sofa.

Another torrent of tears sent Hurley to the kitchen searching for something to blot her wet face. He grabbed a dishcloth from the sink and brought it to her and sat in silence while she continued to cry.

She was quiet now and staring trance-like at the wall her face as drab and sodden as the dishcloth balled up in her fist. Hurley remained at her side, her head tucked under his chin brought memories of their time in his truck, and he knew she was right when she accused him of not having the courage to be there when she needed him.

"Sheriff."

Hurley looked up when he heard someone call from outside. He stood up and went to the front door.

"Sheriff."

Pushing the screen door open, he stepped out onto the porch. Someone was standing not far from the flagpole. Hurley walked to the top of the steps. When he saw Minter Saul, he tramped down the steps and went to meet the old man.

"Minter Saul?"

"Hey there, Sheriff! How you doing today?"

"Not too good," Hurley admitted.

"You got a few people missing from over here, don't ya?"

"So you heard?"

"News travels fast around here, especially bad news."

"What're you doing on this side? I've never known you to come on Taggart property."

"You know, right. Wild horses couldn't drag me over here, but I felt the need to come. Been getting strange urges lately," he said, shaking his head with confusion.

Minter Saul fell silent and Hurley waited.

At last, he spoke up, "Well, best be on my way," and he touched his hat.

"Wait. Did you want anything?"

"Only a feel for the place; that's all." Minter Saul waved his hand and walked toward the cornfield.

Hurley was puzzled at the strange visit. He turned around just as Vicki appeared at the door, her face tear-streaked and puffy. Hurley noticed how tired she was, she needed help, his help. He walked back up to the porch and took a seat in one of the rockers.

When Vicki stepped outside, she handed him a glass of water, which he gulped down and set the empty glass on the table. She sat down in the other rocker, looking out across the front lawn. "Who was that?"

"Strangely enough, Minter Saul stopped by," he said.

"So, he's okay?"

"Why wouldn't he be?" asked Hurley.

She brushed off his question, instead saying, "I met him on the road the other day; he's a strange old coot. What did he want?"

"Said he had an urge to come by."

"Walked all that way for an urge?"

"Seems so."

"Hurley," Vicki said, "I really need to find Trudy and bring her home."

"I'll find her," said Hurley.

"No. I mean me. And I have a feeling she's in the cornfield."

Hurley noticed Vicki's hands trembling and her eyes were filled with something he had never seen in her before—panic.

"Under no circumstances go in there alone, understand?"

She fumbled with her hands before looking into his eyes. "Hurley, I have to tell you something."

"Okay."

"Remember when I told you I saw spirits after the bus crash?"

"Yeah."

"That kid, James, who Trudy plays with. I know this makes me sound crazy, but—he's not alive."

Not amused, Hurley scowled at her. "Vicki, are you still hanging onto that story about the walking spirits? C'mon, now. You're not a kid anymore."

"Please, listen to me before you judge. I need to tell you about something that happened when I was eleven years old. When I first met James."

"You're saying you knew him?"

"Yes! But the thing is . . . he's still a kid."

Hurley could not overlook Vicki's grave demeanor. He leaned back and gave her his full attention.

"When I was eleven, I met some colored kids—a boy named James and his sister Ella—they were at the Crawley farm with their daddy."

"James wanted to be an astronaut," she said, "He knew a whole lot about the stars. He wanted to show me the Big Dipper and the Little Dipper, but it wasn't dark enough to see. We knew he couldn't stay until nighttime because of the Sunset Rule, but he promised to come back before dark and show me where to look. But James was late meeting me and two men on horses rode up."

Hurley watched as Vicki's eyes turned grim and he knew she was seeing the horses and the men and then she said, "It was getting dark."

"That wasn't your fault, you were both kids."

Vicki's face suddenly grew sick with guilt and she could barely look at Hurley when she said, "I got him killed."

"What do you mean?"

"You don't get it, Hurley," she moaned, through her misery. "One of the men asked me," her voice broke and she sobbed, "He asked me if James was messing with me."

As Hurley waited her tears fell and Vicki forced herself to continue. She looked up, her words shaky and strained as she blurted, "I didn't want to get in trouble, so I told the man yes. I said 'yes!' But it was a lie." And with a bleak shake of her head she admitted, "I was afraid they would tell Big Daddy."

"What happened to James?"

"One of the men had a rope and lassoed James and pulled him on the ground behind his horse dragging him through the field. The man kept hitting the horse with a whip forcing it to run faster and farther away until I couldn't see James anymore." Vicki groaned and covered her eyes trying to block the hideous memory that played repeatedly in her thoughts.

"I was so scared," she said. "I ran all the way home and never told anyone what happened."

Hurley was so rattled by her confession he remained unmoving and could find no words.

Her face grave, Vicki said, "James has appeared to me over the years. At times, he's hideously mangled, but other times he's as normal as the boy I first met. I don't know what he wants, but each time he seems bolder, and I'm scared to death. The alcohol helps."

Hurley sat stiffly staring at his hands and going over her story in his mind, trying to rectify her actions. The only thing he could come up with was the fact that she was a child at the time. But the lie she had told caused another child to be murdered and her insistence that the boy's ghost haunted her was difficult to swallow. However, it was curious that Trudy had seen this boy as well and now she was gone.

He was beginning to understand that Vicki's behavior was a result of the guilt she lived with. That awful experience, along with the rape, and having a child, was too much for any one person to carry. Hearing her story enforced how fragile she had been, and still was, and reminded him how much he had failed her. All he could do now was find Trudy, after that, they would figure out how to right the wrong she had done to James.

Chapter 23

The first time Trudy met James, his appearance frightened her. It happened after one of Vicki's threats sent her into the cornfield to hide from another whipping. Trudy wasn't afraid of the hulking cornhusks standing like rows of sentries chaperoning her through the field. In fact, nothing about the cornfield scared her as much as Vicki did. It was a perfect place for hide-and-seek if she ever got a playmate.

Trudy had made her way far into the field when she first saw him. His sudden appearance startled her, and she almost ran away; instead, her curiosity got the better of her and she didn't move. The boy seemed friendly enough, but as he drew closer, she saw that his body was broken and torn, and she trembled with fear. One side of his face was gone; on the other side, only shriveled pieces of skin hung down. His chest was ripped open, exposing shrunken bones. He hopped on one leg; a stick held him upright, the other leg nothing but a ragged stump.

He hopped closer to Trudy and his eyes flickered gold and brown, and something Vicki had once said popped into Trudy's memory.

Tiger-eyes.

"Don't be afraid, Trudy," the boy had said.

All of a sudden, the skin resurfaced over his deformed face. The wounds in his chest shrank and disappeared. His stump dwindled and two healthy legs appeared.

A bright red ball perched underneath his arm replaced the stick. He held it out, inviting her to take it. She stepped forward, captivated by eyes that shimmered gold and sparkled with glee.

"Hi, Trudy! I'm James. You wanna play?" His toothy smile was warm and inviting, and her loneliness evaporated like the morning dew.

Now, Trudy thought about Mama Bertie, she missed her and her flapping slippers coming down the hall. Seeing the kitchen without Mama Bertie, and with Granpa locked in his room, and Vicki always angry kept Trudy away from home. This morning, Vicki had accused her of lying about seeing James, and when Trudy had heard the rage in Vicki's voice, she ran out of the house to the cornfield. She'd hidden amongst the cornstalks and watched the house until Uncle Baby Mitch climbed in his truck and drove away. Still, she remained hidden, too afraid to go home.

After a while, Trudy walked along the edge of the cornfield, worrying about what to do next. Sue Ellen's face suddenly appeared in her thoughts and she smiled. She missed her friend, with her nice dresses and pretty hair ribbons, her big smile and warm hugs. She had smiled a lot when she was with Sue Ellen, until Vicki ruined it all.

When James stepped from behind a stalk, she wasn't afraid. He was her friend too, just like Sue Ellen use to be.

"Hi," she said.

"C'mon," he beckoned. "I have a new game for us to play."

His easy smile pulled her from her misery and she ran freely to his side, never once looking back at the house. He handed her the red ball and she bounced it several times before taking his outstretched hand.

As they moved deeper into the cornfield all motion around them ceased until James reached out and the mummified plants parted allowing them to enter.

Chapter 24

Hurley sat behind the wheel of his patrol car and gripped the radio receiver in a tense hand. "Where was she found, Wade?"

"On the Preecher side of the cornfield, she was deep in; don't know how she got way over there," Deputy Wade replied, his voice crackled with static.

"How'd you find her?"

"An old black man stopped by the office, named Simms. Said he was in the cornfield and came up on her."

"That had to be Minter Saul."

"It couldna been him that done it," offered Wade. "She was hung up in a bunch of cornhusks. A weak old man like that would need several hands to bind her up thataway."

"I'm out here at the Taggart place, talking to Vicki Taggart," said Hurley. "There's a lot going on and she's pretty distraught already. I don't want to add this bad news just yet."

"Do you want me to call the coroner?" asked Wade.

"Damn," said Hurley. "I never thought we would find Mrs. Taggart dead. This is crazy."

"Sheriff, the sight of this woman is one for your worst nightmare. She looks like a doggone tree grew inside of her and sprouted flowers out of her eyes. It's a gory sight, a damn gory sight."

"Yeah, call the coroner. Might as well get him out there as soon as possible."

Hurley glanced out the window at Vicki slumped in the rocker. This was the worst time to tell her they found her mama dead in the cornfield.

"Anything else, Sheriff?"

"No, Wade. Handle things the best you can until I can get there."

He clicked the radio off and got out of the cruiser. Hurley took a deep exasperated breath and trudged up to the house.

"Anything?" she asked, as Hurley mounted the steps.

"Just something I have to check on."

"Is it Mama?" Vicki asked anxiously.

Hurley lied and said, "Wade wants me to come take a look at something; didn't say what, but I'll be back out here as soon as I can. You gonna be okay alone with Big Daddy?"

"He ain't coming outta that room for nobody," she said.

"You call me if anything else happens. But I won't be long."

Vicki stood up and walked to where Hurley was standing.

He took her hands and looked into her eyes. "And no more alcohol. You need to stay alert, focused; ya hear me?"

"I know, Hurley. Please, no lectures."

"All right now." He stepped down to the bottom landing. "Don't worry, we'll find Trudy."

Vicki nodded and sat back down as Hurley rushed back to the patrol car. She pondered on the urgency she saw in his face.

Chapter 25

When Hurley backed the cruiser out of the driveway, Vicki went back into the house. In the hallway, she stopped in front of Big Daddy's door and listened to the eerie silence that rested inside his room. Across the hall was Trudy's room, the door stood open. She went inside and looked around.

Nothing in the room had changed over the years. Trudy slept in Vicki's old bed and used her old furniture. The dusty curtains were the same ones that she'd hidden behind as she watched the murdered dead being carried into the cornfield.

At the window, she gazed at the same view she'd grown up seeing every day, the clothesline strung across the yard, the Air Streamer standing among the weeds, and the cornfield stretching farther than she could see. As a child, she'd imagine she was looking at a field of fairy villages where wish flowers were made and planted by mystical creatures. She smiled as she recalled how vivid her childhood imagination was, and wondered what Trudy saw when she looked out of this window.

As she grew older, the sweet dreams Vicki once had faded, and other activity in the yard nudged her from her sleep. Hidden from sight, she watched with wide-eyed curiosity and bewilderment as her father, brother, and other men, hauled bodies from their trucks, a vision that had been permanently cemented in the far reaches of her mind.

Vicki sat on Trudy's bed, two small dolls were nestled into the pillow and she realized they were her old dolls. She picked one up and the arm fell out, so she stuck it back in and placed the doll back against the pillow. She gazed around the room at coloring books, puzzle pieces, and heaps of clothes lying about. Trudy's schoolbooks were stacked on the floor next to a large weaved basket with toys piled to the rim. It was stuffed with stiff-legged dolls, toy animals, books, and a red fire truck. There was a plastic telescope, a bent hula-hoop and a large doll with no arms.

She knew Mama got Trudy a new toy every time she went to the bargain store. Trudy relished those trips. "Vicki, look what Mama Bertie got me!" she'd say. Her excitement was always the same, even when it was a ten-cent book of paper dolls or a rubber bouncy ball. But Vicki had never paid mind to any of it.

When a cool breeze nudged the musty curtains, Vicki got up from the bed and went to her own room to change clothes. She pulled her shirt over her head, tossed it on the bed, and fished around in the dresser for another top.

In the bathroom, Vicki looked in the mirror at her beat-down face. She splashed cold water and dabbed her eyes with a face cloth. She squeezed toothpaste onto a toothbrush and began brushing her teeth. Then, she stopped and stared into the mirror. Vicki spat the toothpaste into the sink, wiped her mouth and hurried down the hall to Trudy's room. She looked at the basket of toys.

It was lodged between a stuffed dog and a hoola hoop, a telescope. She reached and pulled it from the basket and sat on Trudy's bed holding it in her hand. It was gray plastic, with a scope that slid in and out. She recalled James's words.

I'm gonna save ten dollars to send for a telescope I seen in the Stargazer magazine.

With the telescope in hand, Vicki hurried to the kitchen, grabbed her keys, and rushed out the front door to her truck.

Chapter 26

The smoke from Vicki's cigarette filled the interior of the truck until she cracked her window allowing a slim mist to escape. She leaned forward in the seat for a better view of the house.

The cigarette crackled and the tip glowed when she pulled more smoke into her lungs before expelling a stream into the windshield.

"It's nice," she muttered.

The Preecher house was a solidly built two-story structure with a wraparound porch. A homemade swing suspended from two brass chains swayed in the breeze.

She opened the door and flicked the cigarette butt into the dirt as her feet hit the ground. This house had everything the Taggart house didn't. There was a garden on either side of the front steps that brimmed with pansies; the petals stained with exotic colors mimicked tiny faces. Frilly white curtains at the window conjured a vision of Mrs. Preecher sitting on the swing, carefully hand-stitching the fabric. But today the house sat dark and alone.

"Hello!" she called out, to no reply.

Vicki had felt the need to talk to Minter Saul ever since he appeared in her front yard. He told Hurley he felt an urge to stop by, but she figured there was more to it than that. He was a strange old coot, had been in Piney all his life. When they were together, Hurley encouraged her to go and see Minter Saul about what she saw on the road. But at the time, she wasn't comfortable talking to a Negro, especially a male; she had learned a hard lesson from the incident at the Crawley farm. But now, she was scared and she needed to talk to someone who could tell her something, anything, about what the hell was going on. With that in mind, she thought about Minter Saul; in fact, he stayed on her mind a lot. If he knew about Negro legends and spirits in Piney, he might even know about the boy James, and how to get Trudy back.

Now, here she was, standing in front of the house he owned. But where was he? She regarded the house with careful concern as daylight dwindled and twilight dressed the structure in a late afternoon glow. The stillness around her was soon broken as the crickets reveled in the arrival of dusk with their hearty chirps and an unseen insect buzzed around her head. Vicki scratched the tickle on her earlobe and scanned the landscape. Her eyes settled on a shed perched on a rise not far from the house. A candle flickering in the window beckoned her, and she made her way up the hill. The vigorous trek up the slope had stolen some of her breath. She paused at the door to the shed to allow it to catch up.

"You winded Miss Vicki?" she heard Minter Saul say. "Come on in," he added.

She wondered how he knew she was at the door but decided not to ask; instead, she cautiously pushed the door open and looked inside. The one room shed was dark. Playful shadows leapt from a twinkling candle as Minter Saul sat on a cot peeling potatoes. He tossed the naked ones into a metal pot. An old dog lay at his feet, its eyes lifted when she stepped inside closing the door behind her.

"To what do I owe the honor of your visit, Miss Vicki?" he said, never taking his eyes from his task.

She looked around at the sparseness of the shed, suddenly unsure if this had been a good idea. She fumbled nervously with her hands while trying to find the right words without seeming too forward, "Um . . . if you don't mind, can I ask you something?"

"Yep."

"What kind of name is Minter Saul, anyway?"

His laugh was a series of whoops that bent him over and caused him to slap his knee. Vicki smiled in surprise at his lengthy hilarity. Finally, his mirth eased and a crooked finger flicked a laugh-tear that sprouted from one eye and he sat back catching his breath. "Oh, Lawdy." He chuckled.

"You're the first person to ever ask me, so I'll tell you how it came about. One day," he said, as the whoops subsided, "it's been years ago now, Ned's three-year-old cousin Peggy came to visit with her mama from South Carolina. She was a curly-haired, blue-eyed little thing, as cute as a bug, and she was staring at me so hard that I took off my hat and introduced myself. 'Hello missy, I say, I'm Mister Saul.' But Miss Peggy, bless her little heart, took to calling me "Minter Saul." Miss Rachel felt calling me "Mister" wasn't appropriate anyhow, and she thought Minter was such a cute take on it, and just like that, I been Minter Saul ever since."

He skinned the next potato with his knife and his mood suddenly grew somber.

"Funny how things work out, ain't it?"

Vicki nodded, a distracted smile on her lips.

"But you ain't really here to ask about my name, is you?"

"No, I'm not. I felt I needed to give you a warning."

"Is that so?" he said, and cleaned the paring knife with a rag before picking another spud. "You taken up warning folks these days, Miss Vicki?"

"Look, I just . . . ."

Another potato rattled the pot and Vicki flinched.

"My brother is gonna get this property even if he has to kill you for it."

Minter Saul chuckled, and chose another potato, slicing into the peel. "I always expected to die from something. Mainly these bunions on my feet." He laughed again, and this time the old dog barked in unison.

Vicki waited for him to recover from his own amusement. "Look, a lot is going on around here," she said.

"Seems to me you're trying to ask me something else."

Vicki moved further into the shed. "Can I sit?"

Minter Saul nodded at a crate.

She turned it over and sat down. But she was still hesitant to bring up the subject of spirits, so instead she asked, "Did Preecher really leave his property to you?"

He smirked and said, "That's the first question I thought you would ask. Is it because you think a white man in this county wouldn't leave his property to an old Black man who worked that land for more than fifty years?"

Vicki shrugged, saying, "Honestly, I don't. Maybe you and him had some kinda friendship, but as a white man, in the South? No. That just wouldn't happen."

Minter Saul looked at her for a second and chucked another potato in the pot. "You right, he didn't."

Vicki looked at him, her eyes wide with surprise, "What are you saying?"

"I sent poor Ned on home."

"You killed him?"

"Most would call it that."

Vicki was stunned as she looked into the old man's wrinkled face for any sign of remorse, but saw none.

"Why you shocked, Miss Vicki? You know more about killing than most folks around here."

Taken aback, she blurted, "Why would you say something like that?"

"Because, like I said before, you a Taggart."

"You think my families trash, don't you?"

"Lots of poor white folks don't take to hunting Negroes down and hanging 'em and burying they bodies in some Godforsaken place. It takes an evil kind of person to do that, Miss Vicki. You know anyone like that? Folk, that in the daytime act respectable, but at night runs around hiding they faces under bed sheets to do their dirty work. You know any?"

Vicki's face flushed with guilt and she looked down at the floor. She felt anger creeping and she wanted to explode at the old man and call him every vile word she could think of, but instead, she calmed down and took a few deep breaths and turned her thinking to her purpose for coming there. She needed his help. So, she changed the subject.

"Did you build this shed?" she asked, looking around.

"Sure did. The house and the barn, too." Minter Saul tossed another potato in the pot "You probably don't know that me and

Ned was friends as boys. Spent every day together until he went off to school."

Vicki was still reeling from Minter Saul's harsh words and deep down she wanted to storm out of the shed. But she stayed because in spite of his bitterness toward her family, she was going to ask him to help her look for Trudy. She also wanted to know why he killed Ned Preecher, so she sat back and listened to the gruffness of his voice as he spoke.

"After Ned left, Mister Sherman put me to work in the field full time." The old dog looked up and Minter Saul reached over and scratched its ear. "My Mama and Daddy worked for Mister Sherman first, but after a while, he sent them to work over in Cumming, Georgia. I only saw them once a year on Easter at the church revival. All the workers came, and I got to see Atticus and Patch."

"Your parents?"

"My Mama was called Patch. She was as pretty as a sun shower, and I was proud to have her as my Mama. My Daddy was black as coal with a big friendly laugh. That's all I can remember of them now. Mister Sherman sent them back to Cumming to work even though Mama was gonna have another baby."

Vicki heard Minter Saul's voice drop and his words came with difficulty when he said, "Not long before the next Easter came round, he came and told me that Atticus and Patch was dead. I was eight years old and I didn't believe him. I just knew I would see them come Easter Sunday at the revival."

Moved by the sadness that had crept into his voice, Vicki turned her head to hide an unexpected stir of emotions as she peered at him through the shadows. His solemn face shimmered in the flickering candlelight, and she caught a glimpse of the lonely boy that still lived inside him.

As the wax melted, the flame from the candle flickered, sending twisted fissures of light against the wooden beams of the shed. At the same time, a spark returned to Minter Saul's eyes and he plucked a potato from the bin. He peeled the spud and tossed it in the pot.

"I would like to hear more, if that's all right."

He nodded. "I'm glad to tell what has been leaning against my heart for these past years."

Vicki leaned back against the wall her face hidden in the dimness of the room.

"Funny thing, I waited every Easter for them, even when I knew they weren't coming. Even now on Easter Sunday, I watch the road for their wagon. I don't know why; I just do."

"When Ned went back to school, I worked hard to avoid the loneliness that followed me closer than my own shadow."

Soon enough, Ned's daddy, Mister Sherman, fell ill and died and Ned came home to bury him and see about his Mama. It wasn't long before Miss Rachel joined her husband in Glory, and Ned decided to stay and run the farm. By that time he had a wife, Miss Lily, who was a righteous church lady. She was cordial and spoke friendly whenever she saw me.

"It seemed like me and Ned took up our friendship right where it left off. But truth be told, Ned's take on friendship was like a candle burning bright one minute and then snuffed out in another. One day, I was his good friend, the next just another Negro worker.

"Some days, we sat together under the big Magnolia tree that Ned loved so much, and he would spout on about his future plans. I sat and listened to him brag on his family for hours on end, and also complain about the debt his daddy left behind."

"That's a surprise; we always heard the Preecher's were the richest family in Piney," Vicki said.

"They struggled after that fire, and Ned was a stingy man, he didn't like spending money. Sometimes, he preached from the Good Book and read passages about goodness, trust, and honor. But I suspected those words didn't always live in his heart. For one thing, he never failed to check the money drawer whenever I left the room."

Minter Saul stopped talking and fell silent. Vicki could see that all of this unburdening was wearing on him. She didn't press him further, so they sat in silence for a good while before he started up again.

"After your brother Baby Mitch burnt down his property, Ned was hot as fish grease. He took to pacing the front porch, fists raised, cussing the Taggart family with words he didn't often use. Poor Miss Lily covered her ears and ran upstairs to escape his fits," Said Minter Saul.

"Baby Mitch was let off easy for setting that fire. He only spent a few months in County," added Vicki.

"Ned wasn't happy about that either," said Minter Saul. "When he was into his brandy wine, he stomped around outside under the Magnolia spouting words from the Bible I'll never forget—'Faithful are the wounds of a friend, profuse are the kisses of an enemy.'"

Minter Saul stopped talking when the old dog whimpered. He got up walked to the back of the shed and retrieved a can of water from a corner of the room and placed it on the floor. "There you go," he said to the old dog, and sat back down.

"As we worked to rebuild the farm, Ned grew angrier by the day. The cost of building was high, and he had to sell off most of his livestock to buy lumber. Each month, I seen my pay get short a few dollars, but Ned never offered any words on it. He probably forgot I could count."

"But still, there were times he called me in from the field to have a cup of lemonade with him under his beloved tree."

"You know, Miss, he mused, I truly believe the sweet smell of those melon-size blossoms on that great tree addled old Ned into thinking himself as a man doing God's work."

"Sounds like he was struggling pretty bad after my idiot brother set that fire," she said.

"He was. Ned had been hollering all over town about how he was gonna sue your daddy and press more charges against your brother. I was afraid his anger was gonna get him kilt. But then, Ned did something I never thought he would ever do," said Minter Saul.

"What?"

"I spied Ned and your daddy huddled together having a lively jaw session out on the porch. Not long after that, the prices for lumber and equipment were available to him for next to nothing," he said.

"A lot of people owed my daddy favors."

"Ned was as happy as a pig in slop over the low rates Taggart had arranged for him," said Minter Saul. "Later, when Ned was drunk and spouting all his business, I found out that your father had managed to hornswoggle him into a verbal agreement over his land. It made my heart sick that Ned had made a deal with Taggart; evil should never be rewarded."

"Soon enough, the house and the barn were rebuilt and things started looking up. Ned once again was bragging about all the things he was planning for his family. He was convinced that God favored him highly for his good church work," Minter Saul smirked and said, "I betcha God was having a good laugh listening to Ned's plans."

"However, things didn't turn out like he wanted, and at the end of the planting season, Ned and his wife both came down with pneumonia. It was hard hit and Doc Jenkins visited nearly every day. Miss Lily passed on quickly, while Ned wrangled with his illness for almost a year. Most times, he would bounce back seemingly restored but only a few days later take a turn for the worse."

"Pneumonia can take a person quick," offered Vicki.

"Ned couldn't shake the cough, and Doc's medicine wasn't helping. He took to sitting on the porch most days, trying to get warm in the sunshine. I was up at the crack of dawn each day, feeding the animals and tending to the farm work. I knew he was really sick when he told me to handle the payroll for the day workers."

Without warning Minter Saul bent forward, his face contorted and he grimaced with pain and held onto his side.

Alarmed, Vicki stood up, "Are you okay?"

"Just checking to see if I'm here," he quipped.

"You're here," she said. "You still wanna talk?"

He sighed, and a small burp escaped. "'Scuse me. Miss Lily had a penchant for soda pop. Cupboards full of them bottles, tried me one and it kept me tossing all night."

Vicki smiled and sat back down.

He paused suddenly, and looked at her, "I ain't ever talked so much to a white person before."

"What about Preecher?"

"Heck. Preecher's the one did the talking. I did the listening. Ain't nothing I could say he'd wanna hear."

"Well, I'm listening," she said.

"It wasn't long before sickness swooped down and strapped old Ned in its iron grip. Most of his life, Ned fought strong against sickness and he eventually won the battle. But after losing Miss Lily, he was heartbroken, and his body was weak. This time, pneumonia was more on the winning side."

When Ned started coughing up a thickness, I set a bucket next to his chair. He had this rag that he dragged across his mouth to catch the drool. He'd look me square in the eye, saying, 'I already spoke to Taggart, and he gave his word that if anything happens to me, you can stay on. You got work here until the day you die. What do you think of that, friend?'

"I guess he took my silence as gratitude. Each day, death crept closer, but his strong will always fought for another sun up. Things were so bad that Doc Jenkins no longer came to the house. 'Call me when he's done,' he told me, as he stepped down from the porch. Every morning, I found Ned drenched with fever sweat and weaker still."

"Why were you so loyal?" she asked.

"He was my only friend. It was my duty to look after him when he was ill. I fed him, changed his dirty underclothes, and helped him sit on a bucket so he could relieve himself."

"I wonder if he woulda done the same for you?"

Minter Saul shook his head. "Ned was not a perfect man, but he was all I had in the world. I didn't know what would become of me once he was gone."

"When did he change his will and sign everything over to you?"

Minter Saul quieted. He looked at the shimmering candle, and scratched the old dog's ear. His eyes were full of sadness, but something more daunting claimed his features. It was a presence that caused Vicki to shiver. On the table, the candle pulsed and the flamed jumped higher lighting up his ebony skin. His dark shadow stretched up the wall like a hovering spirit.

"Everything changed for me when I found out that Ned and his family were greedy liars." As he spoke, she noted a change come over him. His gentleness had vanished and a storm raged in his eyes. His jaw clenched and he grimaced as if he were in great pain. Petulance crept through the shed, the old dog whimpered and howled, and the gloom that filled the room was so oppressive she felt her own inner turbulence increase two-fold and her eyes were wet with unforeseen tears.

All of a sudden Minter Saul's hands moved so swiftly all she could see of them was a blur as he skinned the spuds and the pot filled with unfathomable speed. It was at that moment that she knew Minter Saul was haunted.

They sat in silence until he leaned back on the bed and took a deep breath. His eyes found Vicki who was sitting nervously in the corner. "I didn't want you to hear about the horrible things that come outta hate but I keep forgetting, you a Taggart."

Vicki said nothing. Finding his reserve, Minter Saul continued. "On the last day of his life, Ned lay in his bed in and out of consciousness."

"You were the only one with him?"

"Ned was proud, a leader in his church, but he didn't get along with people. He had a short fuse, always fussin' with folk. When he got sick, he said, 'I don't want none of them hypocrites staring in my face. You hear me Saul?' So, I kept folks away just like he wanted."

"That musta been hard for you handling all that alone," said Vicki.

"On his last morning, when I saw his lips dry and cracked, I lifted his head and sprinkled a few drops of water in his mouth. I was surprised when he opened his eyes and took more.

"'How you feeling?' I asked him. He lifted a finger, pointing, and told me, "Bring the papers from my desk."

"Ned's desk was heaped with documents going back years. His Last Will and Testament sat squarely on top of the pile. I picked it up and read through the pages. Sure enough, Ned had named your daddy, Mitch Taggart, as recipient of his home and property. I brought all the papers back to Ned, but by then he had fell off into another deep sleep. I took the papers back to the desk."

"My daddy would never have kept you on," said Vicki.

"I can't be in the same place as the devil," he replied, simply. Vicki had hardened herself against his accusations and she looked at him with no judgment.

"Ned's desk was cluttered with papers, all kinds of legal writing and folders with more papers stuffed inside. I sat down behind his desk and picked through the invoices and letters. I was looking for other documents to see what else Ned had signed over." He paused suddenly, and his face brightened when he said, "Whenever I pick up any paper and read the words on it, I think of my Mama Patch who knew how important reading would be for me. Without her good reasoning for my future, I would never have found things out."

A hard cough suddenly shook his brittle frame; when the spasm ceased, he picked right up where he left off.

"Ned's mother, Miss Rachel was prickly and not happy about the whole thing. Every day, she preached at me saying, 'This is a gift not meant for Negros to have; you one lucky black boy.' One time I was tired from working in the field all day, and I said, 'Miss Rachel, why is it so important for me to read anyway?' She hit me on the head with her ruler and said, 'Because reading reveals the truth!'

"Since she didn't have that many books for me, she took to bringing the family record books, deeds, letters, and invoices to the lessons. I learned my numbers when she showed me how to keep up the payment ledgers."

"It's unbelievable that Sherman Preecher kept his word," said Vicki.

"He did. And that Miss Rachel, he chuckled, she was a pistol. She told it just like she meant it." He chucked another spud, stood up and stretched his bony arms to the ceiling, followed by a satisfied groan.

"Ah, that's better—gotta stretch them limbs before they knot up," he said and shuffled across the floor and picked up a tin can and took a few sips of water; he offered the can to Vicki. "Care for a sip or two?"

"No thanks," she said.

Don't be 'fraid; it won't turn you colored."

At this, Vicki rolled her eyes up to the ceiling and shook her head.

"Okay," he said and sat down. "My curiosity got the best of me and I looked through all of Ned's files. I opened the desk drawers and took note of old photographs and more handwritten papers that he kept. The last drawer at the bottom was locked and I wondered why. Since I knew where all the keys were kept, it didn't take me long to find the desk key."

"When I unlocked the drawer and pulled it open the only thing inside was a single folder. I was curious as to why this one folder got a drawer all to itself; so I took it out and looked through the pages. It was page after page of receipts and invoices for livestock and equipment sales all the way back to Mister Sherman's original building. I could tell that some of the charges weren't right, and from the looks of these invoices, there was cheating going on. I was about to close the file and return it to the desk drawer when another paper caught my eye, probably because the paper was different, high-end and fancy. The name on the top was in big swirly letters pressed right into the paper."

Vicki heard an abrupt change in Minter Saul's voice. As he spoke, his frail body trembled, and she realized he was repeating word for word what he had read on that paper.

Randolph J. Talbot

Attorney at Law

No. 10 Magnolia Lane

Piney, Georgia, Route 10

Sale: Negro infant, healthy male, approximate age: 2 months.

Birth parents, Atticus and Patch Simms (Deceased)

Total: $500 - Cash paid in full to: Sherman Preecher.

"I focused on the words Negro infant, male, and I felt the blood drain from my face and I couldn't move. It was like shock had me stuck in one spot. But still, I couldn't figure why my Mama and Daddy's name would be on this paper and Negro infant, Male. I felt all hot and out of sorts sitting there holding that paper and something hard started pounding inside my chest. It was my heart racing to get somewhere without the rest of me. I fell back in Ned's chair, afraid that the ruckus inside me would drag me to death's door alongside Ned."

"Oh, Jesus." Vicki whispered when she suddenly realized he was speaking about the invoice she had found among Preecher's papers.

"I swear to you, Miss. I ain't cried since I was a boy but I felt water running from my eyes fast, like a river. There were sounds coming outta me," he admitted, "Bad sounds from somewhere deep." Then putting his hand to his chest, he said, "I heard my own voice shouting, screaming, and asking God, why? It scared me when I realized I was cussin at God."

Minter Saul quieted, but only for a second to catch his wind, and he looked at Vicki and said, "I had a brother."

"I sat at Ned's desk for a long time, just staring at that paper. I feared putting it back in that drawer. It was the closest I would ever be to my brother and I didn't want to lock him away again. I felt so weak," he said, "But not a tired weakness from hard work, the weakness in me was like someone had took hold and squeezed my heart tight like a sponge. I think I musta sat there for hours until Ned woke up and was calling for water. I went back to his bedside and stood looking down into his sunken face. His breathing was slow and ragged with phlegm, and I watched his chest rise and fall as his lungs struggled against the pneumonia."

"He opened his mouth for a few drops of water and when I held the cup to his lips, he lapped at it like a thirsty dog. 'Thank you, friend,' I heard him mumble."

"When Ned closed his eyes again I fished around in the pile of dirty clothes on the floor, found a pair of his soiled underwear, balled them up, and shoved them deep into his mouth. In his weakened state, Ned didn't put up much of a fuss when I pinched his nostrils closed. His eyes popped open just long enough for him to see me sending him to his Glory."

Vicki was speechless as she listened to him speak so matter-of-factly about murdering Ned. He had not an ounce of remorse for what he'd done.

"After I knew for sure he was dead, I went back to his desk. I sat down and looked through the bank statements, land documents, and claims and was lucky to find a blank copy of his Last Will and Testament. At that point, I had plenty of time to practice Ned's crooked chicken scratch. I carefully signed Ned's bank accounts and land holdings naming myself as the new account owner, I filled in the blank Will, naming me as sole beneficiary. By then, I had gotten pretty good copying Ned's writing, thanks to Miss Rachel's strict teaching that included a green switch across my knuckles during penmanship."

Minter Saul sighed and took a moment to ponder on his next words.

"When I was satisfied with the looks of the documents, and Ned's signature, I lit a fire in the fireplace and tossed in the Will naming your daddy, and scattered the ashes. Then, I called Doc Jenkins."

"Doc Jenkins, suh, I said. It's Minter Saul at the Preecher farm. I think Mister Ned is dead, suh."

Vicki sat quietly. She looked over at Minter Saul scratching old dog's ear.

"So you just killed him after reading a letter?"

Minter Saul's head snapped around and his angry eyes dragged resentment up and down her body.

"All those years," he lamented, "Ned knew his father had sold my brother like he was one of his animals. A damn animal!"

His eyes bore into Vicki's face and his nostrils flared with anger and he said, "He claimed I was his friend, but he never told me the truth." He looked at her, his face a storm of hatred. "Ned wanted me to be alone. He was gonna take my brother's existence to his grave. When I shoved that rag in his mouth and his eyes popped open and he saw it was me, he knew I had found out. Oh yes, old Ned knew why I was killing him!"

Minutes passed until, at last, Minter Saul calmed and Vicki saw him brush away tears. He looked at her through the eyes of a tortured soul.

"From the time I was a boy, I thought I was alone in this world. Because of the Preechers, I'll never know if my brother is even alive."

Vicki didn't feel it her place to judge Minter Saul. The two sat in stillness, Minter Saul in mourning for his lost brother, and Vicki for her daughter. Time passed, and she watched the candled dwindle down to a pool of liquid wax. She glanced at Minter Saul when he began to cough so hard it rattled his small frame.

"Are you all right, Minter Saul?"

He ignored the question. And when a flame suddenly blazed, she saw another candle had appeared on the table. "I came by the Taggart property yesterday because I felt an urge, but as soon as I reached that old flagpole, I couldn't go no farther."

"Why?"

"That house is evil."

"I don't know why you say that." said Vicki. "I grew up there."

"I can tell you this—get your daughter, and get away from there if you want her to have a chance."

Vicki thought about the house she had lived in all her life and now the strange noises coming from Big Daddy's room and Mama's disappearance.

"I don't have anywhere to go."

"You can have Preecher's house if you want it."

"What about you?"

"Don't need it."

"Why not?" she asked, and again he went silent. Then, she added, "I really don't have a right to ask this . . . ."

"Can I help you find your daughter?"

"You knew?"

"That's what you come here for, ain't it?"

"Well, yes, but . . . ."

"No buts about it. That's what you want from me, ain't it? That's why I told you about Preecher."

"You didn't have to tell me or anyone. Ever."

"Oh yes, I did."

"Why?"

"Truth. I still believe in it. Now tell me about your girl."

Vicki sighed. She plucked a potato from the pot and rolled it over in her hand. "My daughter's missing."

"Oh, she ain't missing."

"You know where she is?"

"C'mon, now, Miss. Quit fooling. You know where your girl is, and you know who took her. Fact, you know more than anyone about what's going on."

Vicki dropped her head. "It's not all my fault."

"Maybe not. The only real problem you got is being a Taggart."

Vicki sucked in her breath and her lips tightened holding back angry words. Instead, she said with frustration, "Can you help me find her or not?"

"Why me?

"Because you know the cornfield."

"You really want to go in there?"

"Yes."

Minter Saul fell silent. "I'm not sure if I'm up to it, Miss."

"What do you mean?"

"You was right about your brother. He shot me."

"What! When?"

"I'm not sure when it was," he lifted his shirt. A bandage was taped to his side. "I'm weaker every day."

She leaned in for a closer look. "No blood; it may not be that bad. You should see Doc Jenkins."

"He don't treat Negroes."

Vicki shook her head with regret and said, "If you're not up to it, I'll go on my own."

"What about the Sheriff?"

"He's looking, but I can't just sit idle. I have to do something."

"The cornfield ain't just weeds and bugs, you know," he warned.

"What's in there?"

"I'm not sure how to explain it. Best I can say is that it's a place for the souls that haven't passed on yet. Like a waiting post; only, they don't know what they're waiting on."

Shaken by the certainty of his statement, Vicki grew silent.

"Miss, answer this. Growing up in that house, what did you see out in your yard at night?"

"Men doing things, and going into the cornfield."

"So you know what that cornfield is, don't ya?"

"I don't rightly know," she said.

Minter Saul rolled his eyes, saying "You know what it is, Miss. A dumping ground for the Klan. Don't you know how many murdered Black folk your family put in the field?"

"I was a kid," she barked at him.

"Yes. You were, but that don't change things."

Vicki was agitated by all of his accusations when she shouted in anger, "What they did is not my fault! All I can think of is Trudy being in that place with James. I have to get her out!"

Vicki's outburst startled old dog from his nap and this time he lifted his head.

"So you wanna be a real mama now?" Minter Saul asked as he sliced the peel from a spud.

Vicki rocketed to her feet knocking the crate over.

"Does every damn person in this town know my life?" she shouted, angrily.

Minter Saul chuckled, "Calm down, Miss. Don't worry; it ain't never too late to make things right."

Vicki swiped the tears on her cheeks, righted the crate and sat back down.

"I have to go in the cornfield, Minter Saul, but I ain't gonna lie, I'm scared as hell, especially being a Taggart."

"What makes you so afraid?"

"I done something a long time ago that I can't fix. I was too young to understand what would happen."

"Where you really that young, Miss?" he asked.

"Yes!" she snapped, stunned by his question.

"Maybe you were and maybe you wasn't, or could be, you only wanted to save yourself."

"Just stop, okay! You don't know me and never will!"

Vicki got up to leave; she crossed the floor and opened the door.

"Just so you know, that boy James, he's been around a long time and he has a strong will," said Minter Saul.

Vicki stopped and looked back, "What else do you know?"

"Here, lately, I can feel his presence. I heard stories about his murder at the Crawley farm. They killed his daddy, too."

"I didn't know that."

"Both bodies never found."

"He's looking for revenge, ain't he?" She muttered dismally.

"I can't say."

"You think he has Trudy in that cornfield?"

"Don't rightly know, Miss. I do know that boy wants something, and he has another strong spirit with him. Something much more vicious."

Vicki's own terrifying experience was seeing the mangled body of James trying to speak to her. She didn't know what horror had caused her father to lock himself in his room, or Baby Mitch to look even more wild-eyed and crazy than usual. As for her mother, she often spoke of facing retribution. Had she become a victim of her own prophecy?

Whatever was going on, Vicki's need to save Trudy was getting stronger, and she felt compelled to find her. With these newfound feelings, she would face James, and make him give Trudy back to her.

"What does James want in return for Trudy; do you know?"

Minter Saul shrugged, and shook his head. "I can feel some loneliness, but I don't know if it's his or mine."

"I have to find Trudy. I can't wait on Hurley. I'm going myself."

"Tread careful Miss, tread very careful."

Chapter 27

The very next morning, Vicki drove her truck into town. She turned right onto North Main Street and cruised past the general store where Big Daddy used to go for meetings. He'd always let her tag along but with strict instructions to stay in the car. As a child, Vicki would look forward to those fifteen-minute rides to and from town, the only private moments she had ever shared with her father, not that he talked very much. His mind was always elsewhere and she rode in silence gazing out the window. Sometimes, he would make a joke and as an afterthought tussle her hair with his rough fingers.

The Piney post office and the courthouse were coming up on the right, and as she drove by the buildings, she saw the Rebel flag flapping beside the Stars and Stripes. She recalled all the times she had driven this road and never paid any mind to those symbols, but today, they loomed, standing side-by-side two powerful symbols with opposing truths. She looked at the American flag, the red, white, and blue hailed freedom for all individuals, while the Rebel flag dictated separation and was often hoisted as an expression of hate against those who were different; this was the flag her father loved so much.

Vicki pushed in the lighter on the dash and tapped a cigarette from the pack. The tip of the cigarette glowed against the coiled heat of the lighter as she inhaled deeply and then released a stream through the open window. She reflected on her long conversation with Minter Saul and tapped the ash from her cigarette on the ashtray. "I can't believe that old man killed Preecher," she muttered, her eyes troubled.

At the next corner, Vicki was caught by the red light. John's Bargain Store was on her left. She thought of the many times as a kid, Mama had taken her to John's for school clothes. She shopped at John's for Trudy, too, but Vicki never did. In fact, she couldn't recall ever buying anything for Trudy. "Idiot," she mumbled, and mashed the gas when the light flashed green.

On the next block was the Busy Bee Diner where she worked. She drove on. No sense in stopping, she wasn't going back to work until Trudy was home again.

At the next intersection, Vicki looked left and right when the truck bounced over the tracks of a railroad crossing and the neighborhood changed dramatically. Stately mansions loomed in opulence and lined each street. The redbrick homes, adorned with colonial-style columns, were beautiful and secluded. Huge Magnolia trees postured in their greatness, and Vicki now knew why the area was called Magnolia Lane. The trees were massive, and this time of year, the air was fragrant with their dizzying sweetness.

Lawnmowers hummed as Negro gardeners manicured the grass to stellar perfection and stone cherubs held huge goblets brimming with colorful flowers. At the end of every driveway stood the statue of a Negro lawn jockey, its cheerful smile honoring the bygone days of plantation life.

As she marveled at the elegance of the homes, she also searched the addresses. She was not there for a sightseeing tour.

She saw the sign first, an old-fashioned shingle hanging from a gleaming brass horse head engraved with the name: Randolph J. Talbot, Attorney-at-Law.

Vicki turned right and followed the expansive drive to a plantation style house that was now an office building. She eased up the path to the parking area and pulled in, gathered the file folder, got out of the truck, and walked up the path to the front door.

Chapter 28

At noon the same day, Hurley parked next to the cornfield, got out of his cruiser, walked around to the rear and popped the trunk. He retrieved the axe he bought that morning at the general store. "Whew!" His eyes swept the sky, "It's gonna be another hot one."

He walked to the edge of the Taggart yard and studied the massive cornhusks. Without a decent breeze, the corn silk drooped, and miniscule insects flitted atop the silk in the muggy air. The stalks themselves were huge, towering over his head. Untouched for years, they had flourished, and he felt a defiance lurking as he stood in their presence.

His plan was to hack his way in and leave a trail he could follow out with Trudy. As he swung the axe left and right, stalks fell all around him, and he moved quickly. When he was a good way in, he stopped to catch his breath and looked back. To his astonishment, the stalks he had split were once again standing erect and the weeds had knitted together consuming all signs of the path he made.

"What the hell!" He looked around. "Where's the damn path? This can't be happening," he muttered, and picked up his speed. He swung the axe again and again until his arms ached and sweat poured like rain on his face.

He stopped once more to catch his breath, then flexed his stiff fingers and rotated his aching shoulders. Another deep sigh and he was ready to continue, but when he looked, he couldn't find where he left off. The cornstalks stood erect on every side of him.

"This is insane," he said, turning in circles. Hundreds of stiff cornhusks were fixed sheath-to-sheath. He felt trapped, and his heart pumped wildly. "Hell no," he said aloud, and raised the axe sending it into the stalks in front of him. A few fell over and he stepped forward swinging again, more toppled and he kept going.

The sun's rays baked his bare head and salty perspiration stung his eyes. His mouth was dry, and he longed for a cold drink of water, and thought of the water hose in Vicki's yard. That would be his first stop when he returned with Trudy. He stood in silence, trying to bring reason to his predicament and when he checked his watch, only ten minutes had passed; that couldn't be right, he thought, he felt like he had been chopping for over an hour.

Then, looking around at the growing vegetation, he said, "This was a bad call; I should've never come out here alone."

Pollen swirled around him and he rubbed his itchy eyes; focusing on Trudy, he raised the axe and swung.

His blade sliced and the stalks were falling more quickly as he gained momentum, until some unwelcome visitors interrupted his progress. A team of insects hung in the air and then landed on his skin.

"Ow, damn! You fuckers think it's dinner time, huh?"

But even while the insect invasion continued, Hurley swung the axe, hustling over broken stalks while dodging and swatting bugs at every turn. To add to his anxiety, the bugs were joined by two large dragonflies the size of Hummingbirds.

"Oh shit!" he moaned.

One dragonfly floated effortlessly in front of his face like it was surveying him. The other circled his head before it joined the first one.

Hurley shielded his eyes from an attack and was relieved when they sped off in another direction, taking the insect swarm with them.

"Damn, those fuckers are big," he muttered.

Scratching his bug-bitten arms, Hurley called out, "Trudy!"

As he continued walking, he came upon a colossal cornstalk with a base as thick and wide as a tree trunk.

"My good God," he uttered, staring at the massive pod.

Without hesitation, and with all the strength he could muster, Hurley swung the hatchet, opening a ragged gash in the base of the plant. However, when he pulled the blade out, a foul odor seeped and a burst of green muck flew into his face sealing his eyelids shut. Hurley screamed with pain as the slime burned his skin, and he struggled to scale the sticky ooze from his eyes. He used his shirttail to wipe the last of the mucus from his face. Exhausted, his eyes stinging, Hurley fell to the ground and sat gasping for air as his thundering heart slowed. For a moment, he felt defeated and wanted to turn back. Instead, he got to his feet and found the axe. Taking a different direction, he hacked his way around the giant plant and called out again, "Trudy!"

Along with the husks, Hurley faced a vast overgrowth of feral plants that he chopped and pulled from their beds with his hands. A burst of strength propelled him forward, and he swung the axe with abandon in every direction. His next swing hit a surface more compact. The plant he'd struck had petrified. The axe blade was jammed into the surface, and when he tried to pull it out, the blade remained, leaving him holding the bare handle.

"Shit!" he exclaimed, and threw the handle into the weeds. Without the axe, how would he find Trudy? How would he even get out of this place?

From the corner of his eye a sudden movement in the bush startled him. A dark man stepped from behind a screen of cornstalks, and Hurley nearly passed out from shock. He staggered back almost falling over, but regained his footing and stood facing the man.

"You scared the hell outta me, Mister. What are you doing here?"

The man said nothing.

"Who the hell are you?" Hurley demanded.

The Negro man was dressed in tattered work clothes, a worn hat pulled down on his head. His skin was dark and his eyes, the color of red clay, were angry and threatening.

"I'm looking for a little girl who is lost," Hurley said.

The dark man's hand floated up from his side and hovered over a pallet of overgrown vines at his feet. The vines parted, revealing a child asleep beneath the creeping plants. It was Trudy.

Hurley was horrified, but relieved to see her alive. He wanted to rush forward and snatch her from the strange cocoon, but the terrible glint in the dark man's eyes cautioned him to remain still.

"Why do you have Trudy here like this?" he asked, confronting the man.

And then, without warning, Hurley was struck by what he thought was a bolt of lightning, but was in fact a seizure so powerful it constricted his body bulging his eyes and causing his jaw to clench. Hurley's knees buckled and he collapsed and lay twitching in the dirt. Only inches from the dark man's feet, his eyes shot open and he saw rotted flesh and insects crawling in open cavities. Unbearable pain twisted his body and he tried to scream, but his teeth were jammed tight. He felt compelled to look up, and what he saw was even more horrifying. The dark man's head was transforming into hundreds of insects until it was an entity of twitching bugs on top of his shoulders. The flutter of a million wings all at once was the rumbling of an unearthly machine that generated a demonic roar, searing Hurley's right eardrum until it burst into a bloody pulp.

He shrieked in agony and his body pulsed and jerked as blood seeped from his ruined ear and ran between his fingers and he stared helplessly at the insects amassing above his head. The steady drumming of wings increased, throbbing the membrane in his left ear. He shoved a finger into the hole, hoping to save it, but it was to no avail. The vicious flutter had inflamed the membrane, and at any moment, his remaining eardrum would rupture.

"Stop!"

At the unexpected command, the rumble subsided and the flies reformed into the head of the dark man. Hurley groaned and rolled over, still clutching his broken ear, but he found the strength to pinpoint where Trudy was, and he inched his way toward her. Closer now, he reached for her hand but recoiled in horror when a horde of feral weeds slinked along the ground with hundreds of fingerlike vines and pulled Trudy back into their world.

"Trudy!" he cried out, as she disappeared into the briar.

"You should go, Mister," a voice said.

Hurley looked over at a Negro boy standing across from the dark man.

"Get out," the boy said. "You don't belong here."

The dark man locked eyes with the boy.

"Not long, Uncle, not long," the boy assured.

Hurley watched the dark man step back into the weeds and then he looked back at the boy, who he was certain was James.

"James," he said. "Can I take Trudy home? Her mother misses her."

"Go!" James commanded, and pointed, and when Hurley looked around the weeds fell apart providing a clear path. A gusty wind picked up, and when Hurley looked for the boy, he was gone.

Chapter 29

Vicki pulled her truck onto the side of the road and parked.

"This is it."

She was certain this was where she'd first met James and Ella. The chicken wire fence was the same and she could see the pine tree forest in the distance. The farmhouse was to her right, the same direction that Ella and James had run before he'd stopped and made funny faces at her. She smiled at that memory.

She reached back and grabbed the telescope off the seat. Once out of the truck, she stuck the toy in her back pocket and ambled down the incline. At the fence, she recalled looping her fingers through the holes and leaning back, gazing up at the sky. But her fingers weren't child-size anymore, so instead she took hold of the railing and scanned the field.

From where she stood, the Crawley farm was as generous as it had been when she was a kid. The grass shimmered emerald with not a hint of brown patches anywhere. The immense pine trees towered in the distance. A coral-rimmed sun sank slowly behind turquoise tree limbs, and in her mind, she heard Ella's warning.

"You know we need to be gone before sunset, James."

Ella had been the cautious one; James wanted to show off his knowledge. At the time, she had thought about the words that Big Daddy used for people who bragged—he called them "cocky sons of bitches."

But Vicki didn't think James was cocky; she liked him and she liked Ella. It had been a long time since she played with kids her age, and it was fun hitting the ball over the fence. James knew all about the stars and he said he would show her where to look to see the Dippers.

Now, as she stood alone at the fence, Vicki looked up into the sky and her inner voice mimicked his words, *Look for the North Star, it's the brightest one and the Big Dipper is never far from it*. Her gaze followed his pointing finger to the shadowy sky, when suddenly and seemingly out of nowhere, two men rode up.

Vicki pushed the gruesome memory away; she didn't want to think about the part she had played. Doing so could easily cripple her and keep her from the task at hand.

But as she stood at the fence looking around the Crawley field, she though about Minter Saul's words, You a Taggart, you know all about killing. He was right; she was like her father in many ways, but she wasn't a murderer who hunted Negroes and discarded the dead bodies without the fear of consequence.

Vicki shuddered at the memory of all the times she had witnessed her father ordering bodies into the cornfield, and with these images seared into the malleable mind of a child, her innocence had slowly eroded and she had knowingly set up a new friend to be viciously slaughtered.

Her recollection of the rape, the brutal and deliberate cruelty that occurred inside the Air Streamer was a tenacious weed that bullyragged its way inside her thoughts and no matter how hard she tried to forget, her wasted existence was sandwiched between dual torments, ready at any moment to push her over the edge into madness.

Vicki touched her face; it was wet, and she was weeping again. Her tears were second nature, streaming without any forethought. She wanted to scream and cry out, curse them all to hell, but this was not about her anymore. She had another purpose that propelled her past her own misery. Finding Trudy was a chance to prove that she could be a good mother, and that, in turn, would help her to heal.

Breathing deeply brought clean fresh air into her lungs and then she exhaled, releasing some of the tension she felt.

Out of nowhere, the tinkle of childish laughter reached her ears, and she looked out over the field, listening. There it was again, voices from deep within the pine trees. Just like that, her pain was replaced by purpose. She climbed over the fence.

Vicki hurried across the vast field to the pine tree forest; and when she stepped past the trees there was a coolness that provided a welcome relief from the sticky heat. The sweet air was crisp and cleansing. She found herself standing under a vast canopy of thick branches teeming with pine needles it was a meadow of fragrant fir trees that conjured memories of Christmas day. She stepped over fallen pinecones and broken branches and huge tree roots emerged from the ground like prehistoric fossils.

She moved on, ducking under low-hanging limbs. It was a perfect place for kids to play hide and seek, so she called out her daughter's name. "Trudy."

Vicki waded through ankle-deep foliage that scratched her legs and eventually reached a clearing where she paused, listening to her surroundings. The birds, hiding expertly in the thick of the trees, chirped loudly at one another, and she heard wings flapping, squawking, and blustering all around. She felt her presence was the topic. The clearing was actually a glade surrounded by pine trees, and when she drew nearer, she saw a red ball rolling across the ground.

To Vicki's astonishment, Trudy ran from between a cluster of pines, and she was laughing. She scooped up the ball and threw it in a high arc. James was there too, running on two good legs. He jumped up and caught the ball in midair.

"See, I told you I would get it back," he said, and laughed.

"Okay, your turn now," said Trudy.

"Trudy!" Vicki screamed, but Trudy, not hearing, ran back into the trees.

James, however, turned toward Vicki. He walked up to her, clutching the ball. "She doesn't hear you, Vicki." His words were mature, but spoken in a child's voice.

"I want my daughter, James."

"You want her now?"

"Yes, right now!"

"But you never wanted her at all, did you, Vicki?"

"You little fuck; give me my daughter back!" she blurted.

James smiled, tossed the ball in the air, and caught it. He turned and ran to the trees where Trudy had gone, and followed her in.

"Wait, James; I'm sorry!"

She rushed across the glade to the opening in the trees, but when she was close enough to enter, she heard a sinister growl and stopped in her tracks.

The animal crept from the bushes. It had the long snout of a reptile and its eyes were hollow black holes that quivered with the movement of tiny insects crawling around the rims. Terrified, she trembled, even as she tried to remain perfectly still. The creature had no eyeballs, but somehow, she knew it was focused on her and she backed up.

"James!" she called out, her voice shaky. "I'm sorry I lied to those men. Please forgive me and give Trudy back."

But James didn't return, and now the animal stalked her. Its mouth fell open and a hideous wail pushed the hair on the back of her neck straight up. The thing inched towards her its back legs curled under as it prepared to leap.

"Gowan now, git!" a gruff voice yelled out.

Vicki stood terror-stricken but her head turned slowly toward the voice and she saw Minter Saul hobbling across the clearing.

The animal looked at him; it lifted its head and screamed into the sky, the sound so human, it shook Vicki to the core. It turned and slipped between the trees.

"Oh God, thank you," she said, falling to her knees.

"That durn thing was gonna kill you."

"Why did it listen to you?" she asked.

"Don't rightly know," he said, as he plodded toward the trees.

"Where are you going?"

"You want your daughter back, dontcha?"

"I thought you weren't up to it?"

"I found some strength hiding in my back pocket," he chuckled.

For an old man, Minter Saul moved quickly, and Vicki hurried to keep up, skirting past tree limbs and stumbling over thick roots and fallen branches. Pine needles scratched her arms. She wiped the blood away and kept going.

After a while, Minter Saul paused as he scanned the surroundings. He sat down on a huge tree root that rose above ground, its length and mass bridged the pine forest to what Vicki recognized as the cornfield.

"Where are we?"

"We're on the other side of your daddy's place." He said, between breaths, his burst of energy lessening.

"I didn't know the cornfield stretched this far over."

"Weeds gobble up the land they want. Don't matter to them who owns it."

"Is that where Trudy is?"

"Could be."

The cornfield rustled against a cold wind and Vicki rubbed her arms. "I dread going in that place; who knows what the hell is in there?" She said, nervously.

"The cornfield is a burial ground, but you already know that, Miss."

Vicki shrugged, resignedly. "I guess there are a few bodies buried in there."

"A few? There are bodies going back fifty years."

Vicki's face paled, but she said nothing.

However, Minter Saul wasn't done talking. "That's when your great-granddaddy, Beasley Taggart started killing Negroes in revenge for his daughter's murder. Only, it wasn't Negroes that kilt her."

"How do you know that?"

"Back then, times were just as bad for Whites as it was for Negroes. Many white folk were struggling to make ends meet and some felt angered that Negroes were earning a wage for work they did as slaves. We became the reason for every bad thing that happened in the county."

"No, that's wrong; it was because Blacks killed a white girl in my family," Vicki assured him, "Something had to be done, so they got an ordinance passed."

"Ordinance!" he laughed, saying, "No real law was passed, that was Klan law. Negroes was lynched for any reason, whether it was a proven crime or not. Your great-granddaddy used his daughter's murder to organize the Klan in Forsyth County, and they came up with the Sunset Rule. After that, the Klan grew in every town, and the biggest one was right here in Piney, led by Beasley, and passed onto his son Cyrus, and onto your Big Daddy, Mitch Taggart."

"Even when the Sheriff found out the girl was messing with a white boy, a drifter she had met up with in Dead Man's Alley, Beasley Taggart wouldn't accept that a White coulda killed his girl."

"They never looked for the boy. Instead, they hung the coloreds that were locked in the barn, and who had nothing to do with the killing. After that, Negroes was run out of the county, and the signs went up on the roads. You seen those signs before, right, Miss Vicki? The ones that said, Nigger, don't let the sun set on you in Forsyth County."

"Not you, though. You stayed," Vicki said, contemptuously.

"Preecher protected his Negro workers," replied Minter Saul.

The shadows of reaching tree limbs crept across the field and Minter Saul looked up at the sunlight shining through the trees. "Did you know the Klan used the Sunset Rule not only to keep Negroes outta Forsyth County, but to catch 'em inside the County?"

"What?"

"That's right," he said, "Some farmers would even hold workers back until after dark, and then call the Klan to go after them. They couldn't leave the bodies to be found, and that's when Beasley said, 'Put them Niggers in the cornfield.'" Minter Saul gestured toward the field. "There's hundreds, maybe thousands of Negroes buried out there."

"That's hard to believe."

"Most Whites in Piney don't know nothing about what went on, but Negroes, we know. The story has been passed down through generations." Then, with a quizzical look, he said, "Miss Vicki, don't you know your family's property is a Negro graveyard?"

Vicki was overwhelmed by Minter Saul's accusations, and she wanted him to stop talking, to just be quiet so she could think. But he just kept spouting more and more about the Klan, and she wanted to scream at him to shut up!

All at once, the sound of someone approaching halted Minter Saul's diatribe, and they both quieted, listening warily to the rustling of the bushes until Hurley pushed his way past the trees. At the sight of Hurley, Vicki breathed a long hard sigh of relief.

"Anybody got any water?" he asked, weakly.

"Oh, my God, Hurley! What happened to you?" Vicki asked.

His face was riddled with bug bites and his shirt was ripped and bloody, one ear was swollen and crusted with blood.

"Vicki," he said, grimly. "The cornfield is evil."

"How did you find us?"

"I was trapped in the cornfield. If James hadn't given me a way out, I would be dead, of that I'm certain." He sat down on the tree root to rest. I saw your truck on the road took a chance that you'd come this way. I'm glad to see you're not alone," he said, looking at Minter Saul.

"I saw Trudy."

"I did too. But I couldn't get to her."

"She's with James."

"Where?"

"In the glade, playing ball."

"Playing ball? I guess she's all right."

"No, she ain't all right," said Minter Saul

"Whattaya mean?"

"I mean, she's in danger. She's with a dead boy, and a vicious spirit that won't be controlled for much longer."

Without warning, Minter Saul's eyes glazed over; he swayed and almost fell over. Hurley caught his arm.

"You need to rest."

Minter Saul pulled away saying, "Plenty of time for resting later, Sheriff, when I'm good and dead." He laughed so heartily the nesting birds took flight. Puzzled, Hurley looked over at Vicki who simply shrugged her shoulders.

"What happened to you in there?" Asked Vicki.

"I was so scared, Hurley admitted, every direction I turned was a wall of corn stalks, I couldn't find the trail I made. And there was a man, strange and terrifying."

Then, with a somber shake of his head, Hurley said, "Vicki, I swear it felt like a nightmare, but I was wide-awake. The man, or spirit, I guess, summoned a swarm of insects and the sound was so loud, it burst my right eardrum. I can't hear." And he touched his swollen ear.

"That spirit is the boy's protector and you're right to be afraid," said Minter Saul. "The boy wants something; we need to find out what it is and give it to him."

"Well, he can't have Trudy," said Vicki. "Wait," she said, her eyes lit up. "I have something he wants." She pulled the telescope from her back pocket.

"He wants a telescope?" asked, Hurley.

"Yes, he wanted to be an astronaut. He loves stars and planets. He told me he was saving to buy one of these."

Hurley shrugged, uncertain. "It's worth a shot."

"Where are they now?" Vicki looked at Minter Saul, who nodded at the wall of cornstalks looming ahead.

"I'm going back in with you," said Hurley. "But at least this time, I know what to expect."

"And we have something to trade," Vicki waved the telescope.

"You should go back and wait in the truck." Advised Hurley.

"No fucking way!"

"It's too dangerous, Vicki."

"She needs to go," said Minter Saul.

Hurley paused and then nodded with uncertainty and glanced at her with misgiving.

"How do you know where to go?" he asked the old man.

"Don't rightly know. I just do."

Chapter 30

A simple touch from Minter Saul parted the cornstalks and he stepped further into the cornfield. But Hurley and Vicki's attempts were not as effortless, the stalks stood unmoving and Hurley had to break them apart to enter.

"Shit! I need another hatchet, he complained as he sucked the blood on his cut finger and wagged his aching hands. These things are like small trees."

As they pushed past the broken limbs the atmosphere began to change. The humidity coated their skin in a film of stickiness that seemed to attract every biting bug in the field. Minter Saul, however, was given a pass and he appreciated that not one insect alighted on his skin. The sound of Vicki and Hurley complaining and smacking bugs tickled his mood as he plodded forward. The two followed Minter Saul deeper into the briar as more bold insects buzzed their faces and an ominous cloud formed overhead blocking the light. It was a swarm of small insects their wings drumming so hard the vibrations rumbled and shook the cornhusks. Minter Saul looked up at the swarm unfazed, but Vicki and Hurley covered their ears against the rumble and Hurley yelped in pain and fell down, a slip of blood trickled from his broken ear and Vicki yelled, "Jesus! It's so loud!"

"Stop it!" Minter Saul hollered, and almost instantly, the humming ceased and the insects scattered.

With Vicki's help, Hurley managed to stand. "It felt like a match was lit inside my ear."

"Is it better now?" She asked him.

"No. I still can't hear a damn thing out of it."

Minter Saul turned and cast a quizzical glance at Hurley.

"Curious," he muttered.

"What does that mean?" Hurley grumbled, holding his aching ear.

"I have a feeling they was just having a looksee."

"Oh, they were looking, huh?" Hurley said, angrily. "If I had a can of bug spray, I'd give them something to see."

Vicki smirked and rolled her eyes when Hurley dodged a lone dragonfly that buzzed his head. "These damn bugs are bold."

"We in their house," said Minter Saul as he set off in another direction and Hurley and Vicki scrambled to keep up.

They continued on their way tramping across more coarse and barbarous brush as they stepped deeper into the cornfield.

"Minter Saul! The weeds, they're growing up behind us!"

"I have noticed that."

"How are we gonna get out?" Vicki's anxiety was increasing as she looked around.

"Don't rightly know, Miss."

Hurley stopped when Vicki snatched leaves from a tree and blotted his bloody ear. As she did so she glanced at the ground, her eyes widening with dread, and she whispered, "We have a visitor."

Hurley looked at a Negro child, no more than three years old, crouched next to his foot.

"Where did you come from?" He asked.

The girl's skin was ebony but covered in road dust. Her ragged dress was hardened with dirt, and her small legs were like saplings. Vicki noticed that the girl's tiny feet were caked with weeds. The child reached a hand toward Hurley, her doll-like eyes sad and pleading.

"Don't touch her!" warned Minter Saul.

"I wasn't planning to," Hurley said. "Is she alive?"

"Not in this world."

"What does she want?" asked Vicki.

"Most of the children have lost parents along the way," he said.

Vicki's face softened and she spoke to the child.

"Hello! Do you know Trudy?"

"I don't think she even sees you, Vicki," said Hurley.

Minter Saul stepped closer to the girl and her eyes shifted toward him. "She's been here a long time."

"How long?" asked Hurley.

"Before you were both born."

All of a sudden, the girl began to weep, then grew transparent and vanished.

"She's gone!"

"She still here," said Minter Saul. "They all are; they can't leave."

"Why not?" Hurley asked.

"When they were living, they tried to get out before sunset but they didn't make it."

"They're buried here."

Aghast, Hurley looked at the ground and back at Minter Saul.

"Don't you know about the Ordinance, son? Negroes had to get out before the sun set."

"I heard about it growing up. My daddy's workers always left early. I thought that would've ended after the Civil Rights Bill was passed!"

"Son, don't you know that law never made it to Forsyth County?"

Vicki interrupted them with a loud sigh; she was growing irritated again. "I'm here to get my daughter not to listen to Klan stories!"

The old man shook his head and continued walking. The terrains were becoming mundane as they tramped over weeds and around hundreds of cornstalks when suddenly Minter Saul hollered, "Watch it!" And they stepped over a toad the size of a small dog. It croaked repeatedly, a monotonous baritone that shook the weeds and floated above their heads on a shifting breeze until it faded with the wind.

Exhausted, the group began to slow down and Hurley stopped, listening closely to the surroundings. "Do you hear that?"

"What?" asked Vicki? "All I heard was that awful frog."

"No, no, listen."

She did, and she heard it too, voices, whispering from every direction.

"It's coming from the cornhusks," said Minter Saul. As soon as the words left his mouth, all other sounds in the cornfield ceased and were replaced by obscure whispers and warnings that rose from within the stalks. The prattle quickly turned into voices, "Watch out! Lay low and keep quiet."

Vicki was startled when something brushed past her, and she gasped, grabbing Hurley's arm. "I'm scared," she uttered. He put his finger to his lips shushing her, just as an abrupt drop in temperature chilled the air.

"Something's happening," he whispered, and looked at Minter Saul who was unmoving except for his roaming eyes. Now the air was frigid and they huddled to stay warm. Without warning, the cornhusks were shoved aside as ghostly apparitions bounded through. The odor of sweaty bodies was strong, and they heard the breathless panting of frightened people on the run. The sound of feet pounding the dirt was loud as the spirits scrambled to hide. Frightened of the ghostly activity that surrounded them, Vicki reached behind her for Hurley, grabbing his hand. "Don't let go, Hurley, please!"

"Just keep still," Minter Saul whispered.

"Keep still?" she muttered, "Is he crazy?" She wanted to bolt and run and get the hell out of there, but she couldn't. She had to get Trudy first. Vicki willed herself to find some self-control and was comforted knowing that Hurley was close to her. She felt him pressed against her shoulder and his finger brushed her cheek as he squeezed her hand.

Suddenly . . .

"Turn it loose!" Minter Saul was shouting.

Her eyes found the old man standing across from her, on his left stood Hurley, the color in his face draining, and he also shouted, "Vicki! Let go of its hand!"

An icy feeling slid up her spine and she suddenly began to tremble, her head slowly turned as she thought, "Whose hand am I holding?"

So deteriorated was the corpse that stood at her shoulder, she couldn't tell what it had looked like in life. Gunshots had opened its chest and its sunken eyeballs glared at her. It was trying to speak and it's mouth moved frantically, but no words emerged, and she heard Hurley shouting, "Let go of its hand!"

But the corpse was gripping her hand so tightly she couldn't pull free. She tugged at the mangled bone that was its arm as it continued mouthing and grimacing in a horrible grotesque manner, it was trying to tell her something with words she couldn't hear. She yanked with all her strength until it released her hand, and then she tumbled backward onto the ground and watched the corpse dissolve into a mist.

Terrified, Vicki scuttled along the ground until Hurley was there and lifted her up. She buried her head in his shoulder crying hysterically.

"It's gone," he said, "You're safe."

"Minter Saul picked up his walking stick and said, "The dead will take you if you let 'em."

Without warning, the sound of a gunshot cracked, sending everyone to the ground. Vicki ducked her head and covered her ears. Hurley and Minter Saul squatted next to her, looking around for the source of the gunfire.

Instead, they heard the ghostly voice of a man saying, "There he is! Catch that Nigger!"

Laughter sailed through the air followed by more gunfire. "Catch 'em; don't let that Nigger git away. Git 'em, dammit!"

Cornstalks fell over and feet pounded all around them as Negro spirits tried to escape. When Hurley stood up, he was immediately knocked back down by something unseen.

"You need to stay down," warned Minter Saul, and Hurley settled next to him, asking, "What's happening?

"Negro spirits running from memories of the Klan."

"Git the rope! String 'em up!"

"No, please! No! No!"

"Hold 'em still! Fucking black scum!"

Terrified shrieks and angry words were followed by the whooshing sound of a whip slicing the air so close to Vicki she could smell leather. It snapped against bare skin, and a gut-wrenching scream echoed through the field. More cries shook the cornfield as the grisly sound of the whip snapped again and again.

Suddenly, a haunting stillness claimed the field silencing the torture. Minutes passed, and Vicki whispered, "Is it over?" But before anyone could respond they heard a disembodied voice cry out, "Please, Mistuh Taggart, please let me live. I have a family."

Hearing her family name, Vicki buried her face in her hands and moaned in misery, she covered her ears attempting to block out the voice of the doomed soul.

Several more minutes passed as she sat with her eyes clamped shut and her ears covered, before the cornfield fell completely quiet, and the warm humid air returned. Hurley and Vicki stood up looking around and Minter Saul announced, "It's done."

"My God," Hurley said.

"God ain't had nothin' to do with this." Stated Minter Saul. And now if you wouldn't mind, help me up."

Hurley took Minter Saul by the hand and pulled him to his feet; he groaned against the stiffness in his legs but quickly shook off the pain and ambled forward. Vicki followed in silence, her nerves frayed; she struggled to control her still trembling body. Every glance in any direction brought her shame. She thought of the corpse holding her hand, his face only inches from her own, and the mouth moving wildly as it tried to tell her something.

She walked on, trying not to feel anything, just walking in a daze like she herself was one of the undead.

Behind her, Hurley brought up the rear in silence. He had witnessed the horror her family was involved in and now she felt ashamed to even look him in the face.

As soon as they stepped into a clearing, they stopped to rest, and Hurley looked around, saying, "What's that sound?"

It was another voice, different this time, a living voice coming from a location not far away. Someone was muttering and cussing, and there was the sound of a shovel hitting dirt.

"Look, someone's over there," Hurley pointed across the clearing, and they all headed in that direction.

Baby Mitch kicked a body into a freshly dug grave. "Get the hell in that fucking hole, Nigger."

"What the hell is my brother doing here?" Vicki asked rhetorically, before breaking away from the group.

"Baby Mitch!"

Startled, Baby Mitch's scarecrow frame jerked, and he almost fell into the hole. "Shit! You nearly scared the life outta me!"

Hurley walked up and stood next to Vicki. "What the hell you doin' Mitch?"

"What the fuck! Ya'll been following me?"

"We're looking for your niece, but it looks to me like you're burying a body," said Hurley.

"This is Taggart land. Ya'll need to keep moving. Mind your own damn business."

"Well, thank you, Mitch, for making my job just a little easier. Looks to me like this could be a murder you're trying to conceal," replied Hurley.

"I'm just burying a dead body I found on the road, giving it a final resting place. No proof I kilt nobody. I know my rights Hurley, so fuck off! Better yet, go fuck Vicki; she been holding it for you all these years."

Vicki paled. "Shut up!"

"So, who you got in there, Mitch?" asked Hurley, nodding at the hole.

Baby Mitch smirked. "Wouldn't you like to know?"

"You mean you're not going to tell us who the poor soul is you took it in your heart to bury in the middle of the cornfield?"

"Oh, so you wanna talk, Hurley? Let's talk." Baby Mitch threw down the shovel and looked at Vicki. "You standing there all pitiful, looking for your kid, and we all know you can't hardly stand that little girl."

"Shut up! You're a damn fool." She shrieked.

"I know who raped you," he snickered. Vicki blanched at his flat-out admission and Baby Mitch cackled and slapped his knee, saying, "I wish you could see your face right now."

"What the hell are you talking about?" Hurley said, his anger rising.

Baby Mitch chuckled some more, saying, "You would've figured it out for yourself if you didn't live in the bottle. Some example of a mother you are, a damn drunk." He spat on the ground.

"Shut your mouth!" Vicki snarled, but Baby Mitch was hyped up and anxious to take attention away from the hole he was digging.

"Ain't you ever wondered why you was attacked in Big Daddy's trailer?" he jeered.

"I said, shut up!" Vicki shouted, her face turning beet red.

"Girl, you're as dumb as a stump. It was Big Daddy that had you brought back to the family. He knew you were fucking Hurley and might even run off with this fool, he said, nodding at Hurley. Therefore, as only a loyal Klan leader would do, he had you damaged. He figured Hurley wouldn't want no damaged goods, and he was right, wasn't he Hurley?" He grinned scornfully.

Hurley and Vicki were shocked by the vile words Baby Mitch spewed.

Baby Mitch was so tickled at the look on their faces he jumped up and down and bent over with laughter. Vicki was mortified listening to him chortle and stomp around the hole with glee.

"That's a lie!" she screamed. "Big Daddy would never do that, and even if he wanted to, Mama wouldn't let him."

"Everybody in town knew you and him were together," he said, looking at Hurley. "Word got back to Big Daddy quick. Baby Mitch wiped his nose on the back of his dirty hand."

"You need to watch your mouth," warned Hurley. But Baby Mitch continued with his revelation.

"Ain't no way in hell Big Daddy would allow you to be with a Nigger-lover."

Hurley's anger surged and his hands tightened into fists. He wanted to pound Baby Mitch's laughing face and shove those words back into his filthy mouth, but he held back.

"I heard him telling Mama about it at the kitchen table; they didn't know I was standing in the front room. I heard it all, and even when Mama protested, he told her to shut the hell up, so yeah, Mama suspected he might do something but she couldn't do a damn thing to stop it. One thing, though, Big Daddy never thought his man would leave you with a kid." He snickered at that, saying, "I guess that was a bonus," and another laugh rattled his spindly frame. He took care of him though – no worry there."

Hurley's police training had taught him how to mask his emotions, but even as he restrained himself he was sickened as he listened to Baby Mitch's hateful details. Every vile word thrown at Vicki cut him deep, as her sorry excuse for a brother revealed the whole story and the weight of guilt sat on his shoulders like a ten-ton boulder.

Sadly, he reached for Vicki, but she slapped his hand away not wanting to be touched by him or anyone else. She crossed her arms over her shaking frame, her mind reeling as her brother's words sunk in. A dizzy headache throbbed and her stomach coiled into a knot, she felt herself spinning like a top and then she was on her knees vomiting into the dirt.

"Oh shit!" Baby Mitch hollered, and snickered behind his hand.

Standing there, Hurley realized how much he could have changed Vicki's life had he chosen to handle things differently. If only he had not teased her about marriage. If only, he had walked her to the back door. If only, he had come to the hospital after the attack. Now, all of his if onlys played over and over in his head like a stuck record.

Always the one to take advantage, Baby Mitch saw the regret in Hurley's face and he hooted, "I knew I was right! Don't cry little sister. You got what was coming; that's all that was. You always acted like you was better than me. Running to Mama and Big Daddy, always getting what you wanted while I went to jail."

He picked up the shovel dragging it on the ground, "Mama and Big Daddy thought I was dumb, but you ain't nothing but redneck trash. Your big-time Sheriff here, he don't want you." He snorted with laughter, and spat another wad on the ground.

"I think you've said enough!" Hurley yelled; his eyes shot daggers at Baby Mitch. At the same time a fierce wind kicked up bending the cornstalks into flapping rags. Vicki got to her feet but the strong current pushed her off balance and Hurley caught her arm. Just as suddenly as the wind appeared, the gust subsided and was replaced by a putrid stench oozing from every direction.

"What the hell is that stinking smell?" Baby Mitch said, and pinched his nose. He looked around just as the stalks parted and the dead came forth.

"Oh shit!" he said, his eyes growing wide with fear and he stepped back, holding the shovel out in front of him.

Broken corpses moved on stilted legs. Some were only burnt stick figures with tattered nooses still dangling, large hateful eyes loomed at him.

Baby Mitch shook with terror, his voice quivered and he whined like a helpless child. "What's happening, Vicki? What do they want?" As they closed in, he swung the shovel left and right at the dead, but still, they lumbered forward until they surrounded him.

"What the fuck?" he screamed. "Hurley, help me! You gotta a gun, shoot 'em, dammit!"

Now, the grisly remains of the long dead blocked any means of escape for Baby Mitch, and skeletal arms reached for him with spindly fingers. An ear-piercing mantra rose up, stifling the air with a spectral chorus, and Baby Mitch covered his ears against the grisly sound. It was the ghostly refrain of hundreds of disembodied voices warbling in misery in a pitch so high, Hurley's broken ear sprouted fresh blood, the pain once again sending him to his knees.

As the dead stood rooted in place, they rocked in unified movement and the stench of decay grew stronger, snaring the surroundings in a mist of rotting waste and causing everyone to sicken and vomit. When Hurley saw the flies appear, he grabbed Vicki and yanked her down next to him just as the insects swiftly spun into the form of the dark man.

The flies whirled like a top near Baby Mitch and then grew in size into a quivering, twitching body of insects that stood over six feet tall, eyes looming large and fixated on him.

Baby Mitch quaked with fear and blood seeped from his nostrils. He cried out to his sister, "Vicki, help me! Please help me! I'm your brother, damn it! Help me!"

In spite of everything, Vicki felt sorry for him and she wanted to do something; she looked at Hurley who shook his head no, and then she saw the dark man reach out and snatch her brother up, his body whirling with a force so great his bones cracked and he screamed with each agonizing turn. The roar of buzzing insects sent her hands over her ears, and she was rooted in place when the dark man spiraled out of the cone of insects. His eyes turned to Vicki, his hateful stare pinned to her face, but the shrieks from Baby Mitch broke his glower and he turned back to his purpose. Vicki saw her brother rise high into the air and suspended over the twisting funnel a great yawn peeled open and sucked his still convulsing body into its rotting carcass. His pleads for his sister sputtered into the depths.

Crippled by what she'd witnessed Vicki fainted. Moments later her eyes fluttered open and she looked up into Hurley's face and realized he was cradling her head in his lap. "It's over, he said grimly, he's gone." His underlying meaning included Baby Mitch. When Vicki passed out she didn't see the dark man's visage burst into millions of fluttering insects rise up and scatter like dust, but Hurley did – it was another sight he'd never forget.

She sat up and cautiously looked around then back at Hurley her entire body trembling.

"Did you see that, Hurley? Did you see what it did to my brother?"

"We can't think about that now, Vicki."

"That thing has Trudy. I know it does!"

"No," Hurley said, still holding her. "It doesn't."

"It's out for revenge against my family. She's probably already dead!"

"I don't think it wants to kill Trudy, am I right, Minter Saul?" he said, looking over his shoulder for the old man.

"Minter Saul?"

"Where'd he go? He was right behind me."

"I lost sight of him in all the commotion," stated Hurley.

"He wouldn't just leave us," Vicki added.

"No. He didn't come all this way to up and leave; something's wrong."

With Hurley's help Vicki got to her feet. "He may have fallen down; I'll look around," said Vicki.

Hurley walked over to the mound of dirt Baby Mitch had piled up next to the grave. He leaned over and peered down into the hole. "What the hell?"

"What is it?"

"You need to see this." He said.

Vicki joined Hurley and looked into the grave, puzzled she fell to her knees for a closer look. "Oh, God!" she yelped, and scooted back on her rear end.

Hurley was quiet as he knelt and inspected the body, his face somber.

"He has a gunshot wound, but no signs of blood. Baby Mitch musta killed him some place else and brought him out here to bury."

Vicki found the nerve to take another look and she peered more closely at the body. She recognized the slimness of the dead man, but it was when she spied the dead dog lying at his feet, she said, "It's Minter Saul!"

"He's been dead more than a few days," Hurley noted dismally.

Bewildered, Vicki looked at Hurley, and said, "But he's been leading us through the field for hours."

Vicki paced in front of Hurley. "Did you notice how he moved so easily through this hellhole while we struggled at every turn? He didn't have one scratch on him." And she held out her own scratched and bug bitten arms.

Her memory flashed back to the first time she'd seen Minter Saul stepping from the cornfield, tapping on her truck window. "You need help?" he'd asked.

A sudden recollection of her time spent in the shed came tumbling back. A candle in the window had summoned her, but once inside, she couldn't recall seeing any windows, only the flame of a single candle dancing wildly on top of a crate. He'd sat peeling potatoes tossing one after the other into a pot that never seem to fill, until a sudden flurry that blurred his hands filled the pot with naked spuds. And the old dog lay on the floor as unmoving as a frayed carpet.

The flame of the candle jumped and twisted at every expression of pain in his life, the loss of his parents, the lies, and discovering a brother who was sold like a slave. But when he described murdering Ned, the flame was at its highest, almost reaching the wood ceiling beams, and she had feared the place would catch fire.

Now, as she looked down at the old man's broken body lying dead in the grave, everything started to come together. He'd wanted her to come to the shed so he could tell her why he killed Ned Preecher. His voice had seeped into her thoughts, allowing her to envision his parents, Patch and Atticus, and feel the love they had for him. She felt his pain over his lost brother and the rage at Ned for keeping the secret. And she realized it was a confession.

Minter Saul told her about the spirits still in the cornfield waiting on something, but not knowing what. Some don't even know they're dead. Like him, she realized.

She turned to Hurley, "He was helping me; even after my brother murdered him, and he was still helping me find Trudy."

"Do you think he's gone for good?" She asked.

"I don't think he's done." Replied Hurley.

Hurley took Vicki's hand as they stepped past the grave.

"So, let's go find him."

Chapter 31

As Minter Saul stepped through the cornfield, the dead stood in silence, watching. He touched his hat at the women, and nodded at the men, all victims of the Klan. Their eyes settled on Minter Saul, but they didn't understand who he was. They didn't even know who they were any longer. Just spiritless souls stuck between two worlds.

Minter Saul knew he'd been murdered, and he was sure it was the night he'd confronted Baby Mitch Taggart on his property. Evidently, the boy snuck back and shot him, and he got old dog too. After that, he had no real sense of time, nor any feelings of hunger or thirst. Still, he had held onto some hope that maybe he was ailing. A fever could easily take away his appetite and mess with a person's mind.

He also had a strong urge to go to the Taggart property, a place he had never been, nor ever wanted to go as a living man. But something pulled at him, an unseen force tugging him, and in a blink of an eye, he was inside the trailer. He remembered looking around at the dozens of Klan robes hanging on hooks. Taggart's rifles and guns covered every surface, and there was rope, yards of rope coiled on the floor, a wicked snake-like yoke lying in wait.

The boy must've loaded his body in his truck and dumped it in the trailer where he lay on the floor, deader than a car-hit possum. He'd looked at himself for some length of time. "Yup," he uttered, "He was dead all right. He shook his head, angered at his stupidity for allowing the boy to sneak up on him like that.

But why he was still walking around in the world of the living, he didn't know. Maybe he was supposed to do something first, and whatever it was, he hoped he would find out soon because his reasoning was gradually fading, and once that was gone, he was sure he would be too.

From the time he was young, he was able to see the dead from time-to-time, but that was nothing in comparison to now. Now, the dead lurked everywhere, even in this trailer. He'd looked away from his own body when he sensed a presence, and located the spirit of a Klansman hiding among the robes. It glared at him. "Cracker," he'd muttered, and watched it vanish.

He wanted to help Miss Vicki get her daughter back; she deserved a chance to be a good mother to the girl. In his mind, that reason was as good as any for sticking around. He had hoped all of this would get fixed before the two of them found out they'd been stomping around the field with a dead man, but when he saw Baby Mitch hovering over that grave, he knew who he was burying. He could smell the dirt; his body was laying face down.

He had decided then and there to leave Miss Vicki and the Sheriff behind. He knew what horror was about to happen to her brother, and as much as he despised the boy, he didn't want that vision to take up any space in his thoughts; he needed all the good sense he could hold onto. There were still so many unanswered questions, and he didn't know if he had time to get all the answers before having to go his way. He felt real sorrow in his heart that he would never find out what happened to his brother. He would never know his name, or if he was even alive. He also wondered if his brother had a family of his own. These were questions he would take with him to his grave.

These days, his mind was full of visions from years ago and yesterday. Voices young and old whispered to him like close friends. He tried his best to shut them out so he could focus on finding the child for Miss Vicki, but it was getting more difficult, his time was growing short.

Chapter 32

Minter Saul walked past more of the dead. He could see them now as clear as day. They were anxious, lingering in the cornfield like passengers waiting on a train that would never come. He walked farther in, scanning the faces, looking at the long dead who in their past lives had been farmers, laborers, and house servants. Some were dressed for church; others wore nothing but rags. A haunted chorus of despair drifted on a breeze and followed in his footsteps. As he plodded forward, he felt a strange sensation, and when he looked at his hands, they glowed translucent and he could see straight through them to ground. Not sure what that meant, he ignored it and kept walking.

By and by, the carefree voices of children at play drifted past his ear and he knew that one of the voices was that of a living child. As he came through the clearing, he observed a white girl sitting in a circle with Negro children; they giggled and rolled a red ball across to one another. There were five altogether—the boy James, Trudy, and three little colored girls. All the children were whole, and except for the clothes some of them wore, which were ragged and from another time, they looked as normal as any child found on any playground. But Minter Saul knew that the four children playing with Trudy were long dead.

"Miss Trudy," he called.

"Yes," Trudy piped up with a smile.

"Your mama's looking for you. Time to go home now."

Trudy didn't move; instead, she rolled the ball to another child.

"C'mon now, your mama's worried sick."

"No!" said Trudy. "She'll hit me again."

James stood up, and Minter Saul saw what a handsome boy he was. Taller than Trudy, his skin was the color of copper and his hair bright red with a bronze hue speckled throughout. His eyes lit up when he looked at Minter Saul; inquisitive and wise, they glinted amber and gold flecks. So strong was the boy's aura that Minter Saul felt even weaker in his presence.

"Trudy is safe here with me, Minter Saul," said James.

"It's fun here. I have lots of friends to play with," added Trudy. James stared at Minter Saul with discerning eyes, unsure of the old man's intent.

Minter Saul suddenly swayed on wobbly legs and his senses entwined like a ball of string that he couldn't unravel, and he felt dizzy and fell down on one knee.

"Are you tired?" James asked.

Minter Saul shook the cobwebs from his brain and tried to focus, "That girl should be with her mother," he said, and James' moved closer to him.

The other children morphed into the corpses they really were and when a sudden breeze passed, they sailed away like wisps of smoke.

"She has to stay and play," James said. "I'm all alone."

All of a sudden a noise coming from the cornfield, branches breaking and corn stalks being pushed aside as Vicki and Hurley broke through and stepped into the clearing.

"Trudy!" Vicki cried out, and ran toward her daughter.

Trudy turned around but didn't move from her spot next to James.

"Don't go near them," Minter Saul warned.

Vicki stopped a few feet from Trudy, her feet suddenly snagged by a mangle of weeds that sprung from the earth. "What the hell... my legs, what is this?"

"Hold on, Vicki," Hurley said, as he caught up to her. "Listen to Minter Saul."

"I want my kid!"

"Just wait," Hurley cautioned.

"No. Enough is enough," her body tensed with anger.

Minter Saul's voice was composed when he looked at Trudy, saying, "There's your mama; she come all this way looking for you. She misses you a lot, and wants to make amends."

But James stepped forward and stood only an arm's length away from Vicki. His youthful face was suddenly frightening and his eyes turned dark when he looked at her and said, "You told those men a lie, and then you ran away and left me!"

Vicki was stunned by his words, her only reply, "I'm sorry James. I was scared they'd tell Big Daddy. Forgive me, please."

"And they took my Daddy. Where is he?" James demanded, his eyes growing darker still.

"I don't know anything about your father. But maybe we can search and find him. I promise. Please let me have Trudy, James, please."

However, Vicki's pleas didn't move James; instead, he extended his hand to Trudy who took it and stepped closer to him.

"Do you want to play tag now?" she asked him, ignoring her mother completely.

Suddenly, Vicki remembered the telescope and she pulled it from her back pocket. "Look, James. Remember this from the magazine? It's the telescope you wanted so you could see all the stars. This is for you, James."

The weeds unraveled from her feet and she took a few steps toward the children and set the telescope on the ground.

"That's mine," Trudy asserted. "Mama Bertie got it for me."

"No, Trudy, it's for James," Vicki said gently and with a forced smile, "We're gonna give him the telescope as a gift."

James didn't move to retrieve the scope and his lack of interest in the toy unnerved her. Unable to think of what to say next, she inched closer to Minter Saul and whispered, "I don't know if you have any power over this kid, but I'm begging you, please get my daughter from him."

"I don't have any say over the dead." Said, Minter Saul.

Vicki's face radiated with anger and she lost her composure and taking her frustration out on the old man she yelled, "What the hell good are you?"

Hurley, angry now, quickly interceded with, "Well, it looks to me like he found Trudy who is standing in front of you, alive."

Before Vicki could respond, the contention between the two was interrupted by a gust of wind so fierce it blew through the clearing ballooning Hurley's shirt and whipping Vicki's hair into a frenzy. Minter Saul staggered backward and leaned into the gust fighting to remain upright. The winds grew stronger and swept through the cornfield shaking the dried husks loose and sailing them upward like hundreds of broken wings snatched from the backs of fallen angels. When the dark man stepped from between the stalks, the whirlwind ceased and Hurley backed away as his crippled ear oozed blood.

"We have more company." He said, grimly.

The dark man approached the group, however, to everyone's relief his frightening appearance morphed into that of a whole man. He was a farmhand dressed in work clothes. A straw hat covered his head and his sparsely used voice was ragged and strained.

"A toy is not what James needs. He needs his father." He said.

"You're not his father?" asked Vicki.

"No," answered Minter Saul. "This is Enoch, the boy's uncle. He was working with James Senior the day his son was kilt. The daddy went to find his boy, and never came back."

"Does he think I know where his father is?" asked Vicki, clearly frustrated.

"Do you?" asked Hurley.

"Of course not!"

"Nothing is settled until the boy's daddy is found," said Minter Saul.

James walked over and retrieved the red ball from the ground and handed it to Trudy and as Vicki watched her daughter go willingly with James and Enoch her anger intensified. She looked at Hurley and at Minter Saul, her eyes questioned their hesitation and then she decided to act on her own.

"No!" she yelled, and bolted forward but Hurley grabbed her arm, pulling her back. Vicki spun around and slapped Hurley in the face as she tried to snatch away from him, screaming, "Let me go!"

And when James disappeared with Trudy into the cornfield, she sobbed and turned her misery on Hurley pounding his chest with her fists.

"She's gone, you bastard, she's gone!"

"She's not," said Minter Saul. "If you want her back, you have to give the boy what he wants."

Hurley's eyes searched the old man's face. "Is there anything you can do to help?"

Minter Saul shuffled forward, his back bent lower now than a moment ago; the old dog had appeared and was following in his steps. "I do know where some very old bones are buried." He remarked.

"You think it's James' father?" asked Hurley.

Minter Saul scratched his head. "I guess we need to find out."

Chapter 33

The heat that night was exhausting, the temperature stuck to the ninety degree mark like a fat tick on a hound dog, and the humidity was as thick as green-pea soup. Sitting in the swing, her hair slicked back with sweat, Vicki fanned herself with a newspaper while Hurley perched on the porch railing – since returning to the Preecher house, no words had exchanged between them. Vicki looked up, sparse gray clouds barely moved and tonight the stars were noticeably absent. She glanced at Hurley's back, he was hunched over the railing, his hand cupped one ear, and she knew he was in pain.

Hurley studied the outline of the massive cornstalks bordering the Preecher property. He noted the stillness -- not a scintilla of air stirred the leaves. His one good ear listened for the chatter of night crawlers hiding amidst the briar but all were eerily mute. He was troubled, how in the world would this entire thing end? He wondered. All he knew for sure was what he had already experienced and hindsight alone would not keep them safe. He had purposefully turned his back to Vicki to hide the terror that worried his face and pushed tears forward in his eyes. He would not let her see how vulnerable he was. That same vulnerability had warned him to stay away from her for all these years. Getting Trudy back was what he could do for her now, what he wanted to do more than anything. But he had no strategy, all he had was an old black man who was a walking corpse and a hysterical woman who might do anything out of desperation. As Sheriff, he hadn't faced real fear until today, and his training didn't include the supernatural. With a dismal sigh, he focused on Trudy. Getting her back would depend on the whim of the dead boy who was obviously in charge. But even worst, was the dark man. Hurley looked down at his trembling hands; it took everything he had left to keep from rushing to his vehicle and driving off.

He sipped from the glass of cold water Vicki had fetched from the kitchen sink and then breathed deeply to relax the tension in his face.

Hurley's head hung down, his eyes squeezed tight as he tried to banish all thoughts of the day.

"Hurley."

He turned around facing Vicki. The look on her face told him she had something to say and he moved from the railing and sat down beside her on the swing.

"Before all this happened, I went to visit Minter Saul in the shed and he told me things." Her hands slid one over the other in a nervous rhythm.

"Is it something you can talk about?" He asked.

She sighed, and pushed a loose strand of hair back behind one ear. "He never said I shouldn't tell anyone and I never will." Her assurance was more for herself than Hurley. But it's something I think you should know."

"What did he say?"

She scooted closer her voice low and secretive as she recounted the conversation she had with Minter Saul. She told Hurley of Minter Saul's years of hard work for the Preachers, and the little white girl who called him Minter a named the Preachers preferred over Mister. She described his parents. His father Atticus, tall and dark, and his mother Patch, whose freckles her boy Saul liked to count and she was pregnant. "Sherman Preecher rented his mama and daddy to other plantation owners and Saul only saw them once a year at Easter, she said. "When Sherman came to Saul and told him his parents were dead and there was no baby, Saul found himself alone except for the Preechers, especially Ned who became his only friend."

She stuttered and her voice trembled a bit when she recounted Minter Saul finding a folder in a locked drawer. "The folder contained invoices going back years, and a letter from a lawyer named Randolph Talbot. It was a written receipt for a Negro baby, a boy Sherman Preecher had sold for five hundred dollars." Vicki paused, shaking her head in a rare display of compassion. She let out an uneasy breath before continuing, "That baby belonged to Patch and Atticus, which meant Minter Saul had a living brother." She tilted her face upward looking directly at Hurley and said tightly, "Ned Preecher chose to let Minter Saul think he had no family left." She stopped talking and now she searched Hurley's face for a reaction.

Hurley listened with a solemnness she had never seen before and when she described how Minter Saul had killed Ned on his deathbed and forged his signature on the Will, Hurley's demeanor turned grave. Vicki got up and moved to the porch railing and leaned against the post. Hurley had no words until finally he broke the silence between them, "I wish I had a drink right now." She looked over her shoulder at him and said, me too." A mountainous sigh pushed his chest outward and he looked down at his hands. Vicki watched as he absently examined his fingernails. "So, what will you do?" She asked. He looked up, "You mean to the old man? She nodded. He paused and rubbed the stubble on his chin, and then, "nothing – the man has been through enough – besides that, he's dead. I'm just glad he's still here to help us."

They both sat in silence until Vicki spied Minter Saul hobbling down from the shed.

Hurley stepped down from the porch with the shovel, and when Minter Saul made it to the house, he said, "Mister Saul, I'm glad you're here."

Hearing Hurley say Mister was a surprise. "Don't know if I can get use to that," he added. "Did she tell you everything?"

"She did."

Minter Saul shook his head, his expression was firm. "I ain't sorry, Sheriff, even if I took one of God's creations, I can't find sorry in me nowhere."

To Hurley's dismay, the old man's visage suddenly faded then brightened right before his eyes and he said, "You gonna arrest me?"

"Uh, I don't think that's necessary at this point, do you?"

Minter Saul's laughter was a merry sound that lightened the task they were about to undertake.

"My times almost up; we need ta hurry."

"Should Vicki come with us?" Hurley asked.

"Can't see how we can stop her."

Hurley glanced at Vicki who was still perched on the railing looking up at the sky.

"Look at her. She's a wreck. Can't we do this without her?"

"She has to be there."

Concerned, Hurley asked, "Tell me this. Can he keep Trudy in his world?"

"I believe he can. And If she's with him long enough, she will cross over and will be his to keep."

Hurley sighed sadly; he looked at Minter Saul's shriveled body. "What's it feel like?"

"You mean this?" Minter Saul gestured at himself. "Sometimes, Sheriff, I can hear the ocean waves revving up and then rolling across the sea like a great freight train. Other times, I seem to be party to the chitchat of the birds flying overhead. The insects are the worse, constantly yammering at each other—it's a damn noisy existence, that's for sure." Minter Saul chuckled and his eyes fell on Vicki as she left the porch.

When Vicki joined them, she too noticed his diminishing size. He ignored her worried face and looked down at the old dog peeking from behind his leg.

"Quit sneaking up! Dang fool dog."

Then, followed closely by Hurley and Vicki, Minter Saul plodded across the field.

"Any idea where these bones are located?" asked Hurley.

"Not with this addled brain I got. That's why I put down the best topsoil Ned had and I added white flowers just like on Atticus and Patch's spot. We'll find those bones, and if we're lucky, James' daddy. I'll put a nickel on that."

In order to cover more ground, the three spread out across the property looking for what Minter Saul described, as "You'll know it when you see it."

After nearly an hour of searching, Hurley called out, "Over here!" and the others hurried to where Hurley stood looking down on a plot of white flowers.

"They're glowing," Vicki, said, as they walked up on a flock of beaming white Shasta Daisies that seemed to perk up and shine brighter as they approached.

Minter Saul chortled with delight saying, "I knew they would make their presence known."

Hurley went to work quickly, pushing the blade of the shovel into the middle of the flowers. With each bite of the blade, the cornfield stirred awake and the stalks shook their prickly crowns tossing streams of corn silk into the air. The heat of the night suddenly turned chilly as he continued shoveling dirt and tossing it onto a mound.

No one was surprised to see the creature slink out of the cornfield. It crouched next to the hole, sitting in silence, watching Hurley dig. As Hurley continued to dig, he glanced at the animal; its tongue lashed out and rolled back over its teeth as it peered at him and just like before his damaged ear leaked blood.

A deathly quiet rendered the cornfield undisturbed and spread out over the field like a creeping fog. Discovering nothing in the dirt, Hurley looked around worriedly, until his eyes found Minter Saul.

"Keep digging," advised the old man, his eyes riveted on the undeviating golem sitting in wait.

Nervously, Hurley plunged the shovel deeper into the ground, and even in the frigid air he was drenched in sweat and his arms ached from wielding the shovel. When he glanced at Vicki the hope in her eyes spurred him on, and he hastened his digging.

As sweat flew from his brow, his breathing grew labored, and the sound of metal hitting dirt was the only disturbance to the frigid night. And then, he stopped.

"Wait," he said, looking into the soil, "What's that?"

Minter Saul hunkered down on one knee, peering into the darkness. "It's a skull."

Hurley stooped and brushed the remaining soil from the skull and gently lifted it out of the dirt placing it on the ground.

The creature crept forward and looked at the skull and without warning; it lifted its head like a wolf spying the moon and shattered the quiet with a piercing scream that caused Hurley's injured ear to throb and more blood pooled inside his ear.

"There's more," he said, and continued freeing the rest of the bones from the earth. When the last of the bones lay on the ground, Hurley scrambled out of the hole and stood back as the creature inspected the unearthed remains. Suddenly, an all too human sob broke the silence and the creature began to weep, the sound was human, a man crying out in pain, and in the time it took to catch one's breath, Enoch stood in place of the creature.

Vicki moved next to Hurley and gripped his arm.

They watched as Enoch lifted his brother's bones from the grave. All of a sudden, the cornstalks parted and James stepped forward holding Trudy by the hand.

"Trudy!" Vicki called out, excitedly.

"Vicki, hold on," warned Hurley.

"No more waiting! Trudy come here, baby."

But Trudy was still fearful of her mother and didn't budge.

"Come, Trudy, come to me; it's time to go home," she implored.

Vicki's words only emboldened James and he pulled Trudy closer to him as they stood next to Enoch.

"She doesn't need you anymore," he said.

Vicki hadn't anticipated that Trudy wouldn't come to her; she ignored James focusing on Trudy. "I'm so sorry, Trudy. Things will be better now, I promise."

But Trudy had never witnessed any compassion in Vicki, and she was confused and afraid. Vicki fell to one knee, arms outstretched, tears flowing she begged, "Please, Trudy, please; give me another chance. I love you so much."

However, Vicki's actions only spurred James to grip Trudy's hand tighter. But then, Enoch stooped down in front of James and said to the boy, "This here is your daddy."

James looked at the bones in awe and dropped Trudy's hand when Enoch placed the remains in his arms. He looked at his uncle, and like the child he still was, he began to cry.

Seeing an opportunity, Vicki quickly dashed forward and scooped Trudy up. "I love you, Trudy," she said, as she ran back and stood near Hurley and Minter Saul. Relieved to have Trudy safely with her, she stroked her daughter's matted curls and looked her over for injuries.

"Are you okay?" she asked, and Trudy nodded. But James, angered by her actions, glared at Vicki.

"No!" Give her back!" he said.

Vicki pulled Trudy behind her and stood her ground, her own anger flared. Hurley, seeing what was happening, was afraid what the boy might do.

He shook his head, "Vicki, don't!" He pleaded, "Calm down."

But Vicki ignored Hurley, and she shouted at James, "You got what you wanted! Now all this needs to end!"

Hurley stepped toward Vicki. "You need to show respect," he whispered to her, "He's holding his father's remains."

"That wasn't my fault!" she yelled.

Suddenly, Enoch's eyes shifted from his nephew to Vicki, his voice was old, worn by time, and somber. "My nephew lives alone, he can't never leave that field and grow up like you did. Your daughter has a pure heart; she's kind and is his only friend."

Panicked, she screamed at Enoch, "No! She's not going with him. Go away!" Her eyes searched the field for a means of escape and then she locked eyes with Hurley. He saw the desperation in her face, and he knew instantly what she wanted of him, and when he looked at Minter Saul, the old man nodded.

In an instant, Hurley sprinted forward and snatched Trudy up in his arms and bounded for the house. The cornfield shuddered as he ran, the stalks twisting and bending over in a furious onslaught of wind and rain, and an angry chorus of voices rose from the depths of the field, warbling in grief and despair. All at once, Enoch began to transform. His body mutating into a horde of flying insects that rose up into a ferocious funnel cloud. Vicki backed away her eyes wide with terror and when she turned to run, she was snatched into the tailspin her screams conjoined with each turbulent spiral, and then her cries were obscured by the thunderous drone of swarming insects and she was gone.

His face wrought with pity, Minter Saul watched Vicki Taggart being spirited away. He nodded with calm acceptance. Although he had hoped things would end differently, deep down inside he knew the bones alone would not serve to appease the boy.

Chapter 34

More than a month had passed since his venture into the cornfield, and Hurley returned to his daily routine, including patrolling the outskirts of town and checking in on the farmers. He gazed out his open window at the cloudless sky and noted the wilted cotton fields in the distance. A morbid heat wave held most folk hostage inside their homes. The farmers called it the "Dog days of August" and they locked their livestock away from the sizzling heat, letting them out only at night when the weather was a bit more tolerable.

Hurley put the word out that a fast-moving fire had destroyed the Taggart house claiming the lives of Big Daddy Taggart and his son Baby Mitch. He went on to explain that they had found Bertie Taggart dead in the cornfield. The coroner's report was incomplete, the cause of her death still under investigation. Hurley instructed Wade that these were the facts they would go by and Wade was only too happy to oblige.

Some folks believed it was the Taggart's comeuppance since many of them disliked what the family stood for. Hurley noticed there was no love lost for any of the family members and opinions as to their ruination ran rapid, some hitting not too far from the mark. When Hurley stopped in the Bargain Store, Margie, the cashier rang up his soda pop. "All them Taggarts wuz took by demons; ain't that right, Sheriff?" she said, matter-of-factly.

The truth was that when he and Wade broke down the door to Mitch Taggart's bedroom, they walked into millions of flies amassing and building bugs nests all around the room. One particularly enormous nest hung down from the ceiling fan, hundreds of flies flitted in and out of the huge cocoon, and when he and Wade took a closer look, they were sickened to see fingers embedded inside the nest and a human eyeball was looking out at them. The eye was alive and it followed them around the room. Hurley had no doubt it was Mitch Taggart inside the cocoon. Wade was so sickened he bounded out of the room, up the hall, and out of the house.

When Hurley found his way back outside, Wade was throwing up in the grass. That's when Hurley went to his truck and got the gas canister. He waited in his cruiser while Wade went for gas and when he returned Hurley threw gas on the nests, and then soaked the room. He lit the match and ran back outside, joining Wade out near the flagpole where they watched the entire house burn to the ground.

The Fire Marshal readily accepted Hurley's report on the fire, and Cecil saw no reason for any further inspection. Bertie Taggart had a quiet burial with only her sister June in attendance. But in Hurley's opinion, the worst thing being said was that Vicki had gone up north to be a prostitute, and took Teeny with her. Most folks readily believed what was said about Vicki, but Pastor Thomas was furious at the talk about Teeny and preached from his pulpit that she was a sweet and naïve girl who was lured away from the safety of her home. Hurley promised the Pastor that Teeny's case would remain open, and they would never stop following any leads that came in. Truth be told, Hurley had no idea what happened to Teeny. Maybe she did go north, but it certainly wasn't with Vicki.

Hurley's vehicle was passing the cornfield, and even in the heat of the day, the cornstalks stood straight and tall, seemingly unaffected by the hot sun. He would never go in there again, not ever. He had wanted to burn it all down and turn it into a real cemetery, but the Town Council vetoed that. For all they knew, it was just an old weeded cornfield, not worth the money needed for something more useful.

Trudy stayed on Hurley's mind. She had been with him for a few days after everything happened, and was constantly asking questions about her family, especially Mama Bertie.

"Where is she?"

Hurley thought the best way to handle things was to be as honest as possible so he told Trudy about Mama Bertie and the house fire.

"Mama Bertie died?"

"Yes, I'm sorry to tell you that, Trudy."

Tears sprouted on her cheeks and a desolate look clouded her eyes. "Where will I live?"

Hurley felt her fear and was concerned that she never asked about Vicki, Big Daddy, or her Uncle and then he understood how lonely Trudy had been.

He tried to brighten and sound cheerful when he told her; "You have an Aunt June, not far from here. I'm going to take you to meet her."

"Can I stay with you?" she asked, despair showing in her face.

Hurley wanted to say yes, but he had no rights to the child; he wasn't a relative.

"I can sleep on the couch. I'll be as quiet as a church mouse, and I won't make a mess; I promise," she pleaded.

"No, Trudy, I have to take you to your nearest relative," he explained, holding back his heartbreak, "It's the law."

Aunt June lived about a mile away from the Taggarts. Hurley pulled onto the gravel driveway and he and Trudy got out and walked the rest of the way. The small wood frame house was elevated three feet from the ground held up by cut logs under each corner of the house. Two mangy dogs rested in the shady crawl space. Only one of the dogs showed any interest when it lifted its head and emitted a cursory woof, then sensing no danger it settled down again.

Miss June was pleasant and her smile welcoming when she pushed the screen door open. "Come on in Sheriff and bring that pretty little girl with you," she chuckled. A heavyset woman who walked with a cane, she said, "I haveta use this stick to get around with, my knee stays swole with the arthritis."

She positioned herself in a recliner and nodded at the worn sofa. "Have a seat Sheriff. I'm glad you sent your deputy to carry me to Bertie's burial – thank you for that."

"No bother," he replied, in earnest, removing his hat.

Aunt June shook her head with remorse, "It was a real sad turn of events, I havta say; whole family gone. Tsk, tsk."

Hurley glanced at Trudy who was standing in the window tracing her finger along the sill. He was glad she was out of earshot, but his heart sank when he saw her eyes heavy and on the verge of tears. Aunt June noticed her too.

"Oh, my goodness. That poor little thing, she's been through a lot."

"It's been tough for her." Said Hurley.

June sighed, and propped her leg on a crate. She uncapped a tube of Bengay and squeezed a dollop on her finger and rubbed the cream on her knee. A pungent smell invaded Hurley's nostrils, and he sat back on the sofa.

"I can keep her for a while, Sheriff, added June, as she massaged the cream into her knee, but I don't have much myself, and it will be hard having another mouth to feed."

"I understand," he said, as he removed his wallet and handed her some money.

"Thank you, this will help." She looked at him as she tucked the money inside her shirt adding, "You do know, I ain't her blood relation."

Hurly balked. "What? You're not Miss Bertie's sister?"

When June winced with pain, he asked, "are you okay?"

"Oh, yeah, it will settle down in a minute." She stroked her knee. "We grew up in the same small town and always played like we wuz sisters."

"That's a problem." Said Hurley.

"What about you? Ain't you her daddy?"

"What makes you say that?"

"Bertie told me her grandbaby's father was a Sheriff."

Taken aback, he said, "Truth is, I don't rightly know."

"She looks like you," June smiled, a knowing twinkle in her eye.

Caught off guard by June's observation, he looked at Trudy and then got to his feet.

"I gotta go," he said briskly, "But I'll be in touch to make sure you have what you need for her, until I can work this out."

"That's fine, Sheriff Hurley. And don't worry, she'll be all right with me."

Hurley crouched in front of Trudy and took her hands in his, but she pulled away and wrapped her slender arms around his neck as the tears fell.

"C'mon, Trudy," June coaxed, "I got some chicken noodle soup on the stove."

When Trudy finally let go, her eyes were flat and dull, and he knew she had resigned herself to another unhappy home. Leaving Trudy tore at his heart and when he got in his vehicle he sat for awhile, not wanting to drive away. But eventually he put the key into the ignition and started the engine. Under the house still resting in the shade the dog lifted it's head and watched him drive off.

Hurley gripped the steering wheel tightly, shaking away his troubled thoughts and continued cruising down the back road. As he peered through the windshield, steam sizzled on the road ahead, creating a rippling heat mirage. He rolled the window down for a breeze.

Farther along, he came upon a car sitting on the roadside—a blue Chevrolet station wagon that leaned to the right. "Flat tire." He mumbled. He pulled up behind the car and got out. Sure enough, the car's front right tire was flat.

"Ya'll need help?" he said, and stepped up to a Negro man pulling a spare tire from inside the trunk.

The man looked at Hurley and smiled. "Sure could use a hand. We're loaded down." "My kids, they think this is an adventure." His laugh was familiar. "Name's, Harold Wilson, Harry for short."

Then he stuck his hand out, which Hurley accepted. They rolled the spare around to the flat, and Hurley helped him change the tire.

After the spare was in place and the flat stored in the trunk, Harry handed Hurley a rag to clean the grease from his hands.

"Thank you so much—Sheriff Hurley, you said?"

"Yup, or you can just call me Hurley."

"By the way, am I on the right road to the Simms farm?"

"The Simms farm?" Hurley thought for a second, and then, "Oh yes, but folks around here still know it as the Preecher farm," he said, and pointed up the road. "Keep going straight on this road. You'll see it coming up on your right."

"Thank you. I wasn't sure," said Harry.

"What brings you to the Preecher, I mean, the Simms farm?"

A broad smile lifted his cheeks when he said, "We inherited the place."

Hurley was surprised by the news, but didn't let it show when he offered the man a hearty, "Congratulations."

"Thanks, we can hardly believe this is happening."

"Where ya'll from?"

"Philadelphia."

"Don't mean to get into ya'll's business, but who left it to you?"

"No harm, Sheriff. Hold on." He looked in the driver's window. "Marian, hand me those papers, honey."

Harry's wife Marian was a slightly built woman with skin the color of honey and her dark hair was pulled into a loose bun. She leafed through a stack of papers on her lap.

"Just a second," she said, and while she searched, he noticed three boys and two little girls giggling and carrying on in the car.

"Ya'll, be still now!" she scolded, and they all quieted down, but when Hurley winked, the five kids giggled softly.

Marian handed a letter to Hurley, saying, "See, it's a letter from a lawyer in Piney."

Hurley looked at the printed logo, Randolph Talbot, Attorney at Law. He quickly scanned the letter, which stated that Mr. Harold Wilson, Sr. had inherited the property formerly belonging to Mister

Saul Simms. Attached was a copy of a Last Will and Testament filled out almost two months ago, the lawyer had signed Minter Saul's name in absentia.

"Harold Wilson, Senior is my Daddy, said Harry, and Saul Simms is his brother."

Hurley's mouth had gone bone dry when Harry smiled saying, "We're Mister Simms's relatives." But seeing the look on Hurley's face he asked, "You okay, Sheriff?"

Hurley found enough moisture in his mouth to speak, he replied, "I knew Saul Simms."

"Did you, now? What sort of man was he?"

"Well, he's a hard man to describe. Let's just say he was a good man who did things in his own way."

"No surprise, Harry chuckled, Daddy's the same way." He shook his head with disbelief. "We still can't get over the shock that Daddy even had a brother."

"He didn't know?"

"Daddy was an orphan. Adopted as a baby and was told his real parents were dead. No mention of any relatives, ever. I wonder if the people who gave him up for adoption even knew my Daddy had a brother named Saul Simms. I'd hate to think anyone would keep that a secret."

"Secrets do a lot of harm," added Hurley.

"I agree."

"I'm just thankful my Daddy's in pretty good shape in spite of years of factory work. This house will give him the chance to breathe fresh air for a change, and my five children will have lots of space to run and play."

"Five children!"

"Yep, an older boy, two girls and a set of twin boys." He grinned.

"I'm certain Mister Saul would be tickled to know his house will be filled with so much family. By the way, can I meet your father?" asked Hurley.

"Why, sure!" said Harry.

Hurley followed Harry to the rear passenger door and watched him lean into the window. "Daddy, this is Sheriff Hurley. He knew your brother Saul Simms."

From the back seat, a crisp, clear voice resonated a sober presence. "Is that so?"

Hurley didn't think he could be any more shocked until he saw Harold Wilson, Sr. lean forward and look him dead in the eye. The man was a younger version of Saul.

"You knew my brother?" he asked, studying Hurley with a keen eye. Harry opened the door for his father who stepped out of the car and sprang to his feet with a spryness Minter Saul hadn't possessed.

Then with gratified relief, his arms stretched high, he groaned long and hard saying, "Kinks, Sheriff, the worst thing about sitting too long is the kinks. You gotta stretch them out before they knot up on you."

When Hurley offered his hand the man's large hand immediately engulfed it, and Hurley felt the roughness of years of hard work as Harold pulled him into a hug.

When at last Harold released Hurley's hand, the two stood and silently observed each other. As Hurley looked into the face of Harold Wilson, Sr., he saw Minter Saul again, and his eyes burned with tears that he quickly swatted away. Not one to miss a thing, Harold, Sr. clapped him on the back saying, "So you did know my brother."

"Yes, sir, I'm proud to say I did."

"Daddy, get in," Harry said, "It's too hot to stand around out here; we only have to go up the road to the house."

Harold smiled and climbed back into the car. "Stop by anytime, Sheriff. I have a lot of questions about my brother. Can you fill me in?"

"I can try."

When the old man pulled his legs in and closed the door, Hurley leaned down and placed his hands on the doorframe. "It was a pleasure meeting you, sir."

"Likewise."

But as Hurley started back to his cruiser, he heard, "Sheriff!" and turned around to see Harold leaning from the window. "Who was the lady that sent me the letter?"

Puzzled, Hurley walked back to the car. "Letter?"

"Uh-huh. I received a letter on behalf of my brother saying he wanted me to have his house and property, told me to contact Talbot."

"Must have been someone in the lawyer's office," said Hurley.

"I don't think so. It didn't have the Talbot name printed on top like the other letter did."

"Who signed it?"

"Um, son," he said, directing his question at Harry who was now behind the wheel, "What's the name of the lady from the first letter?"

Marian looked over her shoulder with the answer. "Vicki, Daddy, Vicki Taggart."

"Do you know Miss Taggart, Sheriff?"

As the reality of Vicki's kind gesture sunk in, Hurley nodded, saying "Uh, yes, sir, I do."

"We'd like to thank her if we could."

"She's not alive anymore, sir."

"Oh! So sorry to hear that."

"She has a daughter," Hurley added. "When ya'll are all settled in, I can bring her around for a visit, if that's okay."

Harold nodded and his smile was bright. "We'd appreciate meeting the young lady."

As Hurley walked back to the cruiser, he pondered on that letter signed by Vicki, and as he watched Minter Saul's family drive up the road to his house, he realized that she had set all this in motion.

Chapter 35

The next day, Hurley stood in front of the desk of Attorney Randolph Talbot. Talbot was a good-looking man, but Hurley guessed he had a bad night because this morning he was a mess. His eyelids were swollen like two puffer fish, his skin was splotchy and he needed a shave. The clothes he wore appeared slept in. Talbot had the look of a man with too much on his plate.

When Hurley entered the building, the secretary wasn't at her desk, which allowed him to stride into Talbot's office unannounced. When Talbot looked up and saw the Sheriff walk in, he physically paled and uttered a curse word under his breath.

"Oh! Is Chyrisse not out there?" He peeked around Hurley, feigning surprise.

"There wasn't anyone at the desk," Hurley said.

"Uh, well, I know we didn't have an appointment, but I do have some time right now—what can I help you with, Sheriff?" Talbot leaned back in his chair, visibly nervous.

Hurley took a few moments before speaking mainly to allow Talbot's obvious tension to heightened just a little bit more. An untamed cowlick sprouted in the midst of his bushy hair and every few seconds he absentmindedly combed through it with his fingers. Talbot sat behind a large oak desk cluttered with folders and law books, and Hurley deemed him an unorganized mess. At first, Hurley wondered where he was from, but when Talbot opened his mouth, his southern drawl made Hurley yearn for a glass of sweet tea—he was definitely a southerner.

"Uh, oh, Lord, where are my ... my manners! Please, Sheriff, have a seat," he said, gesturing at one of two large leather chairs in front of his desk. The nervousness in the attorney's voice challenged his speech and his voice sputtered and stuttered like a stuck car engine. Hurley took a seat and removed his hat.

"Just a few questions about the property at Route 201," said Hurley. "The property owned by Mister Saul Simms."

Hurley didn't think it possible, but he watched the color drain from the attorney's face until it was damn near alabaster. He slumped back in his seat as his fingers waged war with his cowlick. And before Hurley could ask another question Talbot's distress propelled the words from his mouth in a spontaneous exposition. "All of that was before my time, Sheriff. I had no idea Uncle Robbie was selling Negro children to families up north!" Then, he stood up and came around the desk. His blue eyes had darkened, and his face was grave. "The lady agreed not to go to the police, but you're here, so she obviously didn't keep her word," he said, twitching with dread.

"Was the lady Vicki Taggart?"

"Yes, sir. Miss Taggart. She barged in here like a crazy woman holding a receipt for a Negro baby that Uncle Robbie sold for a client. She was cussing and carrying on with all kinds of threats. Shoved all my files off my desk and screamed at me to make things right. Fact is, he revealed, with a nod of his head, I think she was drinking. I asked her, 'How the heck am I gonna do that?' And do you know what she said? That I had to make sure the Simms house and property went to his brother and nobody else, or she would sue me and go to the newspapers. She said she would do everything she could to drive my law firm out of business and send me to jail. Well, hell, I didn't know who this man's brother was. The adoption was over forty years ago. She told me I better find out, and gave me only one day to do it."

Hurley listened quietly as he watched the lawyer pace the floor, his arms flailing about and doing his best to convince Hurley of his innocence.

"Well, sir. I went directly to my Uncle's storage room, and I dug through years of his files until I found the people who adopted the Simms baby. It was the Wilson's in Philadelphia. I swear, Sheriff, I didn't know my Uncle was getting these kids illegally and charging fees."

"What did you do then?"

"I gave Miss Taggart the information, and she sat right there," he said, pointing at the chair Hurley was in. "She demanded I draw up a Last Will and Testament, leaving Mr. Simms's property to his brother, a Mr. Harold Wilson, Sr., who still had a residence in Philadelphia.

Huffing a strained breath Talbot found his way back to his seat and collapsed into it, the leather cushion wheezed under his weight. He looked at Hurley saying, "Am I in trouble, Sheriff? I don't think I should be held responsible for what my Uncle did. I have a good business here, good upstanding clients. Not one single bit of immoral activity since I took over from Uncle Robbie, not one!"

Hurley didn't respond, he stood up and strode to the door.

"Is that it?" Talbot asked, his eyes bucked with anxiety.

All of a sudden, Hurley paused, his brow creased with consideration and he said, "Actually no, Mr. Talbot, it's not."

He walked back and sat down in the same leather chair and crossed his leg. "I'm gonna need you to draw up some adoption papers for me. You see, my fiancée died before we could marry, and I want to legally adopt her daughter. Can you do that?"

The attorneys eyes lit up, and with an overly-ambitious desire to please, he asked, "Does she have any other relatives?"

"She does not."

"Well then, sir, I surely can. No problem at all."

Three months later, Hurley stood leaning against the doorframe of Trudy's bedroom. He had converted a spare room for her. Together, they painted the walls pink, and Aunt June helped pick out curtains and bedding. Trudy sat on her new bed having a lively discussion with her three brand new dolls. He watched her for a few minutes before entering. The pangs of regret he felt every time he looked at her were starting to lessen, and he hoped that soon, the guilt would fade as well.

After Attorney Talbot handled Trudy's adoption without a hitch, he had explained to her that she was legally his daughter and Trudy was elated. Now, her eyes lit up and dimples crimped her rosy cheeks whenever he walked into any room she was in. His heart brimmed with love when she chirped, "Hi, Daddy," and he was amazed at how easily she called him Daddy. In his mind, there wasn't any doubt that Trudy was his daughter, and he told himself that the only thing that mattered now was that the two of them were together as a family.

"Are you ready to go, Trudy?"

"Is it time, Daddy?"

"Yup, if you still want to see the stars, let's go."

"Yes, yes!" she said excitedly and carefully placed her dolls against her pillow.

"We're not gonna be out there too long," he said, "You have school in the morning."

Trudy skipped through the house and followed Hurley out the front door. On the porch, she looked up. "Oh, it's really dark tonight."

"The weather forecast said it would be clear, no cloud cover at all," Hurly reported, as he himself scanned the sky.

When Trudy was safely buckled into the passenger seat, Hurley slid behind the steering wheel and turned the key. Shifting into drive, they took off down the road.

"Will we be able to see the Dippers?" she asked.

"I'm pretty sure we will. Where's that new telescope?"

"On the back seat."

As Hurley drove along, a warm breeze blew through the window. When the truck picked up speed, the wind lifted Trudy's braids and she laughed.

"You smell that?"

"Peppermint!"

"That's right; mint leaf vines grow all along the fences out here. You can catch the aroma on nights like this."

"I smell it! Now, I want a peppermint stick!"

"Me too," he said, "And a tall glass of Mint Julep." He chuckled.

When Hurley pulled up next to the Crawley farm and parked, Trudy jumped down from the truck and inched her way down the slope. The full moon was the brightest that Hurley had seen in a long time. It lit up the farmland like a huge spotlight.

"Be careful now, don't fall on the slope."

"Okay, Daddy."

"Look up there," Hurley said, nodding upward with his chin.

"Daddy, there's so many stars out. I bet there's a trillion stars in the sky tonight."

"Yep, there's a bunch of them up there, that's for sure."

"Is that the Big Dipper?" she asked, pointing up. "It's just like we saw in the Encyclopedia. Now, I know what all the constellations look like."

Hurley craned his neck looking up, "Yup, that's it. Do you see the bowl and the handle?"

"I see it!" she clapped her hands with excitement.

"Look through the telescope."

Hurley stood behind Trudy and held the telescope steady as she pressed her eye to the scope. The night was warm and the air still, and as they stood next to the fence, the crickets warbled and chirruped all across Crawley's field. But then, without warning the field fell silent, all sound subdued, and Hurley felt a chill creep up his back.

He breathed a nervous breath and turned to the line of trees just as two figures came into focus. It was the boy James searching the sky with a telescope, and then Hurley spotted Vicki waiting patiently close by. She sat on the ground leaning back on her arms, her legs bent at the knees. Her long hair hung freely and her face showed no emotion. Her eyes were fixed on James.

Hurley stared at her and then he willed her to see him, and for a brief moment they locked eyes and his heart surged. He missed her so much, and he knew that he loved her. He wanted her to know his heart, but he wondered if that knowledge would bring her peace or even more sadness, so he pushed his feelings aside. And then, Hurley heard the words "thank you" whispered inside his good ear, and he felt tremendous love wash over him. He wanted to go to her, but he couldn't. She was bound to this place and to the boy. Trudy's gaiety pulled him from the vision.

"Daddy, look, I see it! The Little Dipper!" Hurley looked up as an alluring array of stars painted the sky in radiance.

"Look!" Trudy pointed and was delighted when even more constellations appeared in a spectacular presentation including the Hunter, Ram, Twins, Lion and Bear, all splayed their mighty presence across a black surface.

Hurley lifted Trudy into his arms, so together they could enjoy the amazing spectacle.

"Here, Daddy, try the telescope!" Trudy said, eagerly.

When Hurley put the scope to his eye, he used it to search the field, but Vicki and the boy were gone. He did, however, see Minter Saul hobbling up the hillside followed by the old dog.

He chuckled and whispered, "Hello, Mister Saul Simms," and then his thoughts turned to Harold Wilson, Sr. and his family who had settled in Saul's' house, and he said, "Your brother's home."

END